Breakfield and Burkey

Enigma Forced

2

Enigma Heirs
Thriller Series

Enigma Forced
By Charles Breakfield and Rox Burkey
© Copyright 2024 ICABOD Press
ALL RIGHTS RESERVED

Published by

ICABOD Press

ISBN: 978-1-946858-77-1 (paperback)
ISBN: 978-1-946858-76-4 (eBook)
ISBN: 978-1-946858-78-8 (audiobook)
Library of Congress Control Number: 2024906305

Cover, interior and eBook design:
Rebecca Finkel, F + P Graphic Design, FPGD.com

First Edition
Printed in the United States

TECHNO-THRILLER | SUSPENSE

Novels by Breakfield and Burkey in **The Enigma Series**

Out of Poland (novella)	*The Enigma Gamers*
The Enigma Factor	A CATS Tale
The Enigma Rising	*The Enigma Broker*
The Enigma Ignite	*The Enigma Dragon*
The Enigma Wraith	A CATS Tale
The Enigma Stolen	*The Enigma Source*
The Enigma Always	*The Enigma Beyond*
	The Enigma Threat

Novels by Breakfield and Burkey in the **Enigma Heirs**

Enigma Tracer   *Enigma Forced*

Short Stories

Remember the Future	*Hot Chocolate*
The Jewel	*Hidden Target*
Love's Enigma	*Caribbean Dream*
Nowhere But Up	*Fears, Tears, or Cheers*
Destiny Dreamer	*Trusted Friends and Lovers*
Riddle Codes	(a collection of short stories)

Magnolia Bluff Crime Chronicles

The Flower Enigma (Book 5)   *The Killer Enigma* (Book 15)

Acknowledgments

We are grateful for the support of our readers.
Thank you for providing a review.

CHAPTER 1

Promises Failed

Inside the diesel truck, the dashboard and its associated attachments vibrated and rattled from the ride on the uneven road surface. Like an old man wheezing from years of smoking, the air conditioner worked in fits and starts to deliver cool air.

"Stop messing with the radio dial, Miguel," sputtered Toby, not taking his dark brown eyes off the dusty road. "There hasn't been a signal we could grab for at least an hour. Listening to static is annoying."

Miguel slicked back his oily black hair with his fingers, then rested one hand on his grimy knee visible through the worn jeans. "We've been on the road for nearly eight hours for a trip you said would be six hours tops," he whined.

"Hell," Toby grumbled, glancing at his buddy for a second. "We lost time at the weigh station when you decided to teach yourself to drive and killed the engine. These trucks don't always start right up, plus the officials eyed us for the additional smoke we blew. That took an hour. I was surprised they didn't open the doors after looking at the papers, but the inspector did remove the boss's envelope from the clipboard before waving us through."

The truck lumbered through another small, one-gas-pump Texas town with no stoplight. Speed limit signs were present in each rural city, with cruisers strategically positioned to act on speeders. Toby shifted into a higher gear as he fidgeted on the cracked bench seat vinyl.

"Why don't you admit we're lost, Toby? This piece of junk has no tunes, GPS, or air conditioning. I hope those melons and avocados, or what's ever in back, aren't melting, or we won't get paid."

Toby's teeth banged together when he nailed the pothole. "I used the map boss provided when we got the rig at one this morning. It was a lot cooler before the sun came up. I got us from outside Brownsville to San Antonio on a decent highway. If you hadn't spilled your Dr. Pepper on the map, we could have followed his directions to Pflugerville." Toby slapped the seat and caught his finger in the torn vinyl. "Ow." He shook his hand. "Then there was the damn detour that put us on this two-lane road that announces slow as we approach each city limit."

Miguel's head bounced against the seat at the next pothole. "Hey, watch where you're driving. You could miss the holes if you tried. This is one rough ride. In the next town, let's stop for petrol and ask for directions. Maybe we can get food and a couple of bottles of water. It's still morning, and I'm sweating in this sauna."

"You stink, too," Toby stated with disgust, wrinkling his nose. "I hate the idea of stopping and being even later." He toweled his forehead with his filthy handkerchief, then tried to reposition himself on the seat to ease his stiff back. "Maybe asking for directions would help. I'll pull the rig into this adjacent parking lot. I'll walk to the store for water and directions. You get the hot air all to yourself." He parked the rig and set the brake. "Don't touch anything while I'm gone. Don't go anywhere. And don't turn off the engine. I'll take our map. I'm sure they got a pencil."

"Remember, you promised to teach me to drive this big rig when this job's over. I want to drive freight in this country. But not this piece of crap."

Annoyed, Toby opened the door into the inferno of the August morning with the sun blazing overhead. The sweat evaporated from his skin as he hopped down and slammed the door. Smoke randomly billowed from the exhaust stack on top of the cab. He walked around the building to the front door with a view of the regular gas pumps. Toby noticed a few cars were there, but no one was outside refueling. He decided folks must be inside enjoying the cool air. Turning his attention to the paper, he oriented his map to make it a quick conversation.

He started to push the door to enter. Inside, a hand pulled back the door and grabbed hold of Toby, yanking him into the store. He fought to keep his balance, but his worn boot soles slid him into a display rack like a skater on ice. Several items plopped to the floor with resounding crunches. Then, there was stillness. He felt the jarring pain from a solid object banging on his head. His knees gave out as he crumbled to the floor atop several chip bags that exploded from the impact.

A demanding man's voice with a Mexican accent growled, "Stay down on the ground, motherf*****."

Toby's hand reached for his injury as he tried to move into a sitting position. He saw the revolver rising and felt the blow smash down on the same spot.

Toby expelled. "Oof," then he grunted. Lying on his right side, he peered through his eyelashes, but everything seemed blurry. His head pounded, so he shut his eyes, hoping to ease his pain. He heard the voice again.

"Diego, I got another one. What's taking you so long?"

A second accented voice came farther away, echoing as if in a closed area. "I told you not to use names, stupid! You just created another problem. It's bad enough the cashier can't open the damn safe. Now these people know our names, Chico."

"Sorry."

"Never mind; get his wallet, too. We'll take all the money we can, including anyone who stops in before we leave."

Toby figured Chico pulled him up by the armpits and waved his gun. He shoved Toby toward the edge of the checkout counter. Toby noticed several folks sitting near him and holding their knees. They gave him a quick look reflecting fear before hiding their tear-streaked faces against their chests.

"Gimme that wallet from your back pocket, mister. Then sit down and shut up," Chico demanded.

Toby's vision cleared enough to see Chico's hand waiting to receive his wallet while he pointed his weapon to the floor toward the others. Without thinking, Toby grabbed the man's wrist and yanked hard, slamming him into the corner of the counter and knocking out his breath. Toby recognized he stood half a foot taller, so he continued pulling and shifting the tension to keep the man off balance. Chico fought like a ravaged coyote and swung his revolver over, delivering two rounds in deafening rapid succession. Toby released his hold on his killer, falling dead with blood rapidly pooling on the floor.

Multiple screams and cries sounded from the hostages.

Chico bellowed, "Who else wants to be a hero?"

Behind him, the glass doors exploded, followed by three uniformed officers. "Freeze! Hands empty and in the air!" one officer commanded, shifting cautiously to the right. Another officer sidled left while a third maintained her position at the opening.

Stunned, Chico ducked behind the hot grill counters.

A man chuckled from nearby on the floor. "Good. The silent alarm worked. Cops arrived in less than fifteen minutes."

Chico identified the man and grinned. In a blind rage, he shot the man, then turned toward the storefront in time to receive two rounds in the chest from the policewoman. The impact drove him into the hot food area. Several things jarred loose and joined the dead killer on the ground.

Moving cautiously, the other officers methodically walked the aisles. Diego popped up and fired several wild shots. He was shot twice in succession. Once in the chest by the officer, Jose. Again, in the head from the officer, Steven.

Jose hollered, "Who else is here?"

One of the hostages yelled, "We're behind the counter. There were only two of them. Thank you for saving us."

Heat waves radiated from the black asphalt in the parking lot. The three officers huddled in the shady strip outside the storefront, where local citizens placed boards on the broken doors while others swept up the shards of glass debris.

"I hate store shootings. The witness questioning goes on forever," complained Jose.

"At least the coroner loaded up the last of the bodies, and we finished questioning the hostages," Brenda proclaimed.

Steve nodded. "We'll get back to the office, fill out the final paperwork, and see what turns up on the dead guys. According to one witness, the wallet of the man who entered toward the end contained no identification. A rough map located in his shirt pocket was penciled on brown paper. No cell phone on him—strange."

Brenda's shoulder radio barked, "Brenda, have you accounted for everyone? We identified the robber's car, but based on the body count, there should be one or two more vehicles. Can you confirm?"

Jose wrinkled his forehead and fretted, searching the parking lot. "Steve, circle to the back and see if we missed anything. The hostages gave their statements and then left. I only see one vehicle."

Steve returned, shaking his head. The rig parked in the abandoned parking lot belched black smoke, and its idling tone changed, capturing his attention. "Hey," Steve pointed, "that 18-wheeler in the parking lot on the side could be his. It's still running. Let's go take a look."

Jose opened the driver's side of the cab. The stale, hot air took away his breath. Seeing no one, he climbed up and turned off the engine. Leaving the door ajar, he jumped to the ground and walked around to the rear of the trailer. He saw the heavy padlock securing the opening and slapped the metal. "Damn. I hope there's nothing perishable in there. We're going on two-plus hours since the shooting." Wiping his sweaty brow with the handkerchief he pulled from his pocket, he paused. He cocked his head to pinpoint the thud that seemed to mimic his hand slap, but from inside the trailer. No further sounds were heard.

Pressing the transmit button of his commlink, he advised dispatch of the abandoned vehicle, then froze when he heard the thud again. He frantically waved to Brenda and Steve. The two officers rush to his side, meeting at the midpoint of the trailer.

"What's up, Jose?" Brenda asked.

"I heard a thud after I banged my hand on the rear, then again after talking to dispatch. Tell me what you hear, or call me crazy." Jose slapped his hand against the trailer.

A female voice echoed from inside within seconds. "el auxilio."

The officers stared at Jose, who suddenly felt ill.

"Steve, go grab the cutters from our car," Jose ordered.

Steve ran off.

"You're perfectly sane," added Brenda. Beating on the side of the trailer, in Spanish, she yelled, "We're coming to help."

When Steve returned, he and Jose used the tool and had the lock broken in seconds. Jose lifted the rod and swung open the door on the right while Steve grabbed the door on the left. Brenda rushed to the opening and stared at the scene inside. An indescribable stench bellowed from the opening, along with moans and cries. The cargo was heaped in groups, with a few clustered near the side walls.

Jose backed away and took a breath of fresher air. "Dispatch, we need more EMTs here now, with saline drips. Send the coroner, too. We found a freight trailer full of humans, some still alive.

"Steve, go find blankets and all the water you can carry. Tell those workers to help lay blankets in the shade, even under this trailer." Shaking Brenda to get her to focus, Jose said, "Go see if you can find the manifest for this rig in the front."

Jose hopped in and noted random movements of arms and legs. He opened the other trailer door to determine where to place any people found alive for extraction. An anguished cry got trapped in his throat, and tears filled his eyes at the sight of a small toddler lying on the trailer floor with a puddle of blood under her head. Her lifeless, glassy brown eyes stared back at him. It took several beats for him to move on, searching for survivors.

Brenda joined him. Together, they moved several of those breathing so helpers could lower them into the shade to await the EMTs.

"Hey, buddy, are you okay?" asked Steve when the next young victim was positioned for retrieval.

"No," Jose admitted. "I'll never be okay again. That little girl looked like my daughter. I kissed her this morning before school."

He felt Brenda pat his arm. "We're all these people have right now," she whispered. "I'm so glad you heard the first noise and followed your gut."

He nodded and retreated to the depths of hell to find more bodies. "Dispatch," he sobbed into his comm, "we need more help. And we need it now!" He felt his anger and frustration explode as he roared, "Call every surrounding town. We need EVERYBODY! They can't die like this. KEEP the damn media away."

CHAPTER 2

Promised Delivery

A crude, aging trailer parked in front of a decrepit warehouse looked abandoned. Several emaciated dogs wandered alert to every movement while scavenging food. Inside the trailer, Rodrigo kept his temper in check by using his large, beefy fingers to knead the stiff tendons in his neck. He turned his soulless, cold, black eyes toward the seated man. "Miguel, I don't understand. How did you make it to this drop location without the driver, truck, or, more importantly, my cargo?" Rodrigo straightened his shoulder holster to remind the man of the gun under his arm.

Nervous sweat beaded on Miguel's face. "We stopped to get directions," he sputtered. "Toby left me in the cab. He went across to the store for directions and water. It was so hot. A few minutes later, I heard gunshots. Then, police cars raced into the parking lot. Three officers got out. One was carrying a metal pipe. He ran straight for the glass doors, which exploded on impact. They entered with guns drawn. Seconds later, I heard more gunfire, so I ran from the cab. I was scared. I didn't know what to do. I didn't think it was a good idea to hang around and explain to the police. I hitched a ride, telling the driver the area

I needed. He dropped me off a couple of blocks from here. I was glad I remembered the address and found you."

Rodrigo cast angry glances at his two silent associates. He clenched and unclenched his fingers, getting madder by the minute. "Why didn't you drive the truck? You had the keys. The engine was running."

Miguel sobbed. "I don't know how to drive a rig like that. You gotta believe me." He looked at the man, then offered, "Why don't we just go and get it? We aren't that far, maybe half an hour. I can show you. Your cargo should be okay. It wasn't at the store parking lot. Maybe Toby is okay and waiting for me."

Rodrigo sat at the computer and clicked the keyboard, searching for news. His eyes widened as he saw the breaking news story about the 18-wheeler, its cargo, and the shooting fatalities. He shook his head in disbelief at the sudden turn of events.

A long moment of silence was interrupted by Rodrigo clucking his tongue in annoyance. "Too late. You should have tried to leave with the cargo." He shook his head at the turn of events as his stomach soured. "I need to call the shipper and explain this mess. I know the next step, but let's hear it anyway." In a practiced fluid motion, Rodrigo placed a call and put it on speaker.

The man's gruff voice barked in a thick Spanish accent. "Why is my timetable running behind again? You shoulda called two hours ago. What's the hold-up?"

Rodrigo's fingers drummed on the desk. "It's a total write-off. The rig and all the cargo are close by in the hands of the authorities. The news report suggests Toby took one too many bullets in the head."

"What? How the hell did that happen? Why is it a total loss? And who knows the details?"

"I have the driver's riding buddy who ran from the scene. He knows too much or nothing, so not a complete write-off."

"Damnit. Wipe the scene clean. Burn it if you must. We can't use that location as a processing point again. Start looking for another location at least a hundred miles away. I'll destroy the financials and alert the buyers," the man insisted.

"And the runner," Rodrigo asked. "The whiney one?"

"He's useless. Kill him and add him to the fire. Screw-ups and losers aren't needed in my operation."

Nodding, Rodrigo disconnected the call. "Men, you heard the boss. Clean everything with the standard bleach wash; we have to go. But first, take our friend out in pieces so the dogs can eat. Then, add whatever remains of him into the inferno. We leave in an hour."

Rodrigo pulled out his .45 caliber Colt, pointing it at the trembling man.

"You weren't going to pay us, were you?" Miguel whimpered.

"No." He pulled the trigger twice, sending two rounds through Miguel's teeth to make identification impossible if any remains were recovered. "I'm sure the dogs are gathering."

CHAPTER 3

Driving a Hard Bargain

Mateo slowly but deliberately placed his phone on the desk. He recognized that those around him heard his angry side of the conversation with Rodrigo and knew they would leave him alone. Being mad was a luxury he could not afford in this cutthroat business; however, getting even showed strength. Swiping his mustache with his fingers as if caring about his appearance, he turned toward his minions and announced, "All that cargo, planning, and profit is gone. The staging area got liquidated because Toby insisted on taking a stupid kid along who wasn't bright enough to move the cargo out of harm's way. What a mess. The estúpido runs from the truck and staggers to the meeting point in broad daylight. He risked being tracked to us." Mateo's anger flared. He swept his arm across the desk, catching his cell and sending it into the wall. The outer shell protector prevented the expected shattering results.

His lieutenants shifted uneasily from one foot to another. One ventured forward, returning the phone to the desk.

Mateo knew no one expected a thank you from him for anything, but they recognized they could avoid a 9mm bullet in the neck if he didn't get madder. He sat and stared ahead as if to divine the following operational tasks. Sounds from the noisy grind of his teeth alerted the others not to break his concentration. A few minutes later, he issued orders like a machine gun.

"Rodrigo is hunting a new staging area for our next shipment. I need a truck, families for export, and a fentanyl mixture for the next lab, Javier. No, make that two. I want them transported from New Mexico to Arizona across the border, and the inspectors on both sides paid, like always. Santi, alert the gatherers to set the next families up for export. Alvaro, I want teenagers we can provide to Julian for his mail-order service. Javier, tell Chen we need more raw materials tomorrow or the day after. Our drug buyers will be eager for supplies since this shipment got confiscated. Javier, I need standard transport papers after the initial loaded weight and the guards to sign off once they are inside the southern border."

The burley, no-nonsense Santi asked, "Does the import price stay the same or higher to cover the losses?" The others paused to hear the pricing instructions.

Mateo stroked his mustache and tapped a finger on the desk. "Our expenses have risen, and so should our prices. I want concessions from the suppliers and a price premium in advance from the buyers. Bargain hard for higher prices and reduce our costs. Your salaries are based on performance this round."

They nodded and grimly went about their work.

Still simmering about the lost shipment, Mateo grabbed his phone and dialed Rodrigo. The unanswered call went straight to voicemail. Mateo didn't leave a message and slammed the device onto the desk with a thud.

Several minutes later, Mateo's phone vibrated, and the window displayed Rodrigo's weathered face. Mateo snatched it up and accepted the call. "Where were you?"

"Sorry, boss. I was eliminating our current position and its liabilities. Whatcha need?"

"Sorry, Mi amigo. The loss hit us hard. I'm taking it out on the wrong people. How much is needed to reestablish and relaunch our Texas operation in a similarly remote area?"

Mateo was impressed that the scruffy and unkept Rodrigo had a surprisingly good understanding of business with no scruples.

"I have given it some thought, Mateo. This human import business is cleaner since all we have to do is bring 'em in to sell to the organizations who need workers. After we get the money, we hose out the truck before returning it for our full deposit.

"The precursor fentanyl material has a healthy wholesale market. Moving it downstream into manufacturing requires more investment in lab equipment and processing time. We have more exposure until we have finished products for sale.

"I have three possible locations for the human drop points. I want to secure two of them so we have a fallback. I'm securing a couple of smaller trucks to move the base for the drugs to the lab site to minimize exposure. I have two guys who might oversee the labs that you control."

"Rodrigo, enough with the details. What's the cost to restart the labs and two locations? With the right setup, drug processing time is five to seven days."

"To continue to move the human cargo over the border for labor delivery, I'll work the numbers. I'll get prices for the lab equipment and negotiate our purchase with three payments. One-third upon delivery with set up, the second in thirty days, and the third fifteen days later. From our experiences and prior costs, I'd estimate seventy-five thousand would get us going. It is only an estimate until I get the pricing."

Mateo groaned. "That makes this loss worse. Damn. The guys who deliver the equipment, they stay on site?"

"Yes, sir. Like before, we keep the technicians to keep the lab running in tip-top shape. I am using the ones from the location we eliminated with Paulo as their escort. My brother will protect your interests."

"Would it be smarter to stick to the raw materials side at a lower profit?"

"Maybe, but we'd have to triple the business to maintain your same cash flow. I think your control covers you end-to-end better. Your call."

"Crap," Mateo felt torn. "Let's keep the labs for the time being."

"Mateo, we have a little over the estimated amount in the currency pack secured under the truck's cab that got seized. Do you want me to try and retrieve it before it's discovered? I've got eyes on it. Due to its size, the small-town law can't get the truck and trailer into their compound. I should be able to cut the pack free after dark. That cache of funds would take away some of the sting from this failure."

Mateo almost smiled. "Yes, but don't get caught." He disconnected and muttered. "We need a better payment system. Damn hard currency is too difficult to transport reliably and quickly."

CHAPTER 4

Righteous Outrage

From her office in New York, reading the August morning bulletin, Gracie blinked away brimming tears, unable to believe the news flash. She twisted strands of blonde hair around her finger, and the second read jolted her sensibilities.

Fifty miles north of San Antonio, Texas, authorities found an abandoned 18-wheeler. Inside was not the fresh produce suggested by the manifest, but humans packed like sardines. Survivors were transported to undisclosed destinations. Authorities estimated that a third of the undocumented immigrants survived. All reports suggest they remain in critical condition. Dehydration claimed the lives of the aged and infant travelers locked in the box trailer baked by triple-digit temperatures as the summer heat wave continues in Texas.

Reeling from the harsh reality, Gracie leaned back and pressed her fingers to her eyes. "Human trafficking. I don't understand how anyone but a monster could do this," she mumbled. Her thoughts returned to the cruise six months ago, where she was captured and her friends hospitalized, feeling it was related to a similar vicious attacker. They'd all recovered physically, but the memory remained forever etched on her brain. Her fingers pounded a message to JW on the keyboard to engage her European team. Moaning her frustration in not getting a quick fix, she reached for her cell and called her twin brother.

"JJ, I hate being head of our fourth-generation information businesses, the R-Group, and powerless to insist on retribution when atrocities occur like the news reported this morning. Do you ever feel ineffective at times when cases seem aligned?" Gracie took a breath with ideas churning. "Can your CATS resources learn more about the top headlines this morning on the human trafficking event near San Antonio, Texas? As Uncle Carlos would say, my Yaqui Indian senses tingle like crazy when things are too coincidental. I'm afraid Mateo's business model has surfaced again, this time on wheels."

"Yes, Gracie, the team's on it. ICABOD, our best-shared supercomputer asset, flagged the news feed when it surfaced. You're right. It looks like Mateo's handiwork or an evil copycat. We tracked the rental of the rig back to the same money source that rented transport out of Miami months ago. The inside tip Lance Pope shared with you is still paying dividends. We'll work that angle. But Homeland Security is pushing to keep this tragic migrant transport under wraps. With only this one report, I'm not sure why the media isn't outraged by this horrific crime against humanity. Nobody deserves to die like these immigrants did—except for the known trafficker Mateo."

"I sure hope Sophia and Elena are not among those unfortunate victims," she lamented, remembering when she had met the pair during a dinner on the cruise. "Is your right hand, Brayson, aware? He was on the cruise when the girls were traveling with Mateo."

"He checked that angle immediately," said JJ. "Nothing in the info we looked at for the living or dead suggested the girls. I think their captors had other ideas for those two. Remember, the truck came from Brownsville, not Miami, where Sophia and Elena disappeared."

Gracie closed her eyes with relief and sadness that they were still missing. "JJ, we must locate Mateo and end his wretched business model. Recruiting teens for sale or prostitution is bad enough," she spat. "But wholesale importing of people for fun or profit is-is…I can't think of something bad enough to call it."

"I agree, it's outrageous. Can you get your team to start tracing the financial angle? As some reports suggest, victims pay in advance and sign up without seeing the fine print. They can be sold, leased, or forced to smuggle drugs to buy freedom. Payoffs get paid to multiple sources to turn blind eyes to everything. The dangling promises that life in the United States is milk and honey persist. In some third-world countries, people mortgage everything and beg, borrow, or steal to achieve the American dream. The exploitation of refugees is a disgusting business model. Where is the money going, and how do we intercept the endpoints? Mateo and others in the business must have a weak link. What about the credit cards used for the truck rentals?"

"I've asked our cousins, Satya and Auri, to track the information, including rental payments over the last year. JW is supervising. Sometimes, they get stuck, and he needs to write additional computer code to get them on course again. He wants to locate the origin as this is likely not a new business but more likely an expansion. Granger is augmenting ICABOD's processing power in real-time. I suspect Mateo uses cryptocurrency to launder his income, but that's a lengthy search algorithm. We found crypto purchases completed with stolen credit cards bought off the Darknet." Gracie shifted uneasily in her chair and quietly asked, "How's the new contractor doing?"

JJ laughed. "Jeff's doing well. It's nice that he's low mainte-nance, especially while dating you."

"Hey, I'm easygoing, too," she chuckled. "We're working through our issues. Jeff hasn't complained about his work, so thank you for adding him to your team."

"Jeff's smart enough to know we often talk."

"I know," she chuckled. "I need to get back to work."

"Me too. Good night, Gracie."

"Night, JJ. Thanks."

Late afternoon, Jo clutched her tote, entered their cozy Brazilian home decorated in warm, vibrant colors, and locked the front door. "Hey, JJ," she called, "sorry I'm a little late, honey. Traffic was a bear."

Resigned to a standard workout with JJ before dinner, she headed toward their gym, hoping to surprise him. Not hearing a response, she went to their bedroom, buoyed by the welcoming atmosphere of their home. The workday melted as she inhaled the fresh scent of flowers while she put things into the laundry and changed into her exercise clothes.

Jo admired JJ's muscles undulating while he threw spinning sidekicks, elbows carefully aimed backward to halt his imaginary adversary. He added deadly frontal jabs to destroy the punching bag. It spun like a marionette master controlling it for an unseen audience. JJ abruptly stopped, sweeping his longish dark wave away from his eyes. He knelt on one knee and hit a button to initiate a new session.

JJ snapped his head and body up to focus on three spring-loaded projectiles rocketing towards him at ninety miles per hour. Jo gasped, her heart racing while the blunt missiles zeroed in on him like a batter timing the swing against a fastball. She beamed, watching him sidestep each with lightning-swift movements, grabbing them in midair and tossing them to the floor.

Jo walked behind him as he retrieved the objects, knowing he was aware of her presence. "I worry when you place yourself in harm's way, but I love watching you." Reaching her arms around him, she leaned into his back. "Those darts travel like a major league pitcher's fastball. I'll never move that quick."

He spun her around, hugging her back. "Nope, but you are fast enough for everyone to admire your form. Besides, I don't use the programs often. I need to keep my reflexes sharp just in case."

Jo kissed him and gently caressed his cheek. "Sorry to be late again. Do we have time for me to work out before supper?"

"Of course." He waggled his eyebrows and kissed her nose. "I love working out with you anywhere, anytime." He turned on the music she enjoyed while they sparred. "We'll do stretches. Then, let's do an easy session for your muscles and balance. You have another shoot tomorrow."

She nodded agreement and caught her mane of mahogany hair into a scrunchy, centering her mind on her body, smiling at their reflection in the mirror.

JJ laughed. "Honey, even in a gym, you look hot. No wonder you're so successful as a supermodel. Are there any out-of-towners coming up?"

"No, only studio shoots for a few weeks, then maybe a session in Mexico. Let's do this, I'm hungry."

He pulled her limbs, gently insistently tugging to find stress points. "Something weird happened today that sort of relates to our first trip to Magnolia Bluff. I want to discuss it during dinner to get your perspective."

"Sure." She groaned in appreciation as her shoulder popped into the joint. Inhaling, she said, "I knew I held that position too long for that last outfit."

Thirty minutes later, she felt invigorated. "Sweetheart, you're the best," she said, adding a kiss to punctuate her statement. "Let's go eat."

Arm in arm, they went upstairs. Pulling items from the refrigerator, she set up a tray of fruit, cheese, and cut meats while JJ poured wine. He carried the wine and food outside to the patio. The balmy air caressed her skin. She tugged off the hair tie and shook out her mane. She switched on the perimeter lights. The table looked inviting. The garden of fragrant white flowers appeared almost fake. Bending, she smelled a couple and deftly snapped off a few with her manicured nails. She added the flowers to the small vase in the center.

"There. They're perfect."

"Yes, you are, Jo." He pulled out her chair and kissed her shoulder when she was seated.

While toasting one another, Jo asked, "So, what happened today, honey?"

JJ seemed to collect his thoughts but frowned. "We think the human trafficking monster, Mateo, has resurfaced. It appears that he has broadened his business model to include wholesaling."

"Wholesaling?" Jo cocked her head and leaned forward, grabbing a piece of cheese and an apple.

"A large group, nearly a hundred immigrants. From your experiences, I wanted to hear your ideas on the possible end game for whole families."

Chewing the morsels, she thought back to her captivity by invaders in her remote hometown and her harrowing escape after her parents died. She had told JJ all the details of her back-ground when they found the poor souls in Magnolia Bluff. She shook her head to chase away the negative memories. "If my insights could help, then let me try. The leaders promise you a future while starving or beating you to bend to their will. That was how my parents and other families originally got captured."

"We've discovered that most people in this latest fiasco sold everything. They borrowed, jumping at the chance to escape the horrors of their lives only to get trapped in a box truck in the summer heat of Texas. We've found promises to pay and send money back home once established in the states," JJ explained.

She lifted her glass for a sip with her hand trembling. "That must be the incident I heard on the radio. So tragic." A heavy somberness penetrated her heart. "People try, and monsters take advantage. What makes you think Mateo's involved?"

"Some descriptions refer to those we experienced in Magnolia Bluff during our anniversary and what Gracie saw during her Caribbean cruise. Plus, we've recovered surveillance shots from the Brownsville border that appear to show him exchanging packages of what I suspect is money. We're still searching for details." JJ scarfed a few of the delectable tidbits.

Jo wiped her mouth with her napkin. "I recall you telling me after your Miami investigation that Mateo returned over the border to his ranch. Mexican officials were unwilling to divulge details. Did you ever learn more about that location?"

"No, but I love the reminder. I need to follow up on that avenue."

"If the next shoot is in Mexico, perhaps I can learn additional info."

JJ swallowed the last of his wine with the remainder of the meat. "Honey, if you go to Mexico, you'll have company."

"Your Uncle Carlos. I know," she chuckled. "Let's shower and fall into our softer-than-a-cloud bed. I've got a mid-morning start tomorrow."

"I'll do the rubdown, but I promise to wake you early."

Grabbing the tray and flowers, she said, "Deal."

CHAPTER 5

Begin the Attack

JJ reorganized priorities for his daily tasks in the massive office upstairs in his Brazilian house. He messaged Brayson in Luxembourg for a working meal. He could enjoy his lunch while his right-hand support had supper. He launched the video meeting shortly after noon pleased to find Brayson prompt as usual.

"Thanks for this unscheduled meeting. I hope you grabbed something for dinner before you got home. Can we get any more information from the local authorities in Texas? I know you're trying to track the victims' locations. We need to get someone to Texas to conduct potential interviews with survivors when the authorities are finished."

"I can place one or two resources in the hospitals as soon as I can confirm the patients' conditions," replied Brayson. "That way, the access should be better. To support the languages needed and for knowledge of hospital procedures, I'd suggest we assign Ernesto and Marian. We could place them as traveling nurses, giving them flexible coming and going with recognized medical credibility."

"I like that idea," JJ nodded. "Those poor people. It is sickening. Gracie has her team hunting money. Any information we can provide to link the truck and destinations with the payment history would help. Although Gracie wants to get copied, JW leads those efforts."

Brayson laughed. "I'm not certain which of you works the hardest, but you both want to know all the nitty gritty."

JJ glanced at his plate. "We like to bounce ideas off one another when we can't sleep, too. Gracie's taking this event hard. She's worried about whether Sofia and Elena will ever get found and what condition they'll be in. I hope the pair is together because they seemed resourceful, based on your and Marian's reports."

Brayson nodded. "You're right. I don't think the brainwashing efforts worked. Marian gave them hope and some special survival skills training. I think they'll take it if they get the chance to escape. Let me tap into the police files again, and I'll share any updates."

Brayson rose to leave the area, gathering his trash. He patted JJ virtually on the shoulder. "You and your sister are doing great. Give yourself a little slack."

John-Wolfgang, or JW as he preferred, answered the call with a swipe of his finger on the screen without missing a beat on his ongoing program changes. "Hey, Gracie. Is this a follow-up call to the email you sent?"

Gracie laughed. "Aunt Petra told me you were intuitive, annoying, excessively polite, and brilliant like Uncle Jacob. At least you've stopped with the Madam Rodreguiz nonsense when I call."

He tucked his longish dark hair behind his ear. "Mom also says I learn fast. Last time you and JJ were here in Zurich working with us on our martial arts skills, you flattened JJ and me. You are the operating head of the R-Group, technically my boss, and, by day, a director at the World Bank in New York. You have my respect, cousin. I will address you as requested."

JW felt relieved when her image on the screen grinned.

"JW, I need you to round up the rest of your cousins and get into the main room. I want you to set up teams to dig into the money laundering possibilities of that detestable scum, Mateo. I'd like you to determine how many different paths lead in and out of his organization in the U.S., Mexico, and, I suspect, the Caribbean, on one of the last islands from that trip I made. JJ and his team need targets to focus on and potentially put some extra eyes in place on the ground. Mateo is in my crosshairs because of his human trafficking operation. I want to prove if money laundering is related. He got outside help, but we need evidence, including names, places, and, most importantly, money locations. Without funds, his operation is dead."

JW noticed the set to her jaw and the contempt blazing in her eyes as she said their target's name. This was more serious than he had suspected from her email, and he felt worried. He decided to insert a bit of fun. "Mom said I was brilliant like Dad?"

JW laughed at her smirk.

"She said you showed islands of genius between low water crossings of self-doubt and uncertainty. You're on the path. He has more experience. I know you can do what's needed, or I wouldn't have asked. I think you can be better with time. We all can because of how we were trained."

Momentary euphoria swelled in his chest. He sat a little taller in his seat. "Gracie, I'll set everyone up when Auri returns with lunch. When everything is ready, I'll alert Granger and Satya to join the secure Gigazon bridge built by ICABOD. We can run this virtual immersive digitized room twenty-four-seven. The three-dimensional attributes give the sensation of reality, far superior to conventional meeting rooms."

"Thank you, JW. Please notify me of the location of the data and add your daily briefings. Call me if you need anything."

JW smiled as the team joined the Gigazon.

Auri's light brown hair was still damp from his shower. His frown intensified as his bottom lip jutted out. "Why did you ask us to hold off on coffee? When it's this early, we need the super-charging of caffeine and chocolate chip cookies like Dr. Quip used to do."

JW nodded thoughtfully, seeing his uncle in his mind. "True. He appreciated his high-octane coffee and a sugar rush accelerant. He once said he didn't brew coffee but distilled it for maximum potency. It came at a steep price. Early afternoon, he'd retreat for his *power nap*. Whether he was sitting or reclining, you couldn't get his attention. When he crashed on the couch, you couldn't get his attention for at least an hour, sometimes two. Mom suggests we wait until age twenty-five to go full-on with the caffeine and sugar."

Auri nodded, but the frown remained.

"You can have hot chocolate in a couple of hours, though."

Auri flashed a grin.

Granger smiled from his virtual seat. Satya slid into her work chair.

Granger asked, "Are you ready for the immersion in the Gigazon?"

JW nodded as he added his immersion glasses with associated earpieces, which brought his heads-up online, as did Auri. Granger and Satya mimicked the steps.

ICABOD, their supercomputer, advised. "Ladies and gentlemen, the Gigazon is live. I recommend you use your sign-in protocols and authentication steps and begin your collaboration session."

JW nodded at the efficiency of the transition. "Our virtual environment will help bridge our distance with our newest project. Gracie sent me some notes, and we spoke this morning. She tasked us to find the money trail of the slimy, slippery bandit Mateo. JJ crossed paths with him before realizing who he was in Texas. Gracie saw him on her cruise. She suspects he is responsible for human trafficking from and to multiple countries. The web of people involved is unknown, but she thinks if we find the money, the snake itself, and any right-hand leaders, we can significantly slow them down, if not paralyze their operation.

"Auri and Satya, move your virtual workstations together; I'd like you to hunt in tandem. We know Mateo receives funds for his services from multiple sources, but where are those funds going? These days, they have to have a digital trail somewhere. The files from the cruise hinted that bitcoins or some cryptocurrency may have a role.

"How are our new virtual glasses and hearing units working for you? We were asked to evaluate them against the big, clunky headsets we used to wear. If the new generation of devices is inadequate, then we revert."

Satya said, "JW, mine are comfortably seeing details, and the sound is crystal clear. The rendering of the VR screen, keyboard, and visuals is outstanding. I feel like I'm sitting in Zurich."

Auri added a thumbs-up gesture.

"Good. See what you can do and maintain your records. I want to ensure we can operate round the clock but still get our rest."

JW turned, finding Granger nearly in his face virtually. He sucked in a breath. "Granger, I've told you not to do that."

"But I love seeing your reaction," Granger laughed.

"I know. Let's do digital surveillance to identify one of his computers and gain access. I suspect the inventory is tagged and locations maintained online on at least one of the machines. If we get a specific device, we might get the transfer points for the funds. JJ's team can go to the locations once we identify them."

"I'm glad Mateo believes in computer automation," Granger commented. "I'll take the first target on this list and determine if it is active for his human trafficking operations. You take the second. The first one to access a machine and find something useful gets fifty points. That gives us an attack vector that we know how to exploit. We'd be out of work if he were old school using a black notebook and pen."

"You wish, Granger. We don't have time to track points, but I love shoutouts for success." JW laughed as his fingers flew over the keyboard. JW instructed, "Kids, I'm providing some credit card leads we got from Gracie when Mateo rented a fleet of transport trucks. Granger, your target is the old shell corporations out of the Bahamas that Jeff discovered while snooping for records in the Caribbean. I've got the information on the truck used in that terrible incident in Texas. Good hunting."

CHAPTER 6

Brothers in Arms

Julian played the charming escort to Mateo's two wards, Sophia and Elena. He knew they were handled roughly when recaptured at the Miami airport, which made them quiet and scared. It would take a while to gain their trust. He overheard their small private exchanges; he knew they believed the worst would happen.

Julian watched the pair enter the garden area early for breakfast. Both teenagers were striking with Hispanic features and huge, expresso-colored eyes but no energy in their movements like others their age. He knew from the cameras in their rooms that they brushed each other's long, flowing, dark, wavy hair, plaiting thick braids on each side, then joining the twisted hair at the back of their necks. Julian appreciated rituals such as these. They had briefly tasted freedom in Miami before Mateo's people, posing as phony child protective officials, re-acquired them. Mateo suggested they could work as acquisition specialists rather than on their backs. Julian moved them to his Caribbean compound. Mateo wanted him to groom them to attend school if they could be trusted not to run.

"Buen día, my pretty young ones. I am not going to hurt you or force myself upon you. I need your help for our operation to work smoothly. The pay is quite good, and you can earn your education." He noticed small smiles tugging at the sides of their lips. Julian's ringtone announced a call from his half-brother.

Julian didn't hesitate to accept the call. "Ah, my brother from another mother. How are you today?"

Mateo skipped the greeting acknowledgment. "We got hurt when the big shipment got compromised. All the refugees and the precursor opioid material are lost. Two blockade runners with an 18-wheeler are out of reach, and the cargo is in police custody. I suspect the federales are involved. We retrieved the hard currency last night and will set up a new lab in Texas. We are separating the people from the drugs in the future to insulate ourselves."

Julian's brows arched as he sighed. "Running both operations is tougher without our jailed brother's connections. Is there any chance we can get Phillip out? He can stay here. The idiot, Jonas, he hired can die for all I care."

"Not now," Mateo spat the words. "Too many eyes on him. Since I burned my last one with my arranged escape, I have no insiders. Besides, it's the safest place with his current enemies. Word from the underground is that there's a hefty price on his head for partners he screwed. I'm glad you advised that we cut ties with Phillip. No one knows we're connected." Mateo grunted in disgust. "I hadn't thought of the pig Jonas. His side hustle with my wards makes him my enemy, but I can't get him eliminated right now." His voice softened. "How are my wards? I had plans to fulfill a royalty's request when I acquired them. Any improvement after a few weeks of good meals and nice clothes?"

Julian combed his hair with his fingers, fidgeting in his chair. "They're better but still rattled. Fear radiates from their eyes like deer caught in the headlights. They confide in one another in whispers. They have made no effort to run. I offered them a chance at education for a bit of help plus a nice allowance. It might be enough to gain a bit of trust."

Mateo chuckled. "Great idea. They're smart. Keep trying to capture their trust. On another subject, I wanted to speak to you about money options. You recommended cryptocurrency rather than currency. I want to understand it better. We were lucky to retrieve the cash from the truck, but I need something easier for our transactions. How does it work?"

Switching his cell from one hand to the other, Julian rose and stepped away from the girls after motioning them to eat. Julian loved this topic and possessed a deep understanding. "All the business movers and shakers are building their operations using crypto because it's instantaneous. I've researched the technology and various markets we might use. I like the distributed ledger. Transactions get written into the underlying blockchain technology and then echoed to all the hosting servers for a distributed, permanent record. Nothing goes through normal banking channels, which means no regulators or taxes. That's the good news."

Mateo clucked his tongue. "Yes. You understand it, and I trust you. What's the downside?"

Julian smiled broadly. "Everyone can see the transactions." He laughed. "It's like advertising on the Internet, saying check out this digital wallet for money laundering."

Mateo growled. "Then, what's the solution? I thought this was our best direction from what you told me."

"Yes, and I still believe in it. I can create a carefully orchestrated digital dance that moves our funds from one exchange to another. We move it through multiple cryptos, breaking the funds into smaller and smaller amounts, then re-aggregating them into a series of cold wallets we control. We defuse and obfuscate our funds through several doorways to a destination that looks nothing like the initial transaction."

Mateo growled again. "Argh, this sounds like weeks of money laundering finesse just to get us…"

Julian tersely interrupted, "No. The exchanges I'm using operate every day round the clock. We accomplish a single multi-tiered laundering effort in minutes. It takes longer to explain the process. In the digital world, things happen in nanoseconds."

"How can you keep track of all those transactions? It sounds complicated, unlike a pencil and notepad."

"Relax, my brother. All the transactions are available to our accounts at the different exchanges. You and I would have the logins and passwords. I have a sophisticated application to track and record transactions as they occur. I will show you how you can see how much we have any time you want. In my tinkering with these cryptocurrencies on the exchanges, I've even learned how to make money moving from one crypto to the next, free money like interest."

"What about my customers who only use cash?" demanded Mateo.

Julian nodded and brightened as he warmed to the subject. "We go to a digital ATM like I have here. I can locate some near you. You enter the payments or withdrawals in U.S. dollars into a digital wallet. It works like a regular bank. We use both depending on the buyer or sellers' preferences." Julian took a breath. "I know what you're thinking, but there's nothing for you to have to learn. I handle all the income and the payouts with full reporting of the accounting each month. It is a routine in my business. I'll need some new computer gear to keep track of our financial operations if you want this and a week or so to establish a secure environment. I may hire some IT helpers to get it all set up.

Once that's done, those geeks can be eliminated from the payroll. Keep everything operating for now. When I have it ready, we'll turn right into this new financial model. I believe it's in our best interest."

"I'm willing to try this, Julian. I trust you. I will request the details until I understand the processes. Talk soon."

CHAPTER 7

Illuminate the Highlights

JJ finished his workout early and returned upstairs to prepare for the day. He came out of the shower with a towel tucked around his waist and kissed his wife. "I hope you have some fun with the new places you're going for pictures. The camera will love you."

"Honey," Jo said with a grin, "I need to finish packing. Would you mind cooking breakfast? I'll be down shortly."

"I can unless you want me to call and delay your flight."

Jo laughed. "Aunt Lara would be so angry if I showed up late on the set."

"I know, but I'll still miss you, sweetheart."

"I'll miss you too. When are you heading back to Luxembourg?"

"I think tomorrow, but it depends upon the leads. I'll let you know."

JJ dressed and hurried to the kitchen. They both loved fresh fruit and kept plenty on hand. He cut up a wide variety, using the remaining bananas and berries for picture-perfect fruit bowls. Jo maintained caloric count in line with her exercise. He checked her step count and created magic with two poached eggs, sautéed mushrooms, and slices of tomatoes interwoven with fresh avocados. Her plate looked so enticing that he replicated it with double the quantities. She slid into her chair as he added his plate to the table.

"Honey, this looks amazing. I love how you can track my allocations yet create meal perfection."

"I like having fun with fresh foods."

Jo raised her glass of freshly squeezed orange juice. "To us. I love how you spoil me."

He chuckled. "Oh, yeah. Did you wrestle your bag downstairs, or do I need to retrieve it for you?"

"Nope, I got it by the door."

He filled their coffee cups. "I'll let you know the travel plans, but you let me know when you arrive in Greece. Stay close to Uncle Carlos; you know how he worries."

"I also know you check with him daily to ensure I am safe. I have no plans to make you worry." She dabbed her napkin to her lips to remove any residue of breakfast. "Delicious. Thank you."

JJ stood and extended his hand to Jo. "Let's walk in our garden before your ride arrives."

Jo rose, and his arm wrapped around her waist. They walked the path that meandered through the abundant blooms boasting all the rainbow colors. He paused at the bridge in the middle that crossed the stream of the babbling brook water feature, ending in a small waterfall that looped around the area. The lush green and fragrant flowers attracted geckos, hummingbirds, and butterflies.

Jo's watch sounded, indicating her ride would arrive shortly. Without a word, she reached around his waist and pulled him close to stare into his eyes. "Honey, I know you're trying to nail Mateo. Please be careful."

"I will," he promised after a sweet kiss filled with promises. "I'll call you and text often." He guided them back inside and retrieved her suitcase. They walked to the car as it arrived. He added one last kiss before assisting her into the back.

He whistled as he moved toward his office, his step a little lighter. The equipment lit up with a few touches to the keyboard. Three screens displayed the notices he pinned for his morning briefing. A prompt for an incoming call flashed on the middle screen. "Good morning, Brayson. Where are we?"

"JJ, the team's seeing a rising trend in disappearing young teenage girls. Frantic parents are posting rewards for information via social media. They're begging for leads. Some smaller local news channels are interviewing people walking the streets pleading for help. What's curious is the increase in ads seeking male and female models for cosmetics and clothing manufacturers. The logos almost match the well-known brands. Leading manufacturers shut down a few ads their marketing teams spotted that they weren't running. The ads circulate on social media for less than a couple of weeks. Xiamara found two and reached out with a hundred phony names and pictures, resulting in a couple of positive responses. The messaging included confidentiality statements and new contact information for her phony person's exclusive use."

"She loves creating those deep fakes," chuckled JJ. "Did her location have anything to do with the next step?"

"Yep. Arizona and New Mexico were picked up. She excluded Florida, Texas, and Louisiana on this round at my insistence."

"Is there a correlation between the timing of the ads and the disappearances?"

"To a degree. New York, Virginia, and Georgia show increases in vanishing youth; some are classified. We don't have a reliable search profile. There isn't a place on the planet where kids with nice looks and well-sculpted bodies can't find an opportunity.

Most are not legit, nor do they lead to fame like your Jo's without connections. We both know those are few and far between."

JJ tapped his fingers, mentally searching for options. "How does our data relate to the activities of Gracie's team?"

"Our prowling correlates to theirs, but we can't tie in the money trails yet. The hotbeds are in the Caribbean region and spikes in Puerto Rico. Ordinarily, it wouldn't get noticed, but Pliant's henchmen used several digital wallets before his takedown. Now they're active again. However, the transactions are small. We are seeing multiple new wallets opened across different cryptocurrencies inside that region. The IP addresses are going through hundreds of IP address filters, but JW and Granger are getting closer to the origination points. Couple that with new digital wallets being brought online at the same location, suggesting a possible new setup by a bad actor."

JJ shook his head, rolling his eyes. "Could it be that Pliant's old business unit is returning online? I wonder what their level of technical knowledge is. That sort of business is not for a casual consumer, especially with the crypto aspects, if that's a factor. Let's get Judith and Xiamara to contact their Puerto Rico college buddies and see if anyone's changing jobs or seeking consulting support."

"Marian has former services buddies who retired to that region. Do you want her to reach out as well? Marian tends to be less trouble than those two."

JJ sighed. "Sure, let's gather as much intel as possible. No one goes anywhere until we get the ducks lined up. That pair of geeks seem to find trouble, but their native relationships may extend further."

Brayson appeared apprehensive. "Agreed. They'll look more like locals than tourists. Remote intel for now works."

"Yep, Puerto Rico is their old stomping ground. If we determine in-country resource is needed, I'd vote for them first." He grinned at Brayson on the screen. "Then we have you and Marian as a rescue resource, as needed. I'd place your trained ex-special-ops wife beside your equally qualified background anywhere for an extraction. I'm still hoping the beacons on the sandals will pop at some point."

"That would be useful. I'll have Marian reach out discreetly. We might get some noise back."

"Good. I'll fly to Luxembourg tomorrow and stay at my folk's house. Jo left this morning on an extended fashion shoot. I'll ask my aunt and uncle to stay with her until she returns. Keep Judith and Xiamara on track to find more target areas for teen abductions and potential seduction. Sadly, they seem to have insight for people who are perverted shoppers. I'll join you in your office the day after tomorrow; I want us to draw all the elements and do a strategy session."

"Sounds good, JJ. Let me know if you need me to pick you up. As good as our virtual connectivity is, the complexity of this could use a face-to-face so we can play devil's advocate and maybe avoid some."

"Exactly." JJ disconnected and sent a text letting Jo know his plans.

CHAPTER 8

Assignment Updates

Brayson placed a call to the remote team. The call went to voicemail. "Give me a call, please. I've assignment updates."

Before three minutes had elapsed, his video screen rang. "How's it going? You seem to be getting results with your efforts. Are you staying nearly squeaky clean?"

They upgraded their call to video and frowned into the screen. "What do you mean *almost squeaky-clean*?" Judith shook her blonde mane as she scowled. "I'll have you know we stick to the straight and narrow since that last time. We like our life and working with your team, though we miss talking to JJ. Zee gets so sad when she can't talk to him."

Xiamara's brown curls bounced as if she were on a mini trampoline as she play-punched Judith's arm. "Do not."

Brayson added with a tone of sadness as he moved his eyes from face to face. "For the record, he was disappointed when he found you were trying to set up another gaming site on the side. You promised to stay straight if he let you keep your jobs. I hope we can trust you."

With a somber expression, Judith crossed her heart and added, "We learned. We're brilliant, but your team is a lot faster."

"Brayson, we're behaving," Xiamara joined in. "Did you like the pics I sent out? I'm still waiting for more hookups and responses. Judith thinks we'll get some numbers to call to set up location meets. We can trace the area with target landmarks and tap into area traffic cameras for remote surveillance."

"Perhaps you can get enough photos so we can isolate specific persons of interest."

Judith nodded. "These ads target the under-eighteen crowd, and they are gender neutral. We have a meeting later tonight, albeit remote. I verified my access to several area cameras. We might get lucky. The signal is we wear red ball caps turned backward to identify each other."

"Good job. Capture as many images as possible." Brayson admired the young ladies. They were intelligent and attractive, though Judith was a little thinner and curvier than Xiamara. They worked well together, but they always had an angle.

Xiamara grinned and twisted a curl behind her ear. "We will. We want to put a major dent in this business. We are willing to go on-site too if needed."

"Do you still have contacts from your time in San Juan at the university?"

Judith squinched up her nose. "Yes. Is there a problem?"

"Not at all. JJ wondered if your contacts would know if anyone was trying to hire tech support. He thought they might hit up the school."

Xiamara stroked her chin with one hand. "We can ask. I also have a site I haven't visited online since we started working for you."

Judith nodded. "That's right. It had all sorts of job opportunities all over the Caribbean. Is that what you mean?"

"Great. Keep an eye out. It could mean a trip if things line up. However, what you're doing right now is key to mapping the operation."

CHAPTER 9

Where to Look?

Gracie let the call roll to voicemail so she wouldn't have to interrupt her meeting at the World Bank headquarters. She called him back after the live and video attendees had left.

Gracie confessed, "Sorry, JW. I was in a meeting and couldn't take your call. How is the team's progress?"

"It's moving along, though slower than we want. Gracie, I needed to cut back on Auri and Satya's hours. They are still growing and need their rest. They established some perfect programs that ICABOD is monitoring. If anything pops, I can bring one of them back online."

"Good idea. I don't want them to neglect their normal studies." She tilted her chin with a slight shake of her head. "They're amazing. Much more dedicated than when I was their age."

"Their programming skills are excellent. Even ICABOD commented with their latest."

She noticed the brightness of deep blue eyes when he turned his head. "Hey, are you on our video call with the Gigazon? The colors are so vivid."

"Yes. I hope that's okay. Once you're in it, the sensation is like being in a vast work area."

Gracie nodded and raised an eyebrow. "Very cool. How far have you and Granger gotten?"

"We tracked those credit card purchases, but the leads dried up. The cards were stolen and deactivated. We tracked the cards to a Darknet website that sells stolen cards and PINs for twenty dollars a piece with a minimum purchase of a thousand cards. The folks you want intel on weren't using their cards to rent the semi. I can't trace the entire route of the travel from the border. I'm unsure where to take it from here." JW pushed his bangs back with his hand.

"Darn! So, we got nothing?" She wrinkled her nose, frustrated.

"We spotted some cryptocurrency activity on one of the companion cards. Granger's working with ICABOD to locate the crypto wallet he suspects is in the Caribbean. Jeff's research on your trip helped us uncover some data points."

Gracie smiled. "Good news. Jeff will be pleased."

"How is he doing? I like him and think he's a good fit for you. JJ put us in contact with him so Granger and I can clarify some stuff."

"He's still doing some physical therapy from his injury but is improving. We haven't seen each other much lately."

"He is a good professional and easy to work with. Granger thinks so, too. I remembered meeting him last Christmas here in Zurich when you brought him to meet the family. I assumed you were still close. I was slightly surprised when JJ introduced him as a new team member."

"And, Granger, what did he say?"

JW sighed. "You know how Granger works. He's too interested in data intercepts and programming logic to try something new. He likes working with Jeff and gets great answers to his questions. But he's ready to reconnect with ICABOD whenever possible. If I don't say something, he'll work long hours and forget to eat." JW's attention was drawn away from the video. "Uh-oh, Granger is heading this way. He appears anxious."

Granger stepped into the video call. "Greetings, Gracie. Guys, I received a curious lead out of the Caribbean to those new crypto wallets Jeff led us to. I've been watching them. The ones using Monero, I can't read the blockchain transactions, but one of them came in with Bitcoin, which I can read. Transaction activity hits several wallets simultaneously and may be linked to a similar destination. Crypto flowed in, then vanished like a bunch of birds when someone shoots off a firecracker. The one I can read shows going to a pharmaceutical manufacturer in Hangzhou, China."

JW nodded and advised, "We need to dig into this information, Gracie. Not sure why a shady character in the Caribbean would be sending large amounts of crypto to a city in China."

Gracie jumped as ICABOD's voice interjected. "I'm investigating that angle. This region has a high correlation between untraceable cryptocurrency and large pharmaceutical manufacturers. They have developed a *side hustle* selling precursor fentanyl chemicals to semi-legitimate businesses in this hemisphere."

JW mused. "If that's true, then reliable bulk transport is the next logistical hurdle."

"Correct, JW." ICABOD agreed. "I am now shifting through the shipping manifests of the Pliant corporation's ships to see their destinations and cargo."

Granger stated with a thoughtful expression, "I thought we were after this clown's human trafficking business and where the money went. But I'm hearing money is going to China for precursor fentanyl chemicals. Are we dogging the wrong group, or is this a second line of business for them?"

Gracie felt concern growing in the pit of her stomach. "Keep digging, gentlemen. There are several layers to this onion. To your point, Granger, this organization could have more than one line of business. It wouldn't surprise me in the least. Mateo's deranged. I'll tell JJ what we have so far. Nice work. You too, ICABOD."

CHAPTER 10

Hunting the Transport

Jeff appeared well-groomed in his button down collar and striped tie. His green eyes flashed with the lights from the screen. He entered into the Gigazon with an air of confidence. "Sorry, JW. This call is late, but I wanted to review the findings while they're fresh. Granger, did you say you would plug away for a few more hours."

Granger nodded. "Yes."

Failing to suppress a sudden yawn, JW shook his head and wiped his face with his hand. "It's all good, Jeff. I wish I had the stamina of my dad and Dr. Quip. Mom said those two worked non-stop for almost two days straight to break the rampant Ghost Code. I do it, but I am loopy until I've had," he patted his mouth, "six hours of sleep in twenty-four."

Granger protested, "Bro, if you need to crash, go. I'm not going to work much longer myself. Once I point the computer system at this problem, I'm headed to supper. Mama will drag me by the ear if I'm hacking the stack too long."

Jeff chuckled and picked up his pace. "Guys, I've highlighted the list of the dummy corporations and Pliant's shipping assets. Or were. After Pliant's takedown, the ships were sold and donated in a few instances. Start with those transactions to see where the money went. Maybe we can figure out why some hasty sales got top dollar. Usually, when you're in a hurry to sell, the buyer gets a bargain. That was not the case across the board. Most peculiar."

Over the video, Jeff and Granger saw JW's eyes close as his head drifted toward the camera.

Granger raised his voice. "Hey, I've got this, JW. I'll launch the program, and we'll talk tomorrow. Punch out, buddy."

The loud command jarred JW enough for him to bid a good night and disconnect.

Granger smirked. "Some young'uns need an afternoon nap or fold up like a worn-out fan. I've got this, Jeff, if you need to drop too."

Jeff laughed. "Thanks, Granger. It's a few hours earlier here in New York than in Europe. I'll also point out you're a few years younger than JW."

Granger smirked. "True, but I had my afternoon nap."

"Let me finish reviewing the rest of the property. We can key up the recording for JW to review when he returns online."

Granger read the next section of Jeff's report. "Man, you do some thorough research. I will set up the routines to scan for all these terms. Nice."

"Thank you. Call me if you have any questions," added Jeff.

CHAPTER 11

Help Me Trust You

Julian ensured the breakfast table had food dishes to tempt his wards' appetites. He felt he had a good chance to gain their confidence and move forward. The seasonal fruit juices were within easy reach in the middle. The cook delivered the last food of assorted meats as Sophia and Elena timidly entered the dining area with their eyes pointed toward the floor.

"Ladies," Julian announced and swept an arm over the food presentation, "sit and enjoy the cook's culinary delights. I want to talk with you as we eat."

Cautiously, they eyed each other, then the sumptuous-looking meal. They edged closer to the table with hesitant steps. Julian spotted the caution on their faces and suppressed a smirk when their stomachs growled.

He smiled. "Come, come, come, we need to talk. You won't hear what I'm saying if you don't feed those tummies." Julian plopped into a chair and began spooning multiple items onto his plate, which drove the aromatic scents into the air. Like two starving animals who couldn't resist their basic needs, they sat and quickly scooped various tidbits onto their plates.

Amused by the scene, Julian swallowed. "No one will take away your food. So please, use the eating utensils like ladies. The teens at school won't sit next to you during lunch for fear of being bitten while you eat."

Both girls froze their ravenous attack on the food. Their eyes grew wide as they stared at him with disbelieving expressions.

Julian schooled his features to appear benevolent. "I've arranged for you to attend school to continue your education. There is a good school here in St. Kitts. I've decided it will benefit you both to learn with students your age. Would you l ike that?"

Julian got their attention, and they looked stunned by the possibility. Then he saw tears forming in their eyes as they rapidly chattered in Spanish about the fun of making friends and learning. Their excitement grew, making their shoulders appear less slumped, and the corners of their mouths lifted like a burden had been removed. He watched them eat and talk enthusiastically until their plates emptied.

After letting the new opportunity sink in for a few minutes, he continued like a patient father figure, "However, there are a few conditions for this new privilege, and I need your agreement before I proceed."

Sophia and Elena quickly exchanged glances of alarm before returning their gaze to him.

Julian shook his head slightly and then dabbed at his mouth with his napkin. "Oh, do come along. Nothing in life is free. First and foremost, I must have your word that you won't run away. I'm allowing you to learn, and I must believe your promise. I'm trying to do the right thing, and I want you to trust me. Are we in agreement?"

Their guarded expressions eased as they nodded and verbally promised.

"Thank you. I believe you." He smiled. "The next condition is that you tell no one of your past, not even a best friend you find at school. If you discuss your past or anything about me, questions and inquiries will ruin everything for us. Do you understand?"

Again, they nodded and agreed.

Pleased with their attitudes and feeling they trusted him, he announced, "We're scheduled to get school uniforms early this afternoon. Tidy your rooms and complete your grooming to go out. Meet me by the front door at one this afternoon so we can be on time for your fittings. After that, we'll visit the school to speak with the administrator. Remember what you've promised, and everything will be wonderful. Now hurry."

The girls set their silverware on their plates and placed napkins on the side before pushing back their chairs to leave. He heard their giggles and conversation as they returned to their room.

Hearing the door to their room close, Julian called his brother, who answered after a single ring. "Mateo, I was right. Tempt them with food and a chance to learn. Soon, I'll have them eating out of my hand."

"Are you sure they can be alone at school?"

"Yes. Not only did they promise, but the phones I am giving them will track them, and I can randomly listen to their conversations. They ate and laughed; it was music to my ears."

"We'll try it, but you must monitor the conversations closely for a few days. I need at least four but prefer six weeks before we cycle them to another island."

"Yes. As I told you, the school operates on all the islands in the region to accommodate working parents. I can take them to other locations and cycle them. We'll be protected, and they'll have no idea what they're doing."

"All right. Send me names and phones when you're ready. I'll get a team to grab them. Thank you, my brother. Keep them safe."

CHAPTER 12

Houston, We Have a Problem

Alvaro smoothed the young girl's hair as he softly offered, "Remember when we found you? You'd been running from that abusive parent of yours for two days. Take a look around. Many young girls here want to work for a place to sleep and to get cleaned up. This place has food for you. They're nice people."

Pulling her hair harder while he caressed her neck. "You need to do this for me so you don't have to return to that drunk woman beating you."

Fearful tears ran down the well-sculpted fifteen-year-old Hispanic girl's face. "Don't make me go to the hotel. I'm only supposed to clean, but a man ordered me to get naked. I'm so scared I can't do anything. He gets mad and tears my clothes off. The last one used his belt on me, and I'm still bruised. They won't pay me if they see welts, then you'll be angry again. Please don't make me go tonight. Send someone else."

Alvaro pulled hard enough on her hair to wrench her head back. She begged, "You're hurting me." Sucking a breath in, she whispered, "Stop. I'll do it."

Alvaro released the pull on her hair and gently wiped the tears. The other girls watched with terror reflected in their eyes. "It's much easier on you to do what you're told, chicas. Pick three more of your friends to go along with you. I was told it was movie time, and some cooperative girls were needed for some scenes. Remember, no tears, only smiles, and follow the filmmaker's directions. You are to be friendly but only talk to the people we tell you to."

Smiling at the teenagers, Alvaro innocently asked, "Who wants some candy? It'll be a long evening. A little pick-me-up will help get you through the workload at the hotel. Everything will seem like fun with these." He held out is hand with colored pills.

The nominated girls snatched two capsules and swallowed them in a practiced mode with no water.

He added, "Take a baggie each for the customer as a thank-you gift for their business. It's good manners, chicas. Tell them a week's supply is seven hundred dollars if they want more. Here in Houston, we deliver on the same day."

When the girls departed, Alvaro placed a call. "Boss, I can keep fifty of these putas busy weekly with our Houston contracts. We need to cycle more into this region."

"Then get on it."

CHAPTER 13

Buyers and Making Change

Gigazon immersed the attendees into the three-dimensional virtual reality space. When the streamed information ended, Granger and JW stared at one another in stunned silence. The day's research presented by ICABOD on the Pliant Industry's shipping activity left them feeling introspective.

JW slapped his forehead in disbelief and stated the only reasonable conclusion. "Those hastily sold Pliant ships got sold to new shell corporations and were used to haul pharmacy manufacturers outputting precursor chemicals required to build fentanyl. The materials are onboarded into cargo holds from several Chinese ports and then drop-shipped to western Mexican harbors along the coastline. Mateo's group is responsible for bringing precursor fentanyl on leased ships into Pacific ports like Manzanillo. What the hell is his connection to Pliant?"

Granger nodded while increasing the image of the last drop point. "ICABOD, the trail can't end at a seaport. Any thoughts on where the raw materials go? Is it being sold to other cartels for processing before it gets trucked to the Texas border for sale? Or have we identified labs they might be using? What a mess."

ICABOD answered, "Evidence suggests they are wholesaling some portion of the shipment to other cartels but holding some back to process through their labs. A plan like that could be perceived as a conflict of interest if the cartels discover that their wholesaler is also a competitor. I would say that the group who knows the answer to your great question is small and close to the top. I will keep searching for possible locations and identify as many labs as possible for you to share with authorities."

Granger rolled his eyes. "We know cartels traditionally have no sense of humor regarding unapproved competition. Should we start looking for new faces to show up on posters tacked onto telephone poles asking *Have you seen this missing person?* I heard people with gold-crowned teeth get found with a metal detector faster than with dogs."

JW rubbed his forehead and shook his head. "Thanks for that updated forensic technique, Grange. ICABOD, things got murky at the Manzanillo location. I realize cartel members don't file taxation reports, but did you get any hits on payoffs for looking the other way in the dock footage? It might be helpful to identify who's getting a cut of the shipment."

"While it's true that standard government forms are not submitted, cartels balance their product inventory to gauge their profits. The Chinese have also helped our cause by adding QR codes to the pallets and individual boxes for accounting purposes. There is no evidence to suggest that the buyers are storing their inventory numbers with a Cloud provider. They also can't use handheld cell phones to scan everything and transmit with Near-field communication. The method is too clumsy and inefficient.

"I took the liberty of hunting for automated barcode readers of industrial capacity and checked to see if any units were deployed in this area. The region is a rich target market, and high-volume reader units go to the highest bidder."

JW frowned and pulled the data. "The numbers validate that this technology is pouring into the region. We can't identify who's legit or not, can we?"

Granger laughed aloud. "Dude, of course, we'd know. How do these morons do business? They don't use government-insured checking accounts or credit cards. They must use cash or crypto, so it can't be easily traced."

"Granger's correct," ICABOD clarified. "We eliminate them following the usual business rules and concentrate on operatives handling a briefcase full of currency or…"

Granger crowed, "Or fist-bumping after transferring some Bitcoin or Monaro from one crypto-wallet to another. We spot those transactions—voilà! We've identified bad actor suspects."

ICABOD continued, "We already know the ships with the illegal cargo, so we can focus on people taking delivery of the pre-coded boxes using cash or crypto, ignoring the rest."

JW smiled. "I'll get Auri and Satya looking at cryptocurrency transactions time-stamped close to the arrival times. We can work backward to identify the owner if they snag transaction wallet IDs.

"Let's keep these searches going, ICABOD," JW recommended.

Granger exaggerated a high-five without the sound.

CHAPTER 14

From Ship to Shore to Money

Javier leaned against the weather-worn wall of the primary cargo building. The shady spot provided a panoramic view of Manzanillo's non-stop cargo loading and unloading. Ships waited in deeper waters to keep ship congestion at a minimum. He knew each captain was eager to dock at an unloading pier to disgorge the contents from the vessel's underbelly and collect promised bonuses. The longshoremen scurried off the gangways, like ants converging on a sugar donut fallen to the ground. Master sailors plucked juicy assignments that included cash incentives when paperwork got completed flawlessly for specific imported containers. Mistakes, such as dropping priority containers over-board, resulted in immediate seniority shifts due to unexpected vacancies.

Javier re-tied his ponytail and checked his smartwatch. Javier's anxiety became exaggerated when the time for receipt of cargo neared. Parceling the contents to the approved receivers was executed like a Broadway hit performance. At the same time, as director, he kept a practiced eye out for authorities, not on Mateo's payroll.

Javier felt the sweat beading on his forehead and riveting down the side of his tanned face. "I hate waiting for my vessel to dock so my team can unload. This waiting crap drives me crazy," he mumbled.

Shuffling feet startled him as the armed guards of his buyers closed in on either side. No words were exchanged, but each measured the merit of the other with practiced eyes and then shifted their attention to the inbound ship.

Javier sensed sweat rolling down his back, grateful it remained invisible to these killers. He recognized a familiar panic attack symptom as his fingers tapped against his leg moments before his phone vibrated with a call. Recognizing the caller's identification, he stepped away for a private conversation. Catching his breath and inhaling to calm his pounding heart, he answered, "Mateo, I'm at the port. The ship hasn't docked, but our contacts are here. What's up?"

Mateo barked, "What the hell are they doing there already? We need time to unload all our products without unnecessary eyes on our business. Get rid of them."

Javier shifted from one foot to the other without glancing over his shoulder. "Boss, any ideas on how I can do that? These are not patient or polite people."

Javier recognized the annoying sound of Mateo grinding his teeth. "They must have gotten the timetable from the port authority."

Mateo exhaled. "Tell them to return after you've completed the cargo inventory in the early evening when the crowds have thinned. They'll get a ten percent discount on their purchases and first pick to fill their order. Tell them you'll shoot the litter if they disagree, and they'll get nothing. Leave our precursor in the crates with one of your men guarding my products. They do not need to know the content if they can't see it. The discount will make them heroes with Flores, and I will deal with that cockroach. Tell his men that I want the premium in cryptocurrency or no deal. It'll take time for them to get the approval. Call me after you secure my product, and you will get the details to complete the transaction."

"Yes, Boss."

Mateo pounded his fist against the desk, straightened his shoulders, and grinned like a Cheshire Cat. Picking up his phone, he thumbed through his contacts and stopped at Julian—the call connected. "Remember when you said we needed to work in crypto to move money faster? Flores's deal became our first proof of concept. I'll conference you in once Javier calls me back in about six hours. You can explain the steps to complete the transaction. I'll listen, so the next time, it will be smoother."

"Why don't you just have Javier call me?" Julian tried to reason. "That way, you don't have to be burdened."

"I will not be left out of the loop," countered Mateo as he stood, forcing his chair to crash against the wall. "I created this operation, and I know every step, brother. Don't ever expect that to change."

"Of course. But this transaction will be bumpy as things are not set up for volume. With your agreement, I will accelerate the timeline to build out our data center to handle the multiple transactions you expect with both lines of business. I'll make it work. Call me when you are ready for this transaction, but the steps will vary until everything is established."

Mateo nodded and pulled his chair close, then sat. "I'm glad you appreciate my position, my brother."

CHAPTER 15

Feeds and Speeds

Julian glanced at his watch and figured he had approximately four hours until the Mateo and Javier transfer call. He wanted to verify what he suspected before making the final decision and telling his brother. Julian looked at his friend of twenty years. With white hair and a grey pallor to his wrinkled face, he appeared far older than his forty years. He remained cordial while listening to every word.

The island's data center director shared his insights. "The Prime Minister is committed to upgrading the island's data center infrastructure to become a magnet for new businesses. Our weather and location are prime targets for employees wishing to escape the big cities, especially from America. Our first project was the Government Information and Communication Technology Center at C. A. Paul Southwell Industrial Park in the capital, Basseterre. It's been upgraded twice." The man rubbed his hands together and grinned. "But the second project, planned and approved to begin shortly, will dwarf it."

Julian masked his disappointment about possibly changing the girls' school so soon. "Is the Embassy of Taiwan going to fund the new project, too? Also, what are the plans for Internet access speeds of the island's broadband infrastructure? I'm considering expanding business operations. Yet, I read your network's average download speed is approximately forty-four megabits per second, and the upload rate is just over fifteen megabits per second. That places this infrastructure ninety-fifth internationally. I need greater data speeds to locate my business here on the sister islands of Saint Kitts and Nevis."

The director shook his head and raised one eyebrow, looking at Julian. "I see you've done your homework; I've been agitating for gigabit speeds to satisfy a large data center's telecommunication demands. Leadership is maintaining the classic chicken or egg argument. I need more bandwidth to meet customer demands but can't fund the expansions without more clients. A gaming company stopped by yesterday to discuss moving their data center here. They ran for their cars when I said we only had a tenth of the bandwidth needed for Internet gaming competitions."

Julian patted his old friend's arm with a wry smile. "Now, now. You'll find the right combination and get past this bump in the road. Don't be so negative about your modest operation. In the U.S., they are rolling out ten and even forty-gigabit pipes, driving down the prices of gigabit ethernet. It's only a matter of time before the undersea bandwidth you need will be here to feed these hungry data centers. Unfortunately, my business can't wait for those upgrades."

The director banged his fist on the desk, and his face turned red as his lips curled. "That's what I keep hearing from potential customers. I'm going to lose another customer to San Juan. Puerto Rico has an unfair advantage. By default, they have gigabit speeds to support their growing data center business."

Julian, weary of the discussion, checked his smartphone. "I must disengage here and head to my next appointment. I will help you start a fund for a private network provider; the competition might help you gain better traction. We'll talk again soon, old friend."

Outside, with the afternoon sun brightening the colors of the flowers and trimmed walkway, Julian sighed in relief. "I should have stopped the conversation when he said the data center was state-owned. But I couldn't explain I wanted my server farm for illegal trafficking and money laundering in the only island data center that was government owned. Mateo would skin me alive." He pulled a thin cigarette from the package concealed in the inside pocket of his jacket. He lit it with a narrow gold lighter and drew in a breath. Blowing a smoke ring, he considered his options and continued his conversation with himself. "Nothing is ever easy. I need to go shopping for a data center in San Juan. It will be easier to source the needed server equipment and meet my bandwidth requirements. I'll watch them for a couple of weeks and plan my travel. Most of the research I can do from here. We'll make some inroads with young people before moving to Puerto Rico. At least I already have a home there. There's a week-long break coming up, and I'll take them along as a treat for good behavior."

Then, his mind concocted an angle to gain Sophia and Elena's cooperation. With a cruel glint in his eye, Julian softly plotted, "We'll simply bring some of their new friends with us."

CHAPTER 16

Short and Sweet

New York's skyline was visible from the conference room windows. The mahogany table nearly glistened from the bright morning sun, surrounded by comfortable brown leather chairs filled by her talented team. The meeting was half finished with the current topic of interest rates in discussion. Gracie slyly smiled as the familiar image appeared on her phone. Her heart did a backflip as she mentally heard the romantic tune of the muted ringer. Looking up at the group around the table, she said, "I need to take this call." She thumbed the accept slide for the caller. "Please continue the discussions. I'll have Sheniqua catch me up later."

Sheniqua grinned and straightened at being tagged. It wasn't uncommon for Gracie to delegate and level up her team members. The confidence-building tactic was reflected in the team's work. She rose and headed toward the door; hearing Sheniqua guide the conversation to the next topic.

She closed her office door and said, "This is Gracie Rodreguiz; how can I help you?"

"I called soliciting for attitude adjustments and thought you might be interested. Sorry to take you out of your meeting. I could have called you back. I hoped this early I'd catch you between meetings and get your mind off work for a few minutes." Gracie could hear Jeff's smile in his voice.

She slid into her office chair and kicked off her shoes, kneading her toes into the thick carpet. "The meeting was progressing satisfactorily, and I wanted to hear your voice. Frankly, you are a perfect morning respite. Tell me more about your thoughts on attitude adjustment. Is this something I can add to my calendar for tonight? I'll bring the fixings if you cook your wonderful veal parmesan over pasta."

"With my role on JJ's team, can I still call when the urge strikes? I'd love to cook. I have a delightful Pinot Noir we can share. Maybe a luscious dessert, but only if you promise to respect me in the morning before you head to work."

She grinned, her thoughts shifting to leaving in time to pick up some clothes before heading to his place. "Ah, I detect a possible offer of another sleepover, which I'll accept. I'll see you around seven. Have the nice music on, please."

"Nice music?" he laughed. "You said you didn't like the blare of the kazoos or the crashing sounds of my cymbals made of garbage can lids, but sure."

Gracie tapped her fingers on her desk and shook her head, closing her eyes for a breath. "Wow, honey, thanks. With that offer, I'll see you at six. Bye for now."

Later in the early evening at Jeff's New York apartment, he sensed Gracie was distracted as she stared off into space as she gently swirled the wine in her glass.

She softly exclaimed, "Nice meal, Jeff. Thank you."

He frowned. "As my friends in Texas would say, why don't you just put the moose on the table? Please tell me what's playing over and over in your brilliant mind. You're here but thinking of something else."

Gracie struggled to shake off the mental grip that had her thoughts trapped and complained, "I'm sorry, sweetheart. This awful case of Mateo and his human trafficking has grown legs. We thought Pliant was a bad actor, but Mateo is a train wreck. JJ saw him last year when he and Jo decompressed in Magnolia Bluff, Texas. JJ helped break up his human trafficking holding area in that region, but the slimy scum got away. We had a run-in with him on our cruise. He's still trafficking, but he's added fentanyl as a side business. I want to take him down and end his miserable business. At this juncture, he's like a hydra, cut off one avenue, and another grows in its place."

She looked into his eyes. "On our cruise, you saw firsthand how they treat humans as commodities. Thank you for helping. It means a lot to me."

Jeff groaned and reached for her hand, caressing it with his thumb. "I know it bothers you that the girls are still missing. Me too. Watching the buying and selling of humans makes it personal for me, too. If you're worried that I can't handle this operation, don't be. I admit it's selfish of me to work with your brother's team to get closer to you. I hope the combined efforts save those two and others like them. They deserve to grow up without horrible childhoods. Scars like that never quite heal."

She set her wine glass on the table and leaned into him. "I'm glad you're with me and recovered from your horrible beating during our cruise. I'm so proud of how you've decided to help others. I do love and support you, honey." She jumped up with a giggle and reached for his hand. "Come on. Let's listen to the kazoos and trash can lids music while we do the dishes. Then we can take a warm shower before bed."

"Bed? Well, okay, but I get the top bunk this time."

"I didn't bring any jammies, so can I borrow yours? The ones with the feet in them?"

He pulled her into his arms and kissed her quickly. "Isn't it great being us?"

CHAPTER 17

A Change in Plans

Julian held his cell phone in one hand, speaking while pacing the patio length, surrounded by well-manicured white and purple flowers. When he became excited, his speech was often misinterpreted. His English, Spanish, and French words poured into each sentence in a rapid-fire dialogue that confused listeners.

Mateo, no novice to this soliloquy style from his brother, barked, "Stop! Take a breath. I can't understand your problem when you mix French, Spanish, and English."

Julian stopped and pulled out a cigarette. He inhaled deeply after it was lit. He surveyed his surroundings and steadied. "After all my research, we must locate our data center in San Juan. We need the bandwidth I can't get here in St Kitts. I found several data centers we can rent, but I want to see the space to check security and accessibility. We can rent cages to keep our server farm private. San Juan has a point of presence on the Internet from the BRUSA undersea cable runs that connect to the second-largest POP at Virginia Beach. That means we can connect anywhere in the world in milliseconds."

Mateo groused. "I can understand the words, but not the point. You went down the technical rat hole. How does this help our operation? You were looking for data centers in St. Kitts, but now you insist on going to San Juan."

Julian stood stock-still, straightened his shoulders, and took another breath without the cigarette. "St. Kitts has no data infrastructure to host our servers or provide the bandwidth I know we need for the potential volume of buyers. San Juan has what we need to service the cryptocurrency transactions we discussed. I'll need a couple of months and …"

Mateo roared, "Have you forgotten? We've got crypto on its way. You've got about eight minutes before you start the mumbo-jumbo laundering routine you bragged about so it can be used to purchase more products. Also, I thought you enrolled my girls in school to earn their trust. How are they going to react when you tell them you're moving? Those are my wards. Don't screw up, making them run again."

Julian felt his facial features tighten from frustration. "The young ladies will be fine. The school they are enrolled in has a sister location in San Juan to accommodate workers who support the area. As you know, I already have the house, and I alerted the staff to prepare for our arrival." He huffed. "I have enough processing power to handle our modest transactions in the short term. No problem. I want to increase the capability as I believed YOU when you said the business would grow with the drug side. That means repeat business. Sex and drugs are always repeat business. I have in mind racks of servers doing Bitcoin mining and offering laundering services to the other cartels who don't have any technical knowledge. I want to position you to help and control the cartels. If they get their hands dirty with some legal agency, we claim they lied on their application request and move on. We make a percentage laundering our transactions plus their money. I need the data center horsepower I've identified in San Juan."

Julian kept silent but resumed pacing while he heard Mateo's fingers thumping on the desk while processing the information.

"Hmm. If you build the operation you indicated, you will

need additional tech resources. How do you plan to manage that aspect and keep our business secrets? You know I only trust a few people. I don't want any new partners wanting a cut of our action."

Julian chuckled. "I've given that some thought. There are several tech schools in San Juan. I can hire technically competent but naïve technicians for the heavy lifting. I can hire them short-term, then cut them loose before they learn too much. If anyone gets too nosey, you'll get new inventory to sell to those rougher clients you don't like."

"All right. Cannibalize enough of the crypto in flight for your data center. Launder the rest for me. I trust you to cloak all the transactions, brother."

"I'll keep you posted and protected."

Julian nodded approvingly at the larger group of teenagers splashing and laughing in the pool. The afternoon sun brightened the colors with rainbows of light flickering, mixing perfectly with the tiny birds and dragonflies. Sophia looked at him, and he tilted his head with a slight smile, giving her a thumbs up. She turned and grinned at the others. He liked the mixture of boys and girls enjoying his expansive backyard.

Nohea and Ryu, Julian's lieutenants, were preoccupied with Julian's travel arrangements and verifying the San Juan staff was in place with the requested provisions. He walked to the table they worked at while keeping eyes on the teens. "I must leave them here a little longer before we relocate to San Juan. School here is almost over for this semester, so we can move as soon as the break occurs. Gentlemen, I trust you to ensure their safety while I secure my other Puerto Rico transaction."

"Sir," Ryu interjected, "I agree Nohea should remain here. Madam Chloe, your French au pair, keeps an eye out. I can join you to help motivate agreement to your terms."

Julian slapped his trusted support on the back. "Thank you. If I didn't have well-placed officials in the government, I would welcome you. But I need Sophia and Elena carefully observed. I want to arrange to take two or three of these friends to San Juan if their family life is disjointed. Teenagers think they're adults and will help convince their parents. It will require finesse to get them secured. I need you to complete their family background checks. I can make any necessary benefactor arrangements when I return. If they accept, the teens won't return home again."

Appearing hesitant, Julian watched his long-time confidant, Ryu, chew on his lip while he twisted his black mustache.

Ryu finally decided to speak. "Yes, Julian. I will oversee and let you know the likely candidates. I get concerned when I can't ensure your safety."

"And I appreciate that, my friend." He patted him on the back. "Don't forget the girls must believe their friends changed their minds when we leave for San Juan. You can transport them as instructed at that time."

Nohea looked up, showing his five o'clock shadow. "I'll make sure the targets get enticed with moving to San Juan with pictures of the villa and vague, exciting promises. They'll get sedated for transport."

"Any three of these teens should please Mateo. However, I suspect he will tell me to ship them to Alvaro in Houston. Either way, they must be undamaged merchandise to bring top dollar."

"Yes, sir," They commented in unison.

CHAPTER 18

Dead Men Do Tell Tales

Satya wrinkled her nose at the display screen. Auri noticed it right away in their immersive virtual world.

"Satya, I've seen that look before. It's your puzzled look. Whatcha got?"

Satya frowned, feeling annoyed. "The Gigazon is too good at capturing our visual features, giving away our thoughts to other participants. Tell me you can't see the blemish on my face, too."

Auri shifted his eyes downward, confirming her worst fears. She threw her hands into the air. "You see it, don't you? Argh."

"Uh, I don't see anything. I saw you wrinkle your nose. When we are together working on a project, it means something doesn't add up. I've known you forever, cousin."

Enjoying his chivalrous portrayal and kind intentions, she shared her screen. Drawing lines and circles, she explained, "We've been hunting for the crypto wallets that got those funds from Mateo's last transaction before he vanished. I finally opened one and tracked the owner. Something seemed odd. It was too easy. So, I took another avenue to locate the owner."

Auri nodded. "When you think something's wrong, you're usually right. What popped when you used an alternate attack vector to track the owner ID?"

She drew another circle on the screen share to highlight the information. "See this? All the Know Your Customer or KYC is the same. However," she used the tool as a pointer, "the actual ID indicates the holder died a few years ago. Why send crypto to a dead person's wallet?"

"You're right. That's weird. Let's bring JW and Granger into this discussion to see if we missed a step or found a new problem to track. Nice one, Satya."

Moments later, JW and Granger joined their virtual hub space with ICABOD.

JW asked, "What did you two find?"

Satya explained the situation with additional details, such as reverifying each step.

Granger nodded his understanding but asked, "Is there a chance you didn't match up to the correct wallet holder? I'm not saying you did anything wrong, but connecting the same person to a dodgy crypto wallet isn't an exact science."

"That was my first thought." She looked him in the eye. "I've done this identity search several ways, expecting different answers, but the results haven't changed. No, I've got the correct owner from both sides of the digital wallet, except one of them is dead."

JW arched his eyebrows, and one hand rubbed his jaw as he twisted his neck to remove the kinks.

ICABOD interjected, "Think of it from a different perspective. You are chasing the flow of illegally owned cryptocurrency passing through the immutable record of the underlying blockchain technology. Everything is recorded in the blockchain from and connected to owners with amounts annotated with precise time and date stamps. Criminals using cryptocurrency risk being caught if they use their real names on a wallet. The most logical answer is …"

Granger interjected, "To have a dummy ID that can get emptied into some spendable currency."

JW straightened. "Satya, it follows if the crook has a dead person's ID, they don't have to explain or pay a fee for borrowing their name."

Satya grinned, feeling pleased that her hunch was correct. Her nose wrinkled again. "Hundreds or even thousands of scoundrels must be trying to outwit the KYC rules. This can't be the only instance of a dead person's ID being a wallet owner."

JW inclined his head toward her. "I believe it's called Identity Farming. None of us considered this cottage industry could become a high-demand business element for drug or human trafficking."

They stared at one another for several minutes. JW broke the silence. "ICABOD, can you scan the Darknet for Identity Farmers so we can begin a mapping exercise of this distasteful business model?"

ICABOD responded, "I should have a good list in a few hours."

Auri asked, "What are you thinking, JW?"

"If the criminals we're after find a good source for anything, they'll return for more—no need to change something if it's easy and works. We can catch him in a squeeze play if we can map the funds from Mateo's organization to where he gets his bogus wallet holder identities. When we know where the stolen loot is going, we can alert the authorities for an arrest scenario."

Granger agreed. "It would be stupid to reuse farmed IDs, so buyers would use them once and discard them. That means they'd need a reliable source of these IDs to keep the authorities from identifying their operational model."

Satya chuckled. "And all we need is for an Identity Farmer to be careless in his output to help set a trap. I got this, guys."

"You go, girl," they said in solemn unison.

CHAPTER 19

Deductive Reasoning

Appalled, Judith rolled her eyes and twisted a clump of hair with her thumb and forefinger as she looked at the email while Xiamara leaned her chin on her hand and studied the words with a confused expression.

Judith grumbled, "They want us to hunt for what? An Identity Farmer? As in grain-based crackers on aisle two, frozen fruits and vegetables on aisle four, with identities on aisle six?"

Xiamara shrugged, shook her brunette curls, and opened her mouth to speak when her computer screen flashed a 'join this meeting' icon.

"Maybe we'll get a hint from Brayson," said Xiamara as she pressed the not-accept on her phone. "Let's join from your laptop."

Judith frowned and tossed her blonde waves of hair behind her shoulder. She pressed *accept* and shifted the audio to the external speaker.

"Sorry, ladies, but I wasn't sure which of you might be available. JJ and I agreed you needed some contextual framing in addition to the squirrelly email." Brayson chuckled.

"I thought you wanted us hunting for the under-eighteen crowds falling prey to some bogus modeling opportunities," said Judith. She waved her arms, nearly smacking Xiamara. "How does this new hunt fit into the grander scheme?"

Brayson cleared his throat and appeared serious to Judith. Both girls sat a little straighter, waiting for his explanation.

"The notion of an expansion on the identity theft business model surfaced parallel to our human trafficking problem. In the R-Group, our brain trust is tracking the money of illegal trafficking groups. They've accounted for cash movements, but recently verified cryptocurrency exchanges were increasing. For these transactions to flow, they need phony IDs for the crypto wallets used to launder earnings."

Xiamara raised her hand and wiggled her fingers.

Brayson inclined his head, giving her the floor.

"You're suggesting they need a free-flowing supply of phony IDs to use once and discard," she agreed. "Then, it makes sense that the Identity Farmer could take IDs from the people they capture and repurpose the information for laundering."

Judith nodded her head, proud of the logical statement from her friend. "Good one, Zee. We have three business streams with leeches likely overlapping to grab the profits." She raised her hand and counted out the ideas using her fingers. "First, stealing humans. Then, they take the victim's identity because they have a new life. Third, use them once internally for the wallets. But I'd bet my bottom dollar they resell those identities to a secondary market. One hand washes the other. Trafficked individuals willingly surrender everything for a fresh start, and the U.S. is the land of the free 'til it's not. These poor people don't realize what their new life in America will be."

"Wow!" exclaimed Xiamara as she rubbed her hands over her face. "The blockchain data store has real IDs with histories but are dead ends for hunting the whereabouts of the crypto. Trafficked victims have no way to admit that their identity got stolen, making it even harder for the authorities to crack the source."

Brayson nodded with an expression of admiration. "Ladies, your deductive reasoning is whip-sharp plus one step further than we postulated. Impressive. Maybe we should throw half-baked assignments over the wall to you more often. JJ and I may have to knock at your door for work someday."

Xiamara giggled.

Judith tried to mask her pleased look while her chest filled with pride. She curled her hair behind one ear and looked into his eyes. "Thanks, Brayson. That means a lot to us."

Brayson gave a salute gesture with his right hand and disconnected.

CHAPTER 20

Salesmanship

"Hey, Santi. I need some help over here."

Santiago snapped his head toward the hollering worker.

He growled under his breath. "Great. Someone has second thoughts about getting into the trailer."

He was a large, burly man, mostly bald, with a scruffy, puffy beard, making him appear more intimidating than those who worked for him. He lumbered to the small group gathered at the back of the tractor-trailer.

Santi understood Mateo wanted more inventory after their big loss. His job was to calm the people and get them loaded and on the road. Mateo previously chided him for his appearance. He insisted Santiago should dress in something other than his favorite wife-beater tee shirt and jeans. Santi recalled his come-back; *the selling part, not the clothes, closes the deals. I want to look like I work hard to get them over the border, not sell them an appliance.* Mateo valued Santi's success rate and agreed.

He grinned at the group of fish in his barrel. "Does someone want a refund?" He looked at the familiar scenario and grinned. A woman wrung her hands with tears dotting her cheeks. The man beside her fidgeted with his hat, rolling it by the brim, uncertain how to handle the dilemma. Their scared children leaned into their parents for non-existent reassurance.

"Folks, we've got brave families loaded and ready for their new life. Are you going to join them or not? I can refund you if you don't want to go, but you'll have to find your way back to your village. I will retain some money for freeing you from that rat-infested bungalow you called home. But I understand if you changed your mind and want to go back. We need to get on the road. I'm sorry you don't want to get to America, especially when you've come so far. Los Guerra is the last Mexican city before the U.S. Just across the Rio Grande is our destination of Fronton Island. My team and I have gotten you this far. We're all going. I have no one to take you back. You are welcome to walk." He pointed south toward the barren desert.

The man pleaded in hushed tones with his wife. Her tears increased, and the children leaned closer to her.

Santi pushed more familiar buttons. "I'm sure the money you borrowed to get this far will be forgiven when you tell them you lost your nerve at the last minute. A real shame." He reached up and gently caressed the oldest girl's face. "I've seen pretty chicas like her get modeling jobs and even act in movies. Now, she'll return to that pitiful hovel and be married to some poor farmer. She'll spend the rest of her life working like her mother to eat and feed her babies. You can forget about a nice home, good schools, and a film career. Feel free to return to your past and forget the future."

It was too much for the family to bear. The man bellowed at his wife. The children howled and begged not to go back. Suppressing his smirk at having soft-pedaled the border crossing, he held his hand out to the kids to help them into the trailer. The crying woman followed her husband as they thanked Santi for not leaving them.

Santi smiled and patted each in turn like a grandfather to help them settle. Once they were in the trailer, Santi pulled up one of his workers and whispered, "At the first stop in Los Guerra, I want that girl cut out from the family and brought to me. Mateo likes that inventory separate, so we need to get her to Alvaro for processing. Don't be rough. Tell her she'll get to the location a little earlier than the family to audition for a job. Make sure they are all smiles for her new opportunity."

Santi then motioned to the loaders and ordered, "Ensure the produce boxes are fastened tight so they don't fall out at the checkpoint crossing. The inspectors must believe the trailer is hauling Mexican produce, so they clear it faster."

Everyone nodded, completed the loading, and locked the doors.

CHAPTER 21

The Nature of the Beast

Mateo listened to the conversation with a grim expression and shook his head. "Yes, I will be there later this afternoon. Are things quiet, or are you creating more shit, like usual?... No, I won't have time for a celebration with you…No, I am too busy. You, my friend, are invited to my hacienda next Saturday if you want to leave your gun at the door. I have some marvelous Patron I don't mind sharing… Good, I'll bring my men. No surprises."

He disconnected the call, scribbling things to complete on the notepad. He glanced out the window at the flowers in bloom in the gardens and pictured the bleak landscape he would visit later. Los Guerra is a village in Miguel Alemán, Tamaulipas, with 4,570 residents. It is situated near the small community of Fronton Island and the hamlet Guadalupe Guerra Colonia. Three cartels continually fought over the area for domination over drug smuggling, human trafficking, and unlawful migration activities. Mateo often traveled to his staging area to direct traffic and meet with Flores, his prime contact. He was surprised at the remaining residents who received the brunt of the struggles between the fighting cartels.

Mateo sat at his enormous desk reviewing the pending transactions planned for the day, tallying the profits. He tapped his pen on the desk as he reviewed his list. His office was a large recess on the northern wall of his primary Mexican hacienda. It was a short trip to Los Guerra. He had trusted connections on the U.S. side of the border to receive his shipments. His human trafficking and narcotics businesses permitted his lavish lifestyle.

Ego was reflected throughout the property. He was particularly proud of his artwork, including several originals by the masters and some very trendy artists like Michael Goddard. Guests often asked for details regarding his impressive furnishings of finely crafted oak and mahogany pieces, cushioned with buttery soft leather plumped to invite visitors to rest in comfort. Sipping his coffee, recently refreshed by a silent maid, he glanced out the huge picture window to his right at the surrounding gardens of native blooms.

Mateo grinned at the artistic carpenter's careful finishing touches on the magnificent, hand-crafted banister. The man worked methodically, with no wasted moves, which Mateo respected. The craftsman stood to stretch out his back.

Mateo remarked, "Señor, your workmanship is superb."

The man was dressed in lightweight white pants and a shirt, slightly spattered with oil varnish. "Thank you, Señor. Working on such a magnificent spiral stairway to the roofline is a labor of love. This is the third coat of oil varnish, which will last a long time. I'm sorry it's taking so long, but I want to ensure every nook and cranny is coated correctly within all the carvings. The hand application lets me feel for any imperfections."

Mateo chuckled. "I suspect I'll find none. Did you see this in your mind when we first talked?"

"The creatures, yes. The wide spiral stairway in the center of this grand room is more impressive than I initially suspected. I have not done a customized piece like this with this variety of carved pieces supporting this three-foot-high railing." The man wiped his brow and quickly sipped his water bottle. "The spacing between these animals is exactly eighteen inches."

Mateo walked to view the staircase as if arriving via the massive double-door entrance. He silently studied it carefully, pleased when he couldn't spot any flaws. "Sí. It is as I hoped. One can see the animal details from here." He waved his arms. "You captured the intricate details of the rearing Mustang at the start." He laughed. "Almost a warning to an unknown person: *take care if you tread here. The light through the windows on t he forms does highlight the details. Well done, Señor."

The artist nodded and then returned to his project without another word.

Mateo turned as the door opened. Several of his bodyguards entered. He watched the eyes of his ex-military bad-asses scoping out the staircase with admiration displayed in their expressions.

The newest guard commented, "Señor, this is a magnificent addition to your amazing hacienda. But I thought a staircase and railing were for a multiple-story house. Are you planning a second story?"

Before Mateo responded, the lead guard pushed the man toward the door. "You know nothing of finely carved wood. Walk the perimeter until I send for you."

Annoyed at the new guard and his unsolicited comment, Mateo snapped, "What's the schedule for today?"

The lead guard replied, "There was another cartel vote of confidence action last night. We feel it is unsafe to meet the shipment today."

Mateo felt his anger rising and stood. "They're always whacking one another for a claim of power. I spoke to Flores; he failed to mention that tidbit. Flores will say I'm spineless and not worth dealing with if I don't go. Let's leave in an hour to conduct our business. Nobody intimidates me or my people. I want a secure perimeter so my cargo can be processed, so bring enough men." He jerked his chin toward the front door. "Leave him to walk outside while we are gone."

When they left, he returned to his desk and grabbed his list and a sealed envelope. He placed the item on the worktable off to the side. He nodded to the craftsman's soft-spoken, "Gracias, Señor," and continued to his massive bedroom across the great room.

He closed the door, noting the bed was remade with the black and brown velvet covering and pillows. No dirty clothes remained on the floor where he'd left them. Drapes were secured with silken ropes to let light in to nurture the large-leafed plants. Mateo used his handprint to open the sliding entrance to the underground stone passageway to descend into his safe area. Snapping on a light, he grabbed the worn leather shoulder holster that held his 9mm Beretta and a belt filled with fourteen-round clips, sliding them on like old friends. Feeling confident, he briskly ascended to his bedroom and secured the opening, hearing the nearly silent click of the mechanism. He grabbed his dress jacket from the closet. He put it on, covering his armaments and making him appear business-like. Then he returned to the main room with one more appreciative glance at the Mustang, hearing the ominous snort in his mind.

A short time later, Mateo and his entourage arrived at the Los Guerra staging area and established a secure perimeter around the building. Casual foot traffic and cars were discouraged in this area of town. The warring factions had their assigned sections. Police knew better than to respond to shootings or disorderly activities in the regions. Flores controlled the products crossing the Rio and anything destined for Fronton Island.

Fronton Island lay between two channels of the Rio Grande, downstream of Fronton, Texas, across from Los Guerra in Miguel Alemán Municipality, Tamaulipas. It was a contentious piece of real estate that the United States and Mexico both claimed. The strip of land was defendable and remote.

After arranging heavy hits on their personnel, Flores had made an uneasy truce with the other two cartels. The strikes against his competitors were so heavy that local authorities warned Flores to tone down the violence, or the Mexican military would be summoned. A full-scale range war was in nobody's best interest, so Flores negotiated a truce that allowed the other two groups to operate their businesses for a small percentage. Flores even leased some of his large rubber rafts to them to transport product over the river to Fronton Island during specified times. Local Mexican police were paid handsomely by Flores to look the other way.

Mateo was at the staging area, as usual, when delivering precursor fentanyl. All the rubber rafts belonged to Flores, so Mateo bargained to transport his human cargo across the river. Mateo knew his men would receive less consideration than he did in these dealings. In south Texas and into Mexico, men like Flores and Mateo were the dominant authorities that no one crossed if they wanted to live.

The two men quietly faced each other as their bodyguards carefully eyed the situation and their possible opponents. Even as school kids, neither man was friends with anyone else. Each had a level of respect for each other, at least when doing business.

Mateo gruffly stated, "I need rafts for tonight. The usual going rate?"

Flores stared into Mateo's staging area and spat. "More Venezuelans? How are they paying your outrageous fees to get themselves into the U.S.? There's nothing worth staying for in Venezuela and no wealth to buy their way out. Are you branching into humanitarian peace corps work?"

"I run a modest import/export business helping people realize their dreams of the good life in the U.S. Doing these favors gives me great satisfaction and allows me to sleep peacefully at night. My profits aren't your concern."

Flores roared with laughter. "These people you take across the Rio Grande in these rafts are your grade C inventory. The prime B cuts of meat go across the Ciudad Miguel Alemán/ Roma bridge in comfortable buses. I've seen those teenagers wide-eyed and excited about modeling jobs when they reach Houston. Your best inventory gets kept in that compound you call home until customers show up for bidding. You're just like me, importing desired products and packaging them for sale. What happens after that isn't our concern. We only worry about keeping a stock of inventory."

Mateo smirked. "Since you brought up inventory, did you want me to up the precursor fentanyl quantities on my next run? You took all I had, which suggests that business is good. With a small deposit in advance, I can double the quantity."

Flores responded. "We are both in the shipping business. You need my rafts to move your product." Then he laughed. "I need your ships to bring me mine." Flores rubbed his chin and looked into the sky as if seeking a divine answer. "Would twenty-five percent down be acceptable for my next order?"

"Sure, but it must be in crypto." Mateo shrugged with a grin. "My finance manager insists that is the way of our future secure transactions."

CHAPTER 22

Nice Critters Share

JJ and Brayson spent the morning drawing new elements and updating the different segments of the operation on the whiteboard walls in the Luxembourg home office of CATS. Brayson went for a quick workout, leaving JJ to wait for a response. He sipped coffee and eyed their efforts, looking for gaps or steps needed.

JJ's phone rang, and he walked to connect the audio portion via his laptop. Their standing workstations held individual curved monitors. The secured office space had several areas to accommodate training sessions for the team, private offices, and a modest kitchen. Pull-down beds were in the private offices, but he and Brayson usually returned home for a few hours of rest.

He smiled at the rapid response to his request by the Joint Criminal Opioid and Darknet Enforcement (J-CODE) identified with the name on the screen. He accepted the call and opened the speaker to work hands-free. "Good afternoon, this is Juan Rodreguiz. How may I help you?"

The confident voice said, "Sir, this is Agent Gabriela with the J-CODE agency. I am calling to advise that your team has been granted access to our report and research on the tragedy n San Antonio in August."

JJ grinned at the cooperation being granted but couldn't help but needle the agent. "I'm glad you allocated time for us to collaborate on this atrocity. We'll share any new information discovered."

The sound of grinding teeth echoed over the speaker.

She groaned, "Who are you? You're not on any recognized roster in my files. One phone call later, the deputy director rushed to me and insisted we show you every courtesy, so who are you?"

JJ smirked, grateful not to be on a video meeting. "Agent, we are focused on solving this case of human trafficking and, the more recent discovery, precursor fentanyl materials in the tractor-trailer. I assure you that we want to work together. I'm glad we have a collaborative understanding. My people will arrive the day after tomorrow."

Gabriela sighed, sounding exasperated. "We're grateful for the extra help, but no one likes being surprised and questioned by our leaders with no frame of reference."

JJ frowned and became empathetic. "I'm sorry I can't tell you details about my organization due to the strict protocol we have been instructed to observe. When you reply to me, I called to alert people on your team that we assist."

Chuckling, Gabriela added, "Thanks for your honesty. I'll be your contact to make certain you get what you need. I am happy to work with you."

"Thanks."

After disconnecting the call, JJ texted Brayson. Moments later, Brayson walked into the area dressed in workout garb with a towel slung around his neck and sweat beading on the exposed skin.

JJ grinned. "Looks like you had a good workout. Maybe we can spar later; I must practice my kicks."

"Sure," he laughed. "I'm always happy to kick your butt."

JJ straightened with a smirk on his lips. "In your dreams, buddy. I have received cooperation from officials associated with J-CODE. Depending on how you frame the discussion, you may gain access to the trailer and possibly the victims. I had to call in a few favors to get the face-to-face meeting for you. Take your talented bride, Marian, to Texas and see if you can push to the next step. She can do the hospital duty alone if you prefer. Your call."

Brayson replied, "Thanks, JJ. I'll book the flights for the morning. After we finish reviewing assignments and I wipe the floor with you, we'll have dinner."

"Right. Funny man."

Brayson left to pack and work on dinner with Marian. They'd had a good session and called it a draw. JJ felt energized, so he called Gracie. She answered immediately.

"What's up, JJ?"

"I'm mostly checking in. I wanted to let you know Jeff's been busy. He identified the shipping vessels from Pliant's old organization. Using a little satellite tracking with hacking, we placed them in China, picking up chemicals—you know, the addictive, poisonous ones. JW's team located the route the ship's captain requested, which includes a delivery at Port Manzanillo."

"That's fast work. What else?"

"Brayson and Marian are headed to Texas in the morning to see if they can find any residue at the target locations and verify a match on the chemical signature. We're connecting the dots but stuck on confirming the end-to-end financial transactions."

"Will Marian speak to the survivors?" Gracie lamented, "I want to tie Mateo and his associates to the mess."

"I'm right there with you, Sis. We're closer to her gaining access. Detective work like this is tedious. Agencies keep stone-walling us, but I am finding workarounds, using some of our contacts to manage buttons and call-in favors. It would be easier if Mateo and his band of thieves were first-time petty drug dealers who made stupid mistakes. You and I know he's a seasoned pro who is an expert at deception and has a divided organization to protect him. It feels like we're late to the game."

"You're right, JJ. He's as slippery and dangerous as a Moray eel."

"I think if we keep following both avenues, we can put him out of business on the trafficking and the drugs."

"Agreed. The team is making good progress and building a solid case. I'm just impatient. Let me see if I can find anything on the financial endpoints to help the team. I'll review all the transactions that pass-through accounts related to the offshores."

"Awesome. The last time you did that, it helped isolate the area to investigate. Can you target the Caribbean region? I sense we may have more action in that area."

"Fair enough. I know you want to break Mateo, too. His business diversification may make him vulnerable. I'm betting change is hard for him, which could benefit us. He's a smart, greedy pissant out for money and power. I'm sorry I'm so focused on the one part rather than the whole. It's frustrating. I have no right to take it out on you."

"Thanks. We've identified his business model. If we can penetrate the financials, we'll have a clean shot at bringing him down. Send JW any information you get. Brayson and I have identified which team members make sense to go where, depending on where each thread leads. We'll get him the right way. He won't be able to wiggle out."

"I'm grateful you helped me practice patience."

"And you give me new ideas—a win-win. I know you'd feel better if we could find and extract Sophia and Elena. I think we have a fifty-fifty chance."

"I like those odds. Thanks."

"We never do things halfway, sis. Do we?"

"Nope. See you."

CHAPTER 23

Freedom Road

Two days later, Gabriela greeted Marian and Brayson at the sign-in desk. The formality of handshakes was observed; each signed in and received a badge. They agreed to go with first names. Gabriela led them to her vehicle and drove them to the burned-out remnants of the warehouse and the surrounding area. The tractor-trailer had been moved to the side, leaving the area open for inspection.

Brayson began his chemical analysis in the trailer, then moved on to the fire-gutted building.

Gabriela kept an eye on Brayson.

Marian cleared her throat and asked, "May we speak with the survivors? We'd like to know how they get seduced into this import-export mess."

Gabriela shrugged. "That's not my jurisdiction. I can introduce you to the people who have that authority. Give me a few minutes." She placed a quick call and softly made the request. Nodding her head at the response, she concluded the call and noticed Brayson motioning for Gabriela and Marian to join him as he poked at something under the cab. "Brayson needs to show us something." Tapping Marian on the shoulder, she added, "The Texas Border Patrol is in charge of the victims while they're in custody. They'll send me the contact information so you can speak with the ones who will talk."

89

Brayson looked up and frowned. "It looks like vandals found something fastened under the tractor cab and cut it free. Gabriela, did your people find something not in your report? Maybe they added it later."

She rolled her eyes and frowned. "Please show me what you found. I'll find out if someone did a supplement to the report when I return to my office."

They bent down as Brayson pointed out where something had been fastened with duct tape and then crudely removed based on the visible ragged edges.

Brayson stood and brushed off his hands. "Marian, it could have been more drugs."

Marian shrugged. "Possibly or money. I'd wager the traffickers sent someone to get whatever it was before it was thoroughly inspected."

Gabriela shook her head, feeling overwhelmed.

"What did your analysis find?" Marian asked.

Brayson used his hand-held chemical analyzer to show the readout on the screen and scrolled through the results.

"Is it a match?" She questioned.

Brayson nodded. "Same chemical signature as several semi-legitimate pharmaceutical manufacturers based in China."

Brayson turned toward their escort. "How far along are you with determining the source of the precursor fentanyl?"

Gabriela smirked. "It isn't any big secret that this junk is manufactured in China. What else you got?"

Brayson pulled out a short note with several long strings of alphanumeric characters printed on it. "Our think tank mapped these crypto wallets in the Caribbean to wallets used by manufacturers in China. Proof of seller and buyer status for persons now of interest. Will this help your team apply pressure on the Chinese?"

She quickly snatched the piece of paper and read through it. "Nice work. For the data forensics, I need to contact the FBI. I know you won't tell me how you got the information, but I would like a copy for my people."

Brayson smiled. "As promised, it's already in your email, along with our findings. Are we good?"

Gabriela hung her head down for a moment and took a breath. "I wish I'd started working with you sooner. We'd be farther along."

With her usual unassuming smile, Marian petitioned, "The people we're chasing have expanded their business model. Can you get us to the Border Patrol people, please? We need more on the human trafficking angle."

She nodded.

Brayson and Marian, en route to the Mexican border, barely reached the target Farm to Market Road in their Jeep rental when Brayson's phone chirped. He pulled over to determine which way they needed to go. Studying the message, he looked at Marian before connecting to the conference bridge and enabling the speaker. Marian's brown eyebrows arched as he turned off the engine.

Brayson said, "Hey, JJ, we're near the bridge in a deserted area; what's up?"

"We've received an alert about a human convoy beginning in Venezuela and focused on getting to the U.S. on foot. The problem is that Latin American countries called foul on the journey to Mexico. The group is picking up more unfortunates along the way, so it's more like a migration of refugees."

Brayson nodded. "Fine. What does that have to do with us? The Mexican army and the U.S. Border Patrol would have that responsibility, wouldn't they?"

"And," Marian interjected, "since they're desperate to get to the land of plenty, they might be easier prey for the traffickers we're hunting. You don't just walk over the Rio Grande into welcoming arms because your foolish government destroyed their country's economy. Wouldn't it sound seductive after dodging authorities of five countries to hear *I'll get you and your family across the river and past the razor wire?*"

JJ softly chuckled.

Brayson looked at his wife and grinned. "Not only are you cute, but you got the angle faster than me. Sadly, this is like herds to slaughter. Mateo's people offer to help whole families with a slight cost of letting their teenagers head in first to high-paying jobs to pay the passage fees for their families." He shook his head, feeling enormous sadness at the plight of these clueless strangers. "Sounds like we should have someone in this caravan to watch and chronicle everything as it unfolds."

Marian rolled her eyes and stared at her husband. "What a risky idea. You'll be on your own. I'd be pissed if you get hurt—furious if worse."

Brayson did a double take. "Why do you think I'm the best one for this undercover work?"

Marian grinned. "Because, sweetheart, not only do you speak Spanish in multiple dialects, you do the scruffy guy thing to perfection, and you were mentally outlining the plan just now. Plus, if I volunteered, who'd get to see the patients from the trailer, which is why we came to Texas? Dividing and conquering works in this instance. Unless you get hurt, and I have to find you."

Brayson patted her thigh and pulled her hand up to kiss it. "I'd have gotten there sooner or later. Thanks, honey."

Chuckling, JJ said, "Gracie would say the only thing worse than a woman who doesn't understand you is the woman who does. Brayson, you know the drill and the stakes. I've seen your wife mad and wouldn't risk it myself." He laughed. "Take the usual gear for tracking and communications, especially the Zoleo device with your modifications, but keep it light. Our team is already tuned to track the Zoleo, making locating you in the desert easier. Once you determine your attire, sew the beacon signals into your shoes, and we'll map your beaconing signal. Marian, when you finish in San Antonio, let me know. I may need you somewhere else."

Brayson ended the call and leaned over to kiss and caress his wife's face. "Smart ass."

CHAPTER 24

Business Model Dreamer

When Rodrigo arrived at his hacienda before dawn, Mateo was on his second cup of coffee. Fresh coffee and plates of steaming huevos rancheros and chilaquiles sat between them on the table in his office by the windows. The servant closed the door when she left.

Rodrigo loaded up a plate and slurped his coffee. "Mateo, I will need funds to buy this isolated property outside Laredo. It is remote but close to the city for truck transport to the processing lab. I can build without a lot of prying eyes. I've gotten friendly with the truck and rail shippers, which should ease our bulk import of precursor materials across the border."

Mateo dropped the serving spoon on the plate with a clang. He narrowed his eyes. "I told you to set up a lab where finished fentanyl could be cranked out for distribution. This sounds like you're planning a car manufacturing facility. Quit this grandiose planning and stick to our current business model. I want the working model preserved. We need success to recover the funds we lost. We ship it into Port Manzanillo and break it down for truck transport to cross the Rio to Fronton Island. Then, we will send the product to you in Laredo. I've got the local cartels on board for those shipping contracts on the U.S. side."

Rodrigo snorted, and some food sprayed from his mouth onto his plate. "We need more reliable transport than the local cartels and a couple of rubber rafts. We can load the trucks like we currently do, but we can drive loaded trucks onto the rail and let the train haul them straight through Laredo. Our people drive them off the rail cars and come directly to the facility where we run the materials to manufacture finished goods. The same thing happened with human cargo. All we need is some inspectors on the payroll, and we're good to go. No other cartels to deal with."

Mateo, turning red with anger, roared, "Your last brilliant idea almost nailed our asses to the floorboards. You said it would be easy to route our ships to the Port of Altamira on the Caribbean side of Mexico and then jump from there to Galveston. Then, using trucks to deliver the precursor fentanyl and human cargo in Houston could be handled at the same time. That idea went up in smoke when I found out the U.S. forces routinely check for that kind of cargo moving through Panama. Traffic is so botched that shippers are paying a million bucks to jump to the head of the line to meet their timetables. The current drought in the region showed Panama predicting more traffic delays because they are short of water. Rodrigo, I know you're smart, and I trust you. But stay lowkey and make a profit using the routines we know work. If we have no other problems, I'll consider upscaling later. No failures."

Rodrigo shrugged, wiped his mouth, and placed his hands on the table. "I'm sorry, Mateo. I look at things and say, why not? You look at things and say, so? I'll stick with our current business model but won't stop thinking of better options."

Mateo reached over and clapped Rodrigo on the back. "Good; keep focused on what we must do to ramp up the business. Keep your eyes and your sharp mind on the skyline."

"Yes, sir."

"Talk me through this five-acre compound outside of Laredo. You said it had one building for living space, and you think you can convert the other into a manufacturing lab. What sort of security measures do you have in mind? How much is the cost?"

Rodrigo nodded, his enthusiasm growing as he shoveled another bite of chilaquiles and swallowed. "Mateo, I need a new identification before we get to that."

Mateo stared at the man. "Why?" He sipped his coffee.

"To purchase or lease the property I identified, I need to become the buyer of record. You won't want that traced to me, so I need Julian to give me a semi-clean ID to complete a smooth contract. Even with that, I'll need funds to incentivize the county records keeper to fast-track the closing to take possession."

Mateo shook his head. "Rodrigo, I don't want to own the property, so get a lease. Two years if we are investing in lab equipment. For that matter, why can't the lab operation be on Fronton Island? I don't need to buy or lease property there, and with no records or bill of sale to record, we can move quicker to bring the product to market. You could ship from Fronton and meet buyers in Laredo or anywhere else, always moving locations."

"I already thought of that," Rodrigo flung his napkin to the side of his plate. "First, Fronton territory is closely monitored by the U.S. Home Land Security and Texas State Troopers. Trying to run a functional lab to crank out quality fentanyl takes time. We have a higher chance of production being disrupted. I need a safe, quiet, and secure environment with reliable electricity to meet those requirements. Second, the local cartels patrol the area like coyotes vying for scraps to keep their traffic flowing. If they stumble across the lab manufacturing fentanyl, we're in for a blood bath. Fronton Island is a no man's land for what you asked me to provide. If the Chinese lab guys hear automatic weapon fire, they'd freeze or run. You're the one that demanded we use their techs."

Mateo slapped the tabletop. "All right, I'll do it your way. Let me get Julian on the line so you can cover the details. Don't tick him off like you did before. I need you two to get along."

"Yes, Mateo."

Gabriela's windowless office was a typical government issue. The desk was at least fifty years old with scars marring the once beautiful oak finish, topped with a phone, desk pad, personal computer, and a couple of family photos. A gray, four-drawer file cabinet was against a corner with a stack of papers waiting for filing. The three chairs squeaked and creaked at the slightest movement. The faded white walls held a picture of the governor and another of the Alamo. Marian sat to one side with her hands folded.

"Thank you, Gabriela, for setting up this meeting," Marian said pleasantly. She sensed Gabriela's annoyance at being out of control of the situation.

"No problem," Gabriela replied without emotion. "When he arrives, I'll leave so you can complete your business. Feel free to let yourself out."

Marian inclined her head. Moments later, there was a knock on the door.

"Enter," said Gabriela.

One of her staff opened the door. "Your visitor is here, ma'am."

"Thank you." She stood, slung her purse over her shoulder, and approached the tall, uniformed man. "Nice to see you, Austin. I hope all is well with your wife and family."

"All are well; thanks for asking."

"Marian Morris, I'd like to introduce you to Lieutenant Austin Stevens, Texas Border Patrol."

Marian rose and shook hands with the clean-cut man. She loved serendipity situations and knew him in a blink.

Gabriela opened the door to escape. "Austin, as I put in the text message, please extend every courtesy to this lady. She's been vetted. Lunch next week, if your time permits." She shut the door behind her with a soft click.

Austin pushed his Stetson back and studied Marian for a long moment, appearing to access memories. She noticed the second it clicked. His eyes widened in surprise as he slapped his thigh and then ran his hand across his face. "You're that expert. Wow."

Marian arched one eyebrow and smiled yet said nothing.

"You're the long-range sharpshooter Border Patrol brought in to teach the rookies how to shoot a few years back. We thought it was some joke until you dropped five shots into the target center at a thousand yards in under five minutes. None of us believed a pretty blonde gal, under a hundred-ten pounds, could even shoot a fifty-caliber rifle, much less drill shoot to perfection. I'm mighty beholding to your expertise. It's saved me and my team more than once in our scraps with the cartels."

Marian's infectious smile and striking blue eyes never failed to charm the people she met, but her expertise with weapons remained memorable. Shaking Austin's giant hand again, she warmly stated, "Glad to see you again, Austin. Let's sit." They each took a chair, and she continued, "Are you still shooting low and to the right?"

He paused and looked astonished. A rise in red peeked above his collar and headed for his cheeks.

She chuckled, and he laughed.

"I couldn't get close to your thousand-yard record, so I focused on five-hundred-yard distances like you suggested, ma'am. I've held the practice record for four years. Most importantly, it's kept me alive."

"It's good to hear that. The Texas Border Patrol is all over the news these days. Your service is appreciated, even if the country doesn't always say it."

"Thank you, ma'am. Are you still in the service?"

"No, I retired early and went private as a contractor. Which is why I'm requesting your office to let me speak to the illegals who survived the Texas heat in that tractor-trailer."

Austin hesitated. "None of them have told us how or why they got into their predicament. We even had one of our best psychologists try to work with them. He thinks they speak several Spanish dialects, but no one says anything. A couple have recovered, but we are keeping them secluded until we determine where they called home before coming here."

Marian smiled and held her chin in one hand, thinking. "What can I offer if they speak?"

"We can grant limited asylum with a chance to earn citizenship. We can help them connect to support teams."

Marian blinked her eyes and nodded. "That'll do. Please, let me see them. I think I can negotiate on your behalf. Limited asylum means there's a chance to stay. If they don't talk, they will likely be deported to Central America if they don't specify a country of origin. Let's see if this helps get them off-center."

"It's risky, but I'll get approval. We can plan for this afternoon."

"Perfect. Thanks, Austin."

CHAPTER 25

Prized Treasures Shared

The teenagers enjoyed the warm weather and Julian's St. Kitts estate's expansive pool, which graduated from four to twelve feet deep. Elena and Sophia laughed with the teasing banter of the boys and girls from their classes. Madam Chloe watched as the girls huddled, whispering to each other with laughter and pointed comments. "Ah, to be young and so carefree," she thought.

Madam Chloe put up a finger to gain Nohea's attention. When he joined her, she verified, "These teens are the ones Elena was overheard talking with Sophia. They are unhappy at home during the last week per Julian's recordings. That's why she invited them today."

"Outstanding."

"They seem to be having a good time."

"In our research on each family, the parents are often gone. These are the oldest, and they stuck with the chores the parents demanded of them. They are taking parental responsibilities."

She nodded, "Perfect."

Not to be outdone, the boys showed off. They sent waves toward the girls, angling cannonballs off the diving board to cause the most splashes. They had so much fun until a couple of the boys picked up one of the girls who had previously said she couldn't swim and squealed her protest. The boys threatened to toss her into the deep end. Madam Chloe signaled Nohea and Ryu, who moved to end the playful atmosphere. She pointed to her watch as if it was time to get the kids moving.

Nohea whistled shrilly, using his hand to press his lips back over his teeth and mouth. The kids jumped but didn't drop the girl, then grinned at Nohea's whistling ability. They set the girl back on the lounger. The whistle came too late to stop the last cannonball Raul landed, soaked Sophia's hair, making her look like a drowned rat and got out. Sophia turned on the lad and shouted, "Chico estúpido, mira lo que has hecho." Madam Chloe appeared behind Sophia and handed her a towel to let her dry off. "Miss Sophia, he's not stupid; he's just a silly boy." She fluttered her hand and added, "He doesn't deserve to be around you well-behaved young ladies."

"Sir," asked one of the guys, "can you teach us how to do that loud whistle? It gets people's attention."

Nohea smiled, "Perhaps another time. It's time to gather your belongings. Have the rest of the snacks. You can take some home if you want."

Sophia stomped around, visibly angry about being drenched. She dried her body, wrapped the towel around her hair, and slipped on her coverup. Madam Chloe saw her look under the tables, loungers, and pool toys and then watched her anger increase.

Sophia demanded, "Who took my flip-flops?"

Elena joined her friend and displayed hers. "I don't know. These are mine even though they look the same, Sophia. I have the small mark on the inside, see?" She showed her sandals to the rest of the teens.

One of the other girls, Consuelo, held up her items. "I don't have them."

"Sophia," a third girl, Lisbeth, said while holding up the missing items with a slight frown of regret. "I'm sorry. I picked them up to admire them. They're so pretty."

Sophia headed to her with an outstretched hand.

Lisbeth twisted the flower top, showing her friend. "I wondered why these pretty flowers don't light up. I bet the batteries need replacing so they light up when you walk. I was only trying to help get them operating again. I'm your friend. I don't steal. All of us like you and wouldn't steal from you or Elena. These are prized treasures."

Madam Chloe observed as the girl returned the flip-flops just as the flower came off in her hand.

Sophia stared at them and then at Lisbeth, her eyes filling with moisture. "You broke them, " she said.

Elena bent down and pulled off her shoe. She removed the flower and showed it to Sophia. "It pops off but goes back on, " she demonstrated and grinned. "See?"

Lisbeth looked relieved. "Perfect. Get a new battery to replace the one below where the flower sits. Put the flower back in place. Then tap it to make sparkling lights when you walk." She pointed to the area and showed how the battery was removed.

"But they never sparkled, even when we first got them," Elena said.

"Sometimes the batteries go bad in products that sit on the shelf too long. On this model, I think you tap it to activate so you can wear the shoes to school without breaking a dress code with distracting lights. Like bangle bracelets, they don't allow us to wear in class."

Sophia popped the battery into her hand and raised her eyes to gain her guardian's attention. "Madam Chloe, can you give us new batteries to see if we can make them light? It's worth a try. It seems like we need two for each of us."

Madam Chloe took the battery and sent Rhu to find them in the house.

He returned a few minutes later. "I only found one." He handed it to the young visitor.

Lisbeth showed Sophia how to insert the battery properly, replace the flower, and tap it twice.

"Ooooooh!" exclaimed the teens after Sophia put the shoe back on and jumped.

The boys gathered closer to admire them. "Those are so cool."

Maria asked, "Where did you get them? I want a pair, too."

Elena cautiously said, "In Florida."

Madam Chloe said, "We'll put them on the list to buy. But it's time to go, kids." She walked around and whispered in the girls' ears. "Sophia and Elena, Julian sent me a text that we are scheduled to leave for San Juan the day after tomorrow."

A unanimous groan filled the air.

"Sophia, Elena, I need you to please go shower and clean up for supper. I'll escort your guests out."

Four friends filed out with goodbyes and thanks for a fun day. Madam Chloe closed the door, keeping the three remaining teens. "You are invited to join Sophia and Elena in San Juan."

They gave a collective gasp.

She smiled, "Your transcripts will get transferred to the school there, but we need you to return tomorrow with the signed permission slip from your parents. The slip has the school's name. Bring your IDs and pack very little." Sweeping her arms wide, she continued. "Everything will be provided for you. The new school has a different dress code and uniform." She patted each one in turn and grinned. "I'll watch over you like I do for Sophia and Elena. The rules are easy: get good grades. But please don't tell your other school friends. They would be jealous. Perhaps next time, they will be included if they behave better."

They were very excited, which made her smile. Marie asked, "Do you think we could attend college there? My parents told me I'd never get to attend college."

Madam Chloe's eyes filled with moisture. "Every young person should have the opportunity to complete their education. That is the goal. This school shows students how to earn free scholarships. If you don't want that, tear up the paper."

They each looked at the paper, carefully folded it, then slipped it into a pocket.

She smiled at the innocents. "I think you'll like this opportunity. Before you leave, I must take photos to create your travel documents. Ryu, is the camera set up in the library?"

"Yes, we are ready to go, ma'am." They agreed in unison.

One by one, they posed like one does for class photos. Their delighted smiles were wide, and they looked at the camera with hope as she snapped away.

Madam Chloe escorted each of them out. "I need you here by eight at the gate with your IDs, permission slip, clothing, and phone, if you have one. Nohea will let you in, and we'll get busy after breakfast. If you aren't here on time, I'll presume your parents forbade you. Sophia and Elena will reach out to visit when they return during a school break."

Lisbeth twisted her fingers, clearly worried. "My parents may not sign, but they don't care about me. They never let me do anything. I came here, but they think I'm at the library."

Madam Chloe hugged the girl. "No one is checking the signature on this side. It's for the school to keep on file. Consider this your chance to make a grown-up decision to move your life forward."

Maria said, "Thank you so much for this opportunity. I'll be here, no matter what. Lisbeth, I'll walk with you."

The others responded similarly before they departed. She heard their excited conversation as she closed the door.

"Nohea, bring me the film shot today by the pool. I want to select the best for each of our little targets. They are all so lovely."

"I will bring it into the library for you to work on later. The boss will be pleased, and the girls will never know. It's a slick way to get new inventory. We know how to handle it in the morning."

Marian grinned at Austin when they arrived at the guarded wing of the hospital. The white walls, tiled floors, and shiny equipment spoke volumes about the staff's care for maintaining a top-notch environment that promoted health.

"Austin, it might be easier for me to get them to talk if you and your uniform aren't seen. No disrespect intended."

"None taken, Marian. I'll wait in the ward's visitor area we passed."

She looked at the list of four rooms she would access, then reached into her pocket and switched on the recorder. Opening the door, she walked in with a cheerful demeanor and Spanish greeting.

"Good morning, Mrs. Sanchez. My name is Marian. I'm here to help you, but I need some information. I have two options for you to consider."

Fluent in as many if not more dialects than Brayson, she quickly identified the dialect and opened the conversation, empathizing with their struggle. The hardships poured out. No regular work, so no income. Hungry children with no education.

They wanted to have more for their children. Sacrificing every-thing they owned for life in America seemed the best choice. Before crossing the border, they discovered the costs of the limited options too late. One way or another, they had to pay dearly to find that life. One woman had lost her husband on the trek, while another lost her young children. Marian hated the stories and held their hands while they wept.

Travel brokers promised transport through the maze of paperwork to journey from one country to another. Pictures of successful travelers were shared. It looked so much better than their backyard. Running from religious persecution was another driver to have folks hopscotch continents for freedom. Desperate, they took the bait and agreed to be smuggled into the country.

During the conversations with the four in the last room, Marian's phone received a text message chirp she had to ignore. She sighed as she completed her notes for Austin. Fifteen people, six countries, and a number of young people of varying ages. Marian wondered how the teens could reach their parents if they were alive and free. It was a heartbreaking situation. She entered the visitor area, finding Austin alone, thumbing through a sports magazine. He stood.

"Austin, I made notes of the information I received. One woman couldn't speak she was so afraid. I recommend we try to get sketch artists to get drawings of the perpetrators as a start. Each person's dialect is noted, which should make it easier for you to get the right folks to speak to them. I told them that if they continued to cooperate with the drawings and answered questions, they would be helped.

Austin read through the notes. "This is terrific, Marian. We can make some headway. Thank you."

She extended her hand. "No, thank you."

Austin left, and she sat to look at the message she had received. Her fingers rapidly pounded the screen, as she insisted someone could trace the message to its origin. She mumbled, "No. No. Don't tell me you can't because I know you can. It's them. They surfaced, if even for only a moment. Dammit, give me the geo-location. Argh! Somehow, they discovered the batteries needed changing, but they need a strong Wi-Fi connection for me to grab the signal."

She thumbed her contact list and pressed to call.

"Hey, Marian, what's up? Are you okay?"

"I'm fine, JJ. Can you trace the history of the blip I received?" She checked her watch. "Between twelve and fifteen minutes ago, I got an alert with the signature from one of the pairs of sandals Elena and Sophia had. It lasted a nanosecond."

"Really? Let me try."

She heard his fingers rat ta tat tapping on his keyboard. That man could speed type, no doubt.

"Marian, I see the signal, and the signature looks right, but there is no geo. Sorry."

"I think they might have figured out the battery needed replacement. It's only a guess. Someone may have suggested the shoes light up. It is improbably they would find the tracking element under that battery." She sighed and wiped the water from her eyes. "I'd love to tell them we've not forgotten."

"Me too. Since you're on the move, I'll have Satya clone your device and monitor it. She'll establish a program to ping upon receipt automatically."

"Thank you, JJ."

CHAPTER 26

Harsh Comparisons

CABOD opened the video-conference bridge, and JW greeted, "JJ, how's it going? Gracie texted me and suggested we discuss what a couple of your team members were doing."

JJ nodded, and JW noted his serious expression.

"I've got two people in Texas working the human trafficking puzzle, JW. I need you guys aware that Brayson's headed undercover. He has the usual comm equipment for tracking and security. I want his every move watched via satellite signal snitching in case his signal vanishes from our normal channels. I need to track him reliably." JJ fingered back his hair and sighed deeply as he shook his head. "Marian caught a blip from Sophia and Elena, the girls taken from Miami many months ago. I'm sending you the unique transceiver identifier signature in the girls' shoes. The odds aren't high, but if the signal resurfaces anywhere, track it and let me know. I'm guessing it might resurface on an island in the Caribbean or Northern Mexico."

"What's the range for Brayson's and the girls' signals?"

"Brayson should be visible on a low earth orbit satellite in Mexico. I'll send you the coordinates. The transceiver in the shoes is less."

JW tapped the fingers of one hand against his lips, thinking for a moment. "We'll only catch the girls if they stroll near an open Wi-Fi router to have the signal relayed. The alternative is if someone is connected to a private network. We'll drop a little code on every open Wi-Fi router in those areas to grab the nearby signals and echo back to us. It shouldn't be too hard, with only a billion devices likely in the target area. I'll get the kids on it after lunch. Maybe we'll finish by ten o'clock next summer."

JJ frowned and asked, "Has anyone said you sound like Dr. Quip with that sarcastic edge?"

Momentarily staring at one another over the Gigazon, they began chuckling.

"JJ, I'll have Granger work with ICABOD to write and then dump a quick program on all the open routers visible on the Internet in the target area. An automated distribution shouldn't take more than a day. Besides, we'll need something like this to snoop on the cryptocurrency movements we're tracking. A twofer program is better than one. We think we'll get lucky with those crypto wallets that keep popping up and vanishing."

JJ grinned. "Thanks for accepting the challenge. Didn't mean to offend you with the comparison to Dr. Quip."

JW smirked. "It's flattering. And I will mess with Granger that I'm more like his dad than he is."

JW connected to his team's Gigazon huddle area, noticing everyone was busy with their fingers flying across their keyboards and heard multiple tapping sounds like tap dancers practicing for a Broadway musical.

"Hey, all," he announced to gain attention. "I received a new assignment for us to work on. Granger, I'd like us to craft some alerting code to send to all the open Wi-Fi routers in the

Caribbean and Northern Mexico just south of the Rio Grande. One of the field operatives, Marian, swears she got a beaconing signal from Sophia and Elena's flip-flops. I have the identifying signature code. If they wander close enough to be picked up again, we must trap their geo-location and send it to JJ for a rescue operation. Plus, we're adding the tracking of the crypto wallets."

Granger nodded, rubbed his hands together as if plotting the approach, and returned to his keyboard.

"Satya, Auri, another operative, Brayson, is attempting to join the human caravan that has fled Venezuela for the United States. Statistics suggest the human caravan could attract Mateo's goons to take advantage of the migrants' need to gain U.S. entry. Brayson could be in the catbird's seat to identify them and learn what services they're offering. These guys are the big prize, but we must track Brayson's journey with snitched satellite cycles."

"All he has is a transponder signal we need to keep track of?" asked Auri.

"That's too passive," Satya complained. "Why don't we arm him with some crypto loaded with a parasite and have him use it to buy passage? That way, the crypto parasite can alert us as it moves from wallet to wallet rather than us having to guess where it's laundered."

JW felt stunned at her innovative direction. "Satya, you're doing that brilliant, insightful observation thing, and I like it. Your idea would be a game-changer if Brayson could pull it off. You get another hot chocolate for being excessively smart again."

She grinned at the flattery and started quietly chatting with Auri. JW knew they'd have a plan back to him within hours, so he placed a private call to JJ to update him on the timing and logistics.

CHAPTER 27

Accountability or Treachery

Julian listened to Mateo's voicemail and decided to make the first move. He called Rodrigo.

Rodrigo answered the call on the first ring. "Good afternoon, Julian," he said, speaking slowly and deliberately. "Is this a social call or about my business needs for Mateo's project?"

Julian grinned at Rodrigo's cautious tone and imagined his sneer. Adept at dealing with various people, Julian disliked and didn't trust this man. He straightened his shoulders, determined to remain in control of the conversation. "Mateo requested I send you money to build a new lab. Can you explain how you will spend the funds for your project?"

"I need cash to buy the equipment needed for processing the drugs and to secure a lease in a remote area close to Laredo," replied Rodrigo, not hiding his annoyance. "Is this going to be another one of those exercises where you want to see purchase orders before releasing the funds? Didn't Mateo already tell you what to do?"

"Don't take a tone with me. I must justify the monthly spending. My brother left me a voicemail, but his directions were vague. Rather than interrupting his day, I figured you would know the details. If you don't, I'm happy to call him and say you were too busy to explain."

"Just a second. Mateo knows exactly what I requested. Let me remind you that Mateo, not you, runs this operation. When he says build a lab to churn out finished drugs, you need to underwrite it so I can get it done. Add to that a new identity for me to make purchases here."

Julian grinned, planning how to get even with this idiot. "You know as well as I do how Mateo doesn't like to spend without a full accounting. Don't bark at me for doing my job for my brother. Start acting like you care about his best interests as much as I do. If I want details to fund this or any project, I get what I need, or you get nothing. You're not the first person to run point in one of his operations. His business ventures operate like clockwork because things are checked and rechecked. You make me think you're hiding something with your I-don't-give-a-crap tone. I want a line-item list with pricing of what you think you need. If I see any issues, I'll discuss them with Mateo to ensure we are all on the same page. Any questions?"

Rodrigo growled into the phone. Julian knew he was seething. The man inhaled.

"I'll comply. It'll take time to compile the list and shop for low bids, along with terms and conditions for each line item. Then, I'll rank the bids in preferred order based on averaging the weighted responses and then transfer it to a Venn diagram. My analysis and recommendations should be delivered to you in…"

Julian rolled his eyes as he recalled Rodrigo was an ex-university business teacher. Rodrigo and Mateo had a long relationship filled with trust. He interrupted. "Your sarcastic attitude isn't helping. Just give me rough figures, on the back of a bar napkin, of your proposed projects so that you won't be too stressed." The poor ass will think he has the upper hand, thought Julian.

"That's very expedient of you. I'll have something for you by the end of the day. How long on the new identity?"

"Since your tone has returned to polite, give me two days. Text me your address, and I will courier it to you."

After disconnecting from the call, Julian mused, "Ah, good. Disrespectful arrogance, sloppy accounting, and refusing my oversight will do nicely to make my case easier."

Trying to stop this line of conversation, Julian stated, "But Mateo, your wards are doing well in my environment. They're warming to people and their surroundings. This is the wrong time to ship them to you in Ciudad Miguel Alemán. Their confidence will be shattered. We'll have to start over, trying to get them operating like regular teenagers. Besides, they've proved helpful in securing inventory for Alvaro. I am sending three more to the hotel in Houston. I know of your fondness for them, but to troll successfully in San Juan, I need their natural charm and beauty. Their best value is in luring disaffected kids to leave behind their unhappiness. This is a better use of their talents than joining you in your hacienda."

Mateo drummed his fingers impatiently, then snapped, "How much longer in your care? Their buyer added a bonus for a fast turnaround based on their pictures. I can't keep holding him off for too long. He'll go somewhere else."

Julian confidently added, "Let him go somewhere else. Mateo, these two will increase inventory, offsetting the lost sale. It's taken months to get them operating at this level. They are like magnets to the disaffected kids who want a better life. I can't replace what we've created in these two. Give me a couple of months to prove their value. If you still insist on selling them, our harvesting business won't suffer as much."

Mateo relented, "Ah, all right. I'll tell the prince they'll be worthy in several weeks. Continue educating them on social situations so it won't look like I've lied to him."

As an afterthought, Mateo asked, "Did Rodrigo reach out to you on his project?"

Julian smiled like a predator ready to pounce. "Ah, yes, Mateo, we spoke. I need to speak with you about what he isasking for. May we talk tomorrow morning after I finish reviewing the documentation he recently submitted?"

"Fine. I'm sure he's on top of it from our last discussion."

CHAPTER 28

Hitchhiking on Foot

The semi-arid, unforgiving terrain punctuated its power as the wind burst into another vicious swirl, blowing painful grains of dust into his eyes. Crossing the dry arroyo to climb to the other side to gain sight of the vista ahead reminded Brayson of army basic training. He survived carrying a full eighty-pound pack and a rifle. Running his tongue across his cracked lips, he mumbled, "I hope they buy my story so I can join the group. I feel like a refugee with my stomach begging for me to snag a lizard or snake and eat it raw." He glanced around the shadows under the rocky terrain, but nothing moved. He took off his bandana, dragging it across his face and neck, sensing the two days of grit. "At least I'm still sweating. The K-rations and canteen I had packed for maneuvers would be awesome." He smiled a bit and chuckled. "Marian will be pleased I lost the extra pounds in my gut, at least."

Trudging south for nearly two hours without sighting anyone, he paused in the spartan shade of a mesquite tree. Breaking a chunk off today's ration of jerky, he popped it into his mouth. A few heartbeats later, saliva began the extraction of the flavorful morsel he slowly chewed. "I know they dropped me off east of the Chihuahuan Desert, but I haven't seen any demarcation to determine my positioning," he thought. Noting the position of the sun and constructing a rudimentary sundial, he estimated it was late afternoon. Removing his customized Zoleo satellite communicator from inside his baggy pants leg, he opened the foldable solar panel, which allowed a fast charge, and completed a satellite uplink. His fingers summarized his current status. He received the confirmation response. He tucked the eight-ounce device into its holder in his pants leg.

He wiped his brow and continued his trek. He was grateful his position was monitored. Cresting the subsequent rise, he thought he was fantasizing when he heard, "Hey, cabrón, you're going the wrong way."

Hearing an unexpected giggle, he mentally translated the Spanish, then looked around for the source. Squinting, he saw a man's outline against the bright background of the falling sun. The man crossed his arms as Brayson moved closer, but he didn't appear threatening. He decided to stick with Columbian Spanish for the time being,

"I was told to keep walking and look for the caravan going north. Are you part of the migration or policía?"

Brayson saw a woman emerge behind the man, racing after a child. Another figure, shorter with a small sombrero, appeared beside the man. The woman returned to the man's side, holding tight to the youngster.

"There is no reason for the policía to be here. We're joining that group." He looked at the paper he held. "We should meet up with them before sundown. We were told to ask people to get us across the Rio Grande. My family is headed for the land of opportunity." He appeared pleased.

Brayson studied the small group and tilted his head. "I was told to avoid the cities to stay clear of the policía. It's worked. I caught a jackrabbit a few days ago. It was good, but my rations are gone." He patted his stomach. "And I'm starving."

The man reached into his backpack and surprisingly pitched an orange to Brayson. He caught it.

Grinning, the man proudly stated, "There. Now, you owe me a favor."

Brayson was grateful for the piece of fruit but stared at the man before peeling the cool, orange skin. "Do your children need this? I won't take it if they are hungry, amigo."

The man erupted in laughter. "It's all we have left unless we get lucky, like you with a rabbit. I wanted to see what kind of man you are. You have honor. You're welcome to join us."

Chuckling, Brayson nodded to the woman and handed her the orange. "I'm Brayson. Don't let your husband give away food to strangers."

"I am Isabel," she said shyly and quickly peeled the orange; everyone received two sections. Brayson redistributed his to the children with a wink. "My husband is Julio, and our children are Miguel and Daniela."

The group quietly savored the juicy delight until the hot breeze brought sounds uncommon to the surrounding desert. Brayson turned to pinpoint the direction and told Julio they needed to head to the top of the rise. Moments later, they gained the vantage point and spotted a wave of humanity dressed in various colors, some with backpacks, others grasping hands with children or family. Julio turned and waved to his family, who quickly joined them.

Julio's face reflected relief. "At last. Our fellow refugees are approaching from the east, as we were told. We must join them and offer our help. We can help with the old and the ill. We will work for food."

"Yes, Papa," the children replied in unison.

Julio's hand reached around the small of Isabel's back. "Come."

It struck Brayson that this man was willing to work or help anyone to earn food for his family and what he hoped was a promising future. Tears pricked at the back of his eyes as he thought about the threats of the predators ahead to this caring family.

Julio clapped Brayson on the back.

Brayson said, "Let's stick together. Remember, I still owe you a favor."

Julio laughed as they rushed to join the wave of people heading north.

Madam Chloe and Nohea greeted the bubbly teenagers promptly at the gate at 8:00 am. Consuelo, Maria, and Lisbeth excitedly bounced around and chattered like magpies. Nohea opened the gate and ushered in the girls as their friend from school, Raul, raced up.

Chloe and Nohea were instantly on guard, holding the gate shut, but Consuelo petitioned, "Please, Raul is begging to go as well. I…told him I'd miss him. He wanted to apologize for soaking Sophia before we left."

Raul stood tall and admitted, "These are my friends. I have no one here who cares whether I'm at dinner. Please take me with you to their new home. I couldn't bear being left behind. I'll do anything you say; don't leave me behind." He held up his current ID and copies of the requested paperwork the girls had been asked to bring.

Madam Chloe assessed the situation. After staring at Nohea knowingly, she asked, "Nohea, can you please get some photos of this nice young man so he can travel with us?"

With a sly look and a nod, Nohea showed Raul the way, leaving the girls with Chloe.

A long black limousine pulled up to the gate. Everyone was excited. Getting them into the luxurious vehicle took almost no coaxing.

Fifteen minutes later, they were all climbing the gangway stairs to take their seats in the twin-engine King Air 350 for the brief flight to San Juan.

The glamorous travel jazzed the teens to the point that they had trouble buckling themselves into their seats. Finally seated, Lisbeth asked, "Madam Chloe, where are Sophia and Elena? I thought they would be traveling with us."

Chloe delivered her usual maternal smile and flicked her hands in the air. "This aircraft will hold eight people comfortably. For weight considerations, the last two seats were left empty." She patted Lisbeth on the shoulder and continued, "They have a little more paperwork to complete before leaving. We thought it best to take you now. It'll give you more time to acclimate to the new house. The girls will be leaving tomorrow."

Nohea raised a bottle. "To celebrate the journey, we decided everyone deserves a toast of champagne." As he poured into the first glass, he said, "Everyone, take a glass of the bubbly." He raised his glass and said, "A toast to your next adventure." Nohea watched intently as the teens eagerly drained their beverages. Lisbeth asked for seconds.

Madam Chloe politely protested as Nohea filled everyone's glass again. Chloe shook her finger at him as she collected the glasses. Moments later, the plane taxied to the end of the runway.

The young people giggled when the twin engines roared to life, and the plane surged down the runway toward lift-off. Before the wheels were up, the teens were drugged and asleep.

Nohea calmly advised, "They will sleep until we get them on the transport ship. They will put them on a drip link to keep them sedated until they land in Houston. Once we have them on the ship, I'll alert Alvaro to be ready. He is always grateful for males and females for the hotel work." Chloe only nodded.

As an afterthought, he exclaimed, "Oh, I need to get their identification paperwork to Julian. He will be pleased we got four, not just three fresh identities."

CHAPTER 29

Follow the Rules

Travel from St. Kitts to San Juan was smooth sailing on dark blue seas with the state-of-the-art four-cabin catamaran taking the four of them to their new destination. Baby blue skies with fluffy clouds spotted through the windows reminded Julian of the clotted cream served with the fresh cinnamon scones they shared for breakfast. He'd sent Ryu to arrange for the debarkation in San Juan, leaving him to attempt to cheer up the two girls. Sophia and Elena stared listlessly out the windows, each leaning on an arm with no hints of conversation. They appeared sad. He missed their happy chatter of late and wanted to recapture it before they docked.

He pulled the chair closer. "Girls, Madam Chloe and I tried to convince your friends to join us. Unfortunately, even when I spoke to the parents, they said their children changed their minds about going. You mustn't fret about their choices. You'll make many more friends in our new home. Your old friends will remain a fond memory."

Both raised their eyes to him as they shrugged in agreement. He gently caressed Sophia's and then Elena's cheeks. "Let's get ready for the customs checkpoint. I need to see nice smiles to match your photos, or we'll never get off this boat." Standing, he noticed Sophia wipe a tear from her cheek. As he turned away, he heard Sophia comment to Elena in a sad tone.

"They didn't even tell us goodbye on WhatsApp. We should've heard something even if their parents told them no or if they changed their minds. But nothing."

Julian bristled at the statement yet kept his temper in check as he whirled to face the pair. "You linked to each other on a social media app after I told you not to?"

The two exchanged terrified looks after realizing they'd broken the cell phone rules.

Julian pressed the intercom to summon Ryu. He entered and cast a confused expression between his boss and the girls, not seeing a problem.

Julian cleared his throat and took a breath. After casting a saddened stare at the girls, he ordered, "It seems Sophia and Elena have violated our agreement of no unsupervised communications." He conveyed a disappointed expression as he waved his hand. "Take their phones, remove any social media app, and install parental controls. I don't want this to happen again." He glanced at them both with a hurt expression. "I trusted you. You may not install anything on these devices without my approval. Do you understand?"

Tears welled in their eyes, and they nodded in agreement.

Elena held Sophia's hand and pleaded, "Please don't be angry. Our friends said it was the way teens communicated. They loaded the app and showed us how to use it."

Sophia choked back her fear. "Julian, we can't have friends without a social media application to chat."

The tears and pleading were enough to defuse his anger. "I only want what's best for you after your harsh ordeal," he said with a hint of kindness. "But you must follow the rules. I am responsible for your safety." He stilled, considering his option to make them worry just a bit more. "If WhatsApp is a key to modern friendship, then fine, but no other applications without discussing it with me. And you must leave your phones in the kitchen at night. That way either Ryu or I can review the conversations."

The girls both straightened and wiped their eyes.

"Please, don't disappoint me again. I need you to remember your promises so you can attend school and make friends." Julian smiled, offering reassurance after driving home the lesson of obedience. "You both need to remain cautious of what information you share with your new friends. Do not discuss your past or any of my business dealings. Agreed?"

Sophia and Elena offered a handshake. Elena said, "Thank you for the compromise, Julian."

"You're welcome. Go get ready to exit this boat, please."

They grinned and rushed toward their cabin.

CHAPTER 30

Travel Options

Santiago swallowed as the familiar annoyance raced through his body, making his toes twitch. He would leverage his years of experience in reasoning with these naïve young men.

"My friends," he glanced at the ground while he rolled his eyes. "Whoever said you could ride the freight trains over the border for free was lying. Nothing in life is free. You'll be a sadly mistaken fool if you jump atop that boxcar to ride it over the border. The trains make several stops between San Luis Poposi and Nueva Laredo, like the big one in Monterrey. Railroad security guards board at each stop. They make certain all the cars are locked. They'll find you, beat you, and then throw you from the train as it crosses a bridge at full speed. The wild dogs will devour your broken carcass. Hopefully, you'll be too dead to feel the teeth tearing off your flesh." He shrugged and looked at them through half-closed eyes. "We'll take you to Nueva Laredo and over the Rio Grande to America for a fee."

One young man spat on the ground, fortunately for him, not on Santiago. "We're fools if we take the train, but we can pay you to cross the border? That sounds like a food huckster from my hometown who swore the meat was chicken when it was a dog. Everyone told me not to trust people like you."

Santiago grunted and smirked as he pulled up his smart-phone to locate a particular website. Once found, he scrolled to the middle of the screen, started a video, and turned the screen to face the men as he added commentary. "You see this poor unfortunate? He did what you're attempting—hopped on a freight train for a free ride. No one told him about the tunnels, low-hanging traffic lights, or falling rocks that must be dodged or you lose your head like he did."

Seconds became minutes as the sickening video of the officials finding the decapitated body beside the track made one of the young men move to the side to throw up. Several had wild-eyed stares, and Santiago sensed their fear growing. Confident, Santiago announced, "We charge a fee to keep you from ending up dead like that kid. Our trucks aren't comfortably cooled like a touring bus, but we will get you to the border alive."

One of Santiago's men waved at him from across the street and held up his hand twice as he called, "Santi."

"We leave in ten minutes," Santiago said, then pocketed his phone. "Those who want to arrive alive, let's go."

He turned and walked toward the open 18-wheeler with phony produce racks designed to fool inspectors. No one saw the grin growing on Santiago's face, yet he heard their footfalls as one after another followed. He turned and faced the lambs, holding his hand out for the fees as each man mounted the stairs, then disappeared inside. He placed the money into his jeans pocket, then closed and locked the doors when the last man entered.

He noticed two non-conformists lingering by the train's boxcar. Retrieving his phone, he dialed his local contact. It connected. "It seems two guys want to jump on for a free ride. I knew you'd want to protect your corporate property with your normal process."

"Yes, thanks."

As an afterthought, he added, "Thank you for the edited video. It's proven most convincing to all but the most stubborn walking dead." He and the caller on the other end laughed.

"Keep them here," Santi said. "I'll pick them up when I return."

"Do you want us to feed them?"

"No. Hungry, they'll be more agreeable to my terms."

The sunset streamed through the windows at the top of the fifteen-foot ceilings of their Buenos Aires converted loft in the warehouse district.

Xiamara frowned, scrunched her eyes, and tilted her head, confused by the output displayed on her computer's screen. She slid her mouse around the tabletop and moved the content to a different screen. "Argh, that's weird," she stated, arousing Judith's curiosity enough to get a comment.

"All right, let's hear it," Judith snarled. "You're wearing your 'I'm puzzled' look, which means a problem."

Both girls had a pair of panoramic screens and enviable computing power supported by a partition of the CATS team supercomputer, ICABOD. Each enjoyed the flexible work hours supported by the loft environment for work and living space. Vanilla-painted walls held bold works of art of all sizes by local artists that they often found together during forays to town. These best friends had shared living spaces and expenses for years.

Xiamara drew a long breath. "We saw several solicitations for models and acting jobs aimed at teenagers. There have been multiple disappearances of teenagers in St. Kitts. Today, nothing, zip, zilch, nada. It's like someone turned off the spigot. I spotted those same ad campaigns increasing in Puerto Rico. I don't have a reason for the shift."

Judith nodded, her blonde waves matching the movement. "I'm seeing the same thing. I expect teenage disappearances to begin spiking in San Juan soon. I noticed some identity-farming chatter, seemingly linked to teen disappearances. We probably need to alert Brayson and JJ."

Zee reached her arms up after standing and stretched her body. "Maybe we should watch it for a while before raising our hand. We've been at it for fifteen hours straight except for reheating the leftover pasta, which was better the second time."

Judith snickered. "It was good. I prefer it when we cook here. At least we know what we're getting. When do we need to go shopping?"

Zee strummed the calendar on her phone. "Day after tomorrow. That's our day off, too. I love this space as our virtual work area."

"Me, too. I want to make more soup and possibly get the ingredients for a steak, baked potato, and salad supper."

"I can grill steaks to the perfect pinkness." Zee raised her index finger and thumb to her mouth and kissed them. Feeling conflicted, she added, "Let's notify Brayson and send screenshots, then catch five hours of rest." She stared at her screen. "Authorities can't find the missing teens, but their IDs appear as operating identities. Hmmm…Probably means a road trip for us."

Judith flinched and grinned. "You're right, but let's wait until orders come in from Brayson or JJ. Are any interesting IT jobs advertised based on our theory of new crypto-mining companies ready to go online?"

"There are just a few, but only junior-grade tech positions and no heavy-hitting data engineers like us. I find it odd that companies are trolling for people in school. It's almost like they don't want experienced techs. You don't think they are biased against women, do you?"

Judith frowned. "No more Marvel comics for your recreational reading. We have some leads we can report, but I'm more interested in our side hustle with that gaming angle. Did we get any nibbles on our partner propositioning?"

Xiamara's fingers stilled her continuing search entries. "I haven't heard anything in the form of a response. You know what that tells me?"

Judith sarcastically replied, "Umm…we got wax build up in our ears?" She shrugged and added, "Zee, give them a little time to digest our offer. We can help them make more money, and we'll get filthy rich."

Xiamara faced her screen. "Business conversations that stop cold is a warning sign I don't like. Something's wrong, but I don't know what."

"I'm ready to call it a day and heat our leftovers. You're worried we'll have appendages caught in the wringer. Trust me, we'll get wealthy with this side gig."

Xiamara cast an unconvinced look at her best friend before returning to her screen.

CHAPTER 31

Square One, Again

JJ arrived at the CATS team office and checked for updates. His eyebrows rose in near disbelief as he read ICABOD's updates from Argentina and decided it was time to engage with the geeky girls, with Brayson on assignment. He chuckled as he sent a text to the encrypted cell phones of Judith and Xiamara, giving them enough time to tidy up their activities.

I'll call your laptops in five minutes. Hoping you join.

Before three minutes elapsed, JJ's phone rang. "How are our favorite, almost squeaky-clean cyber sleuths?" JJ asked. "Do you have time to discuss our current adventure?"

Clearly on speaker phone, Judith griped, "What do you mean *almost squeaky-clean,* Boss? I'll have you know we have been on the straight and narrow since that last time. We do not want to return to our old ways, looking for a quick buck."

"Hi, JJ, it's Zee. We've had some modest side hustles, but we've been upright and honest."

"Ah, that's good." JJ sighed. "Let's escalate this call to video. I'd love to see your smiling faces."

They accepted the invite from JJ before he continued.

"It's good to know you're not going to partner with that online gaming streaming service that also takes bets on the outcome, right? Argentina has no nationwide gambling commission, so you must get permission from each region. The big players, like Kambi, take a dim view of young entrepreneurs sidestepping the regional laws and setting up a gambling website that takes cryptocurrency without cutting the commissioners in for a piece of the take."

Judith's mouth flapped open, speechless. Xiamara bowed her head slowly; he suspected her eyes were shamefully closed.

She tilted her head up, eyes wide, and inhaled. "We should know better than to lie to you. I'm sorry. It seemed like a good side hustle with little to no downside. Yeah, I know, no excuse, but we've been working hard on our current assignment. Here's what we know so far."

Judith straightened her shoulders and grinned like the Cheshire Cat. "We saw the ads for teenagers in St. Kitts completely stop, then start up in Puerto Rico. We believe teens will begin disappearing there. Also, Zee spotted want-ads for junior technicians from the school we attended. The ads left us wondering why there are no data engineers or network architect openings. We haven't found anything concerning the Identity Farmers you asked about."

"I need you two prowling in your old home grounds of Puerto Rico," JJ requested. "You will be at risk, so please take extra precautions. The issues have expanded to human trafficking, precursor fentanyl supply, and possibly money laundering and identity farming. Can you check the secure Dropbox for the logistics and particulars of your assignment shift? I need you in San Juan in two days."

Judith, always the negotiator, petitioned, "What about our gambling setup? Can we park it in dormant mode for later resuscitation?"

JJ shook his head and put a stern expression on his face. "I recommend you sell it to the group trying to run you out of business. The online sports betting provider, Kambi, or their affiliate, BetWarrior, would be the best-selling choice, and they can utilize their respective war chest of funds. They'll offer chump change, but you should only take cash and forego the percentage you'll be tempted to accept. Arrest warrants are already in process for you both. The authorities will begin the crackdown next week, all orchestrated by your so-called partners. Sell fast and leave with your travel documents. New identities are waiting for you in the Dropbox." JJ sighed, "Behave, you two. Talk later."

Before he disconnected, he overheard Judith complain.

"How is it that he is so much smarter than us?"

Xiamara chuckled, "It's not that he is so much smarter. We're just dumber than him. Get our new buyers on the phone so we can move to greener pastures. I'll get the files and new identities down and printed. Then we blow this popsicle stand. Get us top dollar."

"Say goodbye to Argentina," said Judith.

"Do we do the, *don't cry for me* song too?"

"Nah."

Travel to Puerto Rico was uneventful. The attractive ladies stood at the airline arrival carousel with two hundred of their newest friends, jockeying to the front while waiting for their baggage in San Juan. Xiamara felt nostalgic, thinking about their college days here in San Juan and the small tour guide business they had created to pay for their tuition. Waiting impatiently, Judith tapped her foot and checked her watch every few minutes, making sarcastic comments about the time they wasted waiting for the luggage.

"Zee, how much longer are they gonna take?" Judith moaned as she shook out her blonde hair. "How hard is it to run our bags through the baggage chopper and give us our stuff? I feel like we're being held hostage yet again."

Not quite listening, Xiamara recalled the multiple jobs they took to complete their degrees. Without working those jobs, their lives would be far different. She absentmindedly reminded, "What are you so upset about? Don't you remember everything moves leisurely in Puerto Rico until the bill arrives?"

"Hey, my friend, I know that look in your eye. You're thinking about the good old times. Those are gone, and this is a new day. We can improve on what we know and learn what we need to. Everything is a glass half full for you, and I worry about where the hell is the rest of my wine."

Noise from the carousel interrupted their familiar exchange of Xiamara's calm logic versus Judith's take-charge action when their bags approach.

"I'm so glad you are with me, Zee." She looked down at the wobbly, torn bag and groaned, "How am I supposed to file a claim with a bogus passport while on a secret mission? Crap!"

Xiamara giggled, "I bet the baggage handler was tearing through your suitcase to check out your underwear. You have all the unwanted attention I'd pay money for."

Judith tried to keep the laughter at bay, but Zee's comment easily overtook her anger. "Thank you for helping me keep things in perspective. Come on, let's eat and plan our next move."

Xiamara insisted they hit the old café they used to frequent while attending school.

They grabbed a taxi to take them to the San Juan bistro.

"Look how bright the building is. I bet they painted the exterior after the last hurricane." Grabbing their bags, they landed on the sidewalk. Judith chuckled and started to move to the familiar calypso music, with her toes stepping around her bag matching the beat, then hip-bumping Zee. "I missed this, Zee."

"I can tell." The music reached them as they exited the vehicle with their luggage.

Once they got there and pressed through the doors, Xiamara looked at the crowd of teens and lamented, "Wow, did we pick the right place at the wrong time?"

"I guess school let out, and this is the place to meet. Sheesh."

"Come on; I see the last and only table where we can sit. It'll be fun to watch the kids. Teens know the beat of the community."

Winding through the noisy teens, they secured seats and jammed their bags under their feet. Judith tried to gain the attention of one waitress but was ignored.

Xiamara sighed and rose. "What do you want? I'll place the order. Maybe I can get our drinks since they're probably swamped in the back."

"The usual, please. I know you haven't forgotten my faves."

Zee elbowed her way over to place their order. Standing in line, a pretty teenager with long, dark brown waves chatted with the others her age. Zee noticed that the odd glasses the girl wore seemed excessively large and bulky. Her tight capri pants and midriff top matched the pink and green on the glasses. Then, the girl stepped back and began using her hands in the air as if entering something on a keyboard.

"You're all set," the girl commented in Spanish. "I've booked you for an interview with our senior recruiter tomorrow." Then, as a parting tip with a wink, she added, "I recommend you dress smartly. They'll be impressed by that."

Zee asked, "Say, is that one of those computers in the eyeglasses with a heads-up display? It watches your kinetic movements. Those movements execute what's being projected, right?"

The young girl blushed prettily at being noticed. "Yes, it does. At first, it was a little creepy, but now I don't know how I'd ever use a stationary desktop."

Xiamara brought the drinks to the table, set them down, and commented to the teen. "How cool is that? Jude, take a look at her heads-up eyeglasses' computer."

Judith took a sip and cleared her throat. "Excuse me, is your company looking for some IT support to work in your tech environment? We're looking for fun geek work. Anybody with this kind of cool technology would be a blast to work for."

The girl's eyes widened, seemingly impressed. "You know how to program this sort of stuff? I want to go to school and learn how."

Zee asked, "Can we have your manager's number to call and ask if he's hiring?"

The girl stepped back and looked side to side as if expecting someone. "Uh, I'm not sure…"

Xiamara smiled and patted the girl's arm gently. "Take my number. If they're interested, they can call. I'm Xiamara, and this is Judith."

The young girl's face bloomed with an admiration smile as she nodded and slipped the handwritten note into her jeans.

"Thanks, Ms. Xiamara."

CHAPTER 32

Being Agile

White noise provided a calming sense as JW connected to the Gigazon. He was pleased the group was present. "Good day. I need each of you to update your status. We are in Agile Mode, so we must provide progress or obstacles. If you start boiling the ocean with endless details, I'll use the digital flyswatter on your avatar."

Everyone laughed, and Satya added an unexpected giggle.

"Granger, go first, please."

Granger nodded and grinned. "Ahem." He sat straighter. "Per our discussion, ICABOD and I have worked tirelessly to assemble snooping code to be delivered to any open Wi-Fi router in the target areas, hoping the missing girls will pass in proximity. We calculated there are more than one thousand open routers with no keyword for access or secured routers with the factory default entry of PASSWORD. These targets will soon receive our highly engineered yet undetectable code. We set the application to check in once every..."

A loud buzzer sounded, stopping Granger's soliloquy. An animated image of Granger's avatar getting swatted by a large flyswatter was prominently displayed on everyone's screen. Satya and Auri couldn't suppress chortles and snorts, mainly when the business side of the device covered the avatar's mouth. Granger visibly pouted, then sent a glare toward JW.

JW ignored the attitude. "We're using the Agile programming method to focus on progress toward our assignments or to petition for ideas from the team. Each of you has the skills needed to achieve our overarching project goal." He paused and looked at each of them. "Granger, you're a master programmer I can't do without. However, long explanation is not necessary to share your points. Let's stick to the points we all know the background of the discussion."

Granger nodded with an expression of understanding.

"Satya, your turn," said JW.

"We locked onto Brayson's signal signature using our satellite snitching technique."

Auri added, "We alerted him to the crypto wallet we staged and briefed him on how to use the cryptocurrency loaded into the wallet. He was advised of the parasite code on the tail of the Ethereum crypto and its purpose."

Satya grinned and said, "Auri and I debated the possibility of trafficking victims being relieved of their identities. We believe those credentials are repurposed for bogus crypto wallets. We found several wallets matching teens who disappeared in St. Kitts."

"We determined this was a good news/bad news scenario." Auri frowned, appearing somber, then continued, "The good news is we can confirm their abduction based on the launch of the new crypto wallet. The bad news is the victim is now in transit to their new vocation."

Granger admitted, "Nice and concise, you two." He saluted them each in turn. "If you had let me finish, JW, you would have your answer. As I was saying before, I was so rudely interrupted..."

Again, the buzzer sounded, and the large flyswatter flicked several blows on Granger's avatar.

JW shook his head. "Just say the code was delivered to every open router. We all know you're brilliant. Net it out so we can keep moving."

Granger's shoulders slumped, and he looked up with puppy-dog eyes. "Sorry to be so pedantic in my delivery. Thanks for trusting me to do the task correctly. Sometimes, I worry something was missed in the process. Finding a mistake early is much better than later."

JW smiled. "Point taken, Granger. Don't boil the ocean to convey your progress.

"In the name of transparency, Gracie's occasionally used that annoying flyswatter on me. We can all improve. Let's get back to it. Thank you."

The blazing noon sun highlighted the cracks of the desert, and sweat dried the moment it formed. Santiago was tired after clearing forty to take along. He separated a dozen he said could walk if they wished because they could not pay. It was too bad that the old father would not give up his daughter. She had potential, he mused. He approached the last scruffy man, who seemed out of place.

"Buenos días, Señor." He continued in Spanish. "I'm here to help migrants safely enter the United States. Hundreds of thousands of people are trying to escape their wretched past. I see age lines etched on their faces before they are forty—threadbare clothes stained with dirt covering scarecrow bodies. You look better fed than the whole lot this month. Why?"

Brayson licked his cracked lips and replied, "Buenos días, Señor. Some of this caravan had nothing left to lose. Some lost everything." He gazed at the ground and shuffled his feet. "Sorry, I'm not as malnourished or as destitute as others. But I don't have the possessions that some of them do. I sleep on the ground in my jacket. One tends to travel light when running in the middle of the night to avoid capture."

Santiago considered the story's viability and searched for a way to trip up the stranger. "So, authorities came for you in the middle of the night? Too bad you would be a valuable worker on a ranch. I help those who can pay me. This is no charity." He laughed. "If you ran that fast, you probably don't have funds to cover your travel." He turned away, ready to load and go.

"Wait," Brayson begged, wiping his dirty hand across his filthy skin. "I have digital currency to pay my way. Can you take cryptocurrency, or must it be dollars?"

Santiago faced Brayson again with a smile pasted on his lips. "A smart Columbian not to bring cash that can be stolen or beaten out of you. I prefer dollars, but the crypto offer has possibilities." He gestured his arms and hands to encompass the lack of desert amenities. "We are far from town or machines for a digital transaction. Let me ask a friend if we can accommodate your request." Santiago stepped away from the people and dialed Mateo.

"Mateo, I have a Columbian here saying he has a crypto wallet. He promises to pay in crypto to enter the U.S. Can I accept this?"

Mateo whistled. "Yes, for ten thousand, or we kill him if he lies. I'll text you the instructions for you to use in Monterrey."

"Thank you, sir."

Santiago lumbered back to the immigrant. "I can do this. There will be a fee for the special effort."

Brayson released a breath. "Gracias, Señor." He bobbed and bowed, appearing grateful. "How much? I barely got out alive, but I have my crypto wallet. I'm not rich, but I've saved my whole life for when I marry and get a family."

"Ten thousand to get you to the border and another ten to cross into the U.S."

Brayson cringed as if a whip struck his back; his shoulders slumped, and a wince escaped his lips. Tears filled his eyes as he took a breath. "Crypto won't get me freedom if I'm left here. Take me to a computer with Internet access, and I can transfer Ethereum to pay you."

Santiago smiled like a wolf with access to the henhouse. "Which means you get to ride free until then. You might be a little too smart for your own good. Humph." Santiago twisted his body and savored how happy his boss would be with the windfall. "Francisco, your job is to ensure we get paid before we cut him loose." He jabbed his index finger into his worker's chest while he continued, "If he gets away before I get payment, you will regret it."

"Yes, sir," Francisco replied, grabbing Brayson's bicep. "You will be my shadow."

Santiago bellowed to the people he collected. "Time to go toward freedom."

"Señor," Brayson pleaded. "I will pay for my new friend and his family. Surely you have enough room for four. I will make it worthwhile?"

Santiago turned his gaze to the family with the pretty daughter. "Relations of yours?" he demanded, thinking of what he'd like to do to the girl as soon as possible.

"No. They befriended me and shared their last piece of food with me. I am in their debt. I will pay their passage."

Santiago whipped his head to face Brayson, stunned. "Same terms as you. When we reach Monterrey, you can make the transfer. Twenty thousand each before we go over."

"I don't recall seeing Monterrey on the border when I memorized the map in Columbia."

"You and your friends want a ride or not?" he shrugged with disinterest.

Brayson wiped his face, and Santiago knew he'd won.

"Yes. I will transfer twenty thousand in Ethereum for the family and me in Monterrey to get us to the U.S. border."

Santiago smiled broadly, his gold molar reflecting the light. "If all goes as agreed, we'll exchange the second payment to cross. You won't screw me in this deal. Now I have your precious friends as uh…collateral."

Brayson flinched and nodded in agreement. "I need a few minutes to relieve myself before getting into the truck."

Santiago nodded, and Francisco escorted him to an area with a modicum of privacy. Five minutes later, Brayson was tightening the rope holding his pants. He was the last to enter the cargo trailer.

CHAPTER 33

Introductions

Judith exhausted her local contacts from the university they attended, looking for anyone who was hiring. Two days later, dressed in casual slacks with floral patterned blouses, they visited the university and left copies of resumes with the school in case inquiries for qualified graduates came to the technology department head. Xiamara volunteered to be a guest in one of the upcoming classes to increase the visibility of their desire to work for a local company.

The pair returned to the Swordfish bistro to look for the girl with the virtual eyeglasses access computer. Judith grabbed the back table with the circle bench seat in the corner to keep an eye on the crowd. It seated four comfortably and six with shoulder to shoulder.

The waitress brought drinks and the empanada of the day.

Judith sipped her cool beverage and broke off a small bite to munch. "These empanadas are great, Zee. We may need to get a second round."

Xiamara grabbed the remainder of the one Judith started and savored each bite, licking her lips. "Yummy,"

"Dammit, no phone call on the techie gig. The girl probably forgot even to mention it."

Xiamara nodded, swallowing another bite and tasting her drink. She dabbed her mouth with the napkin. "You know how teenagers are. When we started our jobs, we were ignored. The only thing that ever got anyone's attention was that deep fake adult entertainment business we launched."

Judith chuckled. "That got too much attention. Why does the universe seem to conspire against us winning?"

Xiamara snickered and stated, "Jude, your high-octane bod and signature blonde mane are only enhanced by your impatience for time delays. If I'm not mistaken, the girl is back. It looks like she's bringing someone along- maybe her employer or her handler. The guy looks almost too smooth to be her employer. I'm thinking…"

The teen spotted the pair in the corner booth and linked her arm around the elderly man's, pointing in their direction.

Judith noticed the girl was wearing a stunning floral sundress she had spotted in the window of one of the exclusive women's stores they had passed on their walk here.

The girl stopped at the table and said, "Julian, I told you two ladies were looking for techie work. They spotted the kinetic eyeglasses I used and asked to speak with you. They seemed educated to me."

The man patted the teen's hand. "Thank you, Sophia. I didn't doubt you for a second." He inclined his head and nodded. "Ladies."

Xiamara blushed shyly, then glanced at Judith as if to share a secret.

"Good afternoon, Julian, is it?" Judith smiled while she racked her brain to recall why that name was familiar. "We spotted the cool tech your daughter was using and hoped we might have arrived as innovations are being brought to San Juan. My friend, Xiamara, and I attended university here. We have advanced computer sciences and programming education and experience."

Julian retrieved each of their hands to kiss them gently and, in French, said, "Enchantée, mesdemoiselles. My Sophia indicated your interest in technology. Your background seems interesting. My name is Julian Lafleur. I have a home here and on other islands in this region. I am a businessman working on expanding a private data center for some creative applications."

"Applications are my specialty," Xiamara gushed. "I love making the final product easy but almost addictive to the users."

Julian appeared impressed as his mouth formed a half-smile. "We do need to chat. May I join you?"

Judith slid over and patted the vacant spot. "Please."

"Sophia, my dear. Please show a few teens how easy it is to activate the computer. You might get some eager takers from this young crowd."

Sophia nodded and dashed to the far end of the dining area, extracting her glasses from the pocket in her dress.

Judith wasn't surprised to see that the pattern of the frames matched the dress. This man had money, she thought. "Can you provide more details regarding your business and what skillsets you need? If Xiamara and I can't help, we'll tell you immediately."

Zee recognized the bubbly persona of her friend, who was excited to move the assignment forward. "Mr. Lafleur, we've returned here to help local entrepreneurs, but Judith and I are interested in tackling the challenges of technical innovators. We're more experienced in high-end technology than anyone else in San Juan. We can be your go-to-geeks if you have data center technical work requirements, from racking and stacking operating systems installation, network configuration, perimeter security, to even data center hosting."

Judith used her napkin to conceal her expression, proud of Zee's attitude as the man leaned forward, undeniably captivated by the hook, line, and sinker story audition.

Julian leaned back against the cushioned bench, signaled for a drink, and asked, "Do you ladies have any expertise in digital currency hosting and crypto mining?"

Judith straightened up, ready to do her part to get the job. "Mr. Lafleur, as Xiamara explained, we can build any infrastructure in your data center. The head technology professor at the university will vouch for us. We ran the lab environment and dabbled in crypto during our studies. It was a capstone activity. We can adhere to budgets, manage data lakes, optimize energy consumption, ensure secure crypto transactions, and host crypto wallets."

The waitress brought his beverage, and he took a long drink. He cupped his chin in his hand and remained silent.

Judith felt she had the winning hand, so she said nothing.

Moments passed before he seemed to reach an internal decision.

"Ladies, I'd like to continue this discussion, but not here." He finished his soda and handed them a business card with his name and number embossed with raised lettering, "I have your number. I'll check at the college and text you in a couple of days. Adieu."

Judith heard him tell Sophia it was time to leave. Scooching closer to Zee, she asked, "Do you recall the name Sophia from the files JJ sent to us?"

Xiamara's face brightened, and she pursed her lips together. She tapped the side of her head and closed her eyes. "Yep, from a trip JJ's sister took in the Caribbean. Julian's face looks familiar. I don't recall seeing the name, but his face was in one of the pictures in the background. I never forget a face, but it could have been a coincidence he was in the photo."

They ordered one additional empanada and iced teas from their waitress. "We might have ended up in the right place at the right time," said Judith smugly.

"I'll send a text to JJ with the highlights of the discussion."

"Perfect. I wish I'd snagged a photo of the pair."

Xiamara grinned. "I got her picture as Julian was headed toward her when he left. I'll send it along."

Outside the cafe, Julian's phone chimed with an incoming call. He opened the car door for Sophia, instructing her to wait for a few moments before he answered. "Alvaro, did you receive the new merchandise? I trust you were pleased with the young man and the girls."

"Yes, thank you for the new acquisitions. They do require a great deal of training on pleasuring the patrons. One of the girls balked at the instructions and tried to run. We tried additional medication to make her more agreeable to her new job, but she started to slide under."

Julian frowned and started pacing behind the car, waving one hand. "You didn't take her to the hospital, did you? You know the rules about trying to save inventory."

"Of course not. But with her potential, I didn't want to write her off. I called our veterinarian contact to see if he could help. Though he tried, she was too deep into a coma and stopped breathing. I need more inventory."

"You need to take better care of what we are sending you," Julian angrily argued. "It takes time to sift through the teens looking for the right profile to extract. Call Mateo and ask if Santiago can fill the gap sooner if you are in a big hurry."

"The assets Santi sends are undernourished castoffs. They take longer to make presentable and sellable. Yours are a healthy weight, attractive, and almost marketable as soon as they arrive. They are quick learners once we have their medication dosage correctly sized."

Julian clenched his fists and paced behind the car. "I'll see what I can do, but I'm not altering my harvesting techniques to help your carelessness. If you don't want to accept the substandard bodies you get from Santiago, treat my shipments better."

"Yes, Julian. Thanks for helping me. I will call Santi to remind him that anything suitable would be appreciated. I have gotten a few diamonds in the rough from him."

Julian remarked, "Make sure to tell Mateo of your need and the steps you are taking. He likes it when people tell him how they are solving problems. Leave out the lost inventory information unless you like him mad." He disconnected the call. "That man is a careless imbecile," Julian muttered as he opened the driver's door.

CHAPTER 34

Get Connected

When Judith and Xiamara arrived at four-thirty in the afternoon, Swordfish was crowded with a mixed crowd of teens and young adults. They were stunned to discover the back booth empty and rushed to grab a seat. The menu indicated happy hour started at five, and locals seemed well aware.

"I wonder, Zee, will the teens stick around or leave when the bar opens?"

Xiamara fought to connect to the Wi-Fi and grumbled, "This is a more popular place than when we lived here. Everybody's on their smartphone talking, texting, or streaming photos. The conversations almost drown out the music."

"JJ seemed to believe we were onto something when we spoke last night regarding Sophia. I think he appreciated the details, especially Julian's description. He said he'd research the man to learn how connected he is in this region and send additional details today." She looked at her watch. "I expect we'll hear from him soon."

Xiamara placed their order for three different appetizers and club sodas with the passing waitress. "I figured out why no one sits back here. It's too removed from the crush of people. Look how they move between one another, chatting and laughing."

"Friends are like that," Judith remarked as she looked around the area. "Look toward the far end of the bar; Sophia's here. I was worried she might not be here two days in a row."

"She seems comfortable with the younger people; look at how she engages. See if you can get discreet pics while I get connected."

Judith palmed her phone as if playing with it, nimbly capturing shots. Now and again, she would hold it to check the results or pretend she was taking selfies in the corner. "See if you can use your phone as a Wi-Fi hotspot and connect your tablet. We can capture some details for our next report. I can send you a few of the better shots."

Xiamara enabled her phone to work as a Wi-Fi hotspot, selecting the admit-all as she connected. The device completed the electronic handshake, and Judith sent a few photos.

"Got them. I will quickly test to ensure they go to the Dropbox JJ assigned us." She created a document entitled Finding Work Day Three, summarized the information with an excellent new photo of Sophia talking with another pretty girl, and completed the file transfer.

Judith noticed Zee intently watching the screen and looked at her while delivering a thumbs-up at the results. At a sudden lull in the noise level, Judith breathed for a second until she heard Zee's phone chirp, acknowledging a new connection. "What's that?"

The color drained from Xiamara's face as she turned the phone screen toward her. She saw the new signature identity on the display. "Zee, didn't you restrict the connections? Looks like we've got a hitchhiker helping themselves to our hotspot. Better kill the process."

Xiamara shook her head, making her curls bob. She laid the tablet so Judith could see the screen, albeit upside down. She rapidly selected monitoring software to snoop on the transgressor's data traffic. When she looked at Judith, her face appeared confused.

"What's the matter? Did you shut down the process?"

"No. Jude, this is so weird. It's not a regular stream of data but a repeating signal or beacon. Are we being tracked or identified as a target?"

Alarmed, Judith demanded, "Zee, shut it down. I don't want us identified by some beaconing program that happened to come online. I'd better alert JJ. We might show up on the wrong radar system or be targets."

Excitement rushed through Granger when the alert sounded. "Hey! He shouted. "The signal we're monitoring just lit. It's beaconing from a hotspot in San Juan, Puerto Rico. It lasted long enough for a geo-location, then vanished. JW, are you online?"

JW's nose appeared on the screen, designated for the Gigazon.

"Right here, Granger," he replied loudly.

Focused on the screen, Granger jumped in his chair, startled, as he saved his cup of tea from tipping onto the desktop.

JW chortled. "See why it's not funny to do that to anyone unexpectedly? Whatcha got?"

Trying to catch his breath, Granger grumbled, "Not funny, man. It's okay for me to do it, but you're supposed to be the team lead." He took a deep breath and held it momentarily, pressing his palm to his heart to slow the racing. "I got a hit on the beacon for the girls Marian wanted to be located. I mapped a positive spot in Puerto Rico before it disappeared."

ICABOD quietly interjected. "Team, we have the signal from one pair of footwear. That does not mean we have one of the girls spotted, only their shoes."

Granger frowned, feeling the excitement drain with the reality check from ICABOD.

JW nodded with a serious expression. "A disappointing but appropriate observation, ICABOD. I'll let JJ and Gracie know, but I'll suggest more work before we send a rescue team. Well done. Keep a focus on a twenty-mile radius of that location, Grange."

CHAPTER 35

Catching a Break

Judith's heart dropped as her phone vibrated, indicating a call from JJ. She picked it up and swiped to answer.

"Where are you? Who's by you?" he cleared his throat.

"We're at the Swordfish. Zee used an open Wi-Fi connection; sorry to make you angry."

He laughed. "All good. Your alert echoed on our board. I can confirm that the girl you mentioned, Sophia, is someone we're trying to locate along with her friend. The signal Zee just picked up is connected to them. I'll send you a couple of lousy pictures of the girls. They aren't in focus, but it's the best I have. You can almost see the bruised face of one of them."

Moments later, Judith scanned the photos and showed them to her buddy. She raised her fingers to her eyes and pointed them toward the crowd to get Zee to get her eyes on them if possible. "Judith, tell me about that beaconing signal that Zee just picked up. That signal is from people who were kidnapped. Are they both there, or is there only one?"

"JJ, this place is filled with teenagers of all colors, shapes, and sizes. Sophia walks around, showing her kinetically activated computer inside three-dimensional eyeglasses. The kids are wild about how it works. She's signing them up to buy one or something. Her device got us into the conversation with Mr. Lafleur yesterday."

JJ interrupted, "You need to stay alert and hyper-cautious. We're still researching Mr. Lafleur. If you can snap a photo of him, it might help."

"Zee uploaded some photos to the Dropbox. Mr. Lafleur's not here; we didn't get his photo yesterday. If he asks to meet with us, we'll try." She bit her lip, waiting for his response.

"Marian gave the girls sandals with flowers that light up and planted a beacon inside. She swore she saw it deliver a short burst of signal a few days ago, but it wasn't located in Puerto Rico. It's the same signal signature that Xiamara has piggybacking. One or both of them have the sandals."

"Okay, we'll keep sending photos and look for shoes that light."

"Good. I'm going to authorize Marian to head your way. I think you need some backup. Plus, she knows the girls. You could have discovered a key link. The girls were originally with Mateo, who we are trying to locate in Mexico or possibly the U.S. Is the man you met Hispanic with dark hair and speaks with a Spanish accent?"

"No, JJ. He has blonde hair, is well-mannered, and has a French accent. He's refined, which is typical of the connected and the rich in this region of the world."

"Humm, interesting. Keep looking. When you learn the job details, let me know if Mr. Lafleur contacts you again. I'll call you later. Thanks for your efforts."

"It's gone. The beaconing stopped, Jude. I'm sorry," complained Xiamara.

"You're fine. We're looking for light-up sandals with flowers."

Zee inclined her head and cupped her mouth with her hand. "Sophia is headed this way."

"Hi, Ms. Xiamara. Julian said I was perfect to share your information with him. He told me he was proud. I wanted to thank you and hope you can get the job. He's a nice man who treats me and Elena nicely. Anyway, I gotta go."

The young teen hurried away, talking to others and laughing. Judith considered Sophia a thoughtful individual. If she had been kidnapped, perhaps Julian found a way to manipulate her with kindness. She thought maybe he was a good guy. Xiamara pulled Judith's arm to get her attention.

"Did you see her shoes?" Xiamara asked.

"No, I was speaking with her. Why?"

"They weren't lit, but they have flowers."

Judith slapped her forehead. "Let's get the snacks bagged and head back to the hotel to write up additional details for JJ. Thank goodness you're being vigilant."

CHAPTER 36

The Breadcrumb Trail

On the outskirts of Monterrey, Santiago pulled the 18-wheeler to a stop in an unmanned rest area. Climbing out, he walked to the back of the truck, stretching after hours of driving. He took a swig from his water bottle and then lit a cigarette. He stomped out the butt when a black SUV with tinted windows pulled in behind the trailer and stopped. Santiago sauntered over and motioned for the driver to lower the window.

"We timed that well. I've got him in the back. You know what he needs?" commented Santiago.

The man nodded. He raised his left arm and thumbed toward the rear. "I've brought two security men. We'll take him to Internet connectivity, and he can use the portable device we brought. We are to watch him make a funds transfer to the crypto wallet address Mateo provided example photos of how it is supposed to look so he can't do anything funny. Then, I phone the number Mateo provided to hear a verbal confirmation."

His smile broadened, and Santiago added, "Try remembering the total amount in his account. He has to deliver another twenty thousand to cross."

The man raised his eyes in indifference. "If there isn't enough, what do you want me to do?"

Santiago's smile vanished, and his face reddened like an incoming thunderstorm about to erupt. "Cut out his lying tongue, shoot him through the head, and dump the body in the desert for the scavengers. I'll sell the teens anyway."

The man nodded.

Santiago approached the trailer and unlocked the doors. "Señor, step down. I have friends who will drive you to connect to make the transaction. Everyone else, please wait until the car takes him away. Then, I give you a chance to stretch. We've water and a snack for you." Hearing no complaints, his mind pictured lambs being led to slaughter.

Brayson climbed down, and the two men strolled to the SUV.

Brayson said, "I wouldn't mind a bit of water if you have extra."

Santiago chuckled. "Of course, there's some in the vehicle."

"Do I need to add a tip for the water?"

Santiago slapped him on the back. "Only if you want a ride back to finish your journey and see your friends again."

Brayson clucked his tongue. "I can transfer another five thousand US from my crypto wallet. Would that make the transport officer happier?"

"If you insist, Señor," said Santiago as he opened the rear door.

After Brayson entered, Santiago returned to the trailer, signaling his men to join him. They let the migrants out to stretch for a few minutes.

Santiago's phone played Vios Con Dios, and he answered, "Yes, Mateo. The man is on the way to complete the transaction."

"Good, get moving. Wait just past our favorite fuel stop on the other side of Monterrey, about seventy-five miles. We met there two trips ago. Let the others know to head there when the transaction is completed. I may have other plans for the man you don't trust. I'll get back to you."

Santiago disconnected and shouted, "Time to load up. Give each person water and a snack bar or two." He turned toward his captives. "We will pick up your friend closer to the border."

Satya exclaimed in an excited tone. "Finally, I've tracked Brayson to the outskirts of Monterrey. I've been so worried. Auri, please confirm?"

Auri acknowledged, "Oh good. I was concerned after his signal went dark hours ago. Better alert JW that Brayson's surfaced and provide the current coordinates. It'll be a starting point if we lose his signal again. Good one, Satya. He was probably traveling in a metal transport, so we lost him."

JW joined the Gigazon bridge. "Nice work grabbing Brayson's location. Perhaps he'll transmit another message. The day would be golden if we caught another signal from those missing girls."

Granger came off mute. "They surfaced once. It's only a matter of time before we pick them up again. Practice patience, gang. We all know I need it." He chuckled and returned to work.

Satya remarked, "I'd like to see that crypto parasite we loaded on Brayson's wallet surface in a transaction. That would be sweet."

JW cautioned, "Team, we have several traps set. Stay the course. We will catch them. They'll make mistakes. Unless I miss my guess, we should see that crypto parasite jump to a new wallet soon. When that happens, we start geo-tracking to see the next destination. Then we can whoop it up a bit."

CHAPTER 37

Character Assassination

Mateo's agitation rose as the conversation progressed. Holding the phone with a death grip, he gulped and growled through gritted teeth. "You can't be serious, Julian. You can't believe Rodrigo has gone into business for himself?"

Julian smoothly offered, "My dear brother, I'm having difficulty receiving the necessary justification for his requests. I promised you a full accounting of your operations. Trying to get an accurate spend from him is…well, I'm not getting it. I noticed duplicate receipts but figured he was moving fast to complete the lab project. Is there a way to get a proper accounting of his purchases without hurting his feelings? I can't understand why he is buying material to set up another lab if you didn't order it or mention a backup facility to me. The only other explanation is that we're being double charged while he's lining his pockets."

Mateo stood in his office and began pacing, making angry grunts between what he was hearing.

Julian continued. "Each time I try to talk to him, he gets argumentative, telling me I'm slowing down your request. I don't like bothering you with simple accounting issues, but his demands for more funds are a worry. Can you talk with him and find out what I'm missing? I'm not getting anywhere."

Mateo paced back and forth. He switched the phone to his other hand and raked his hair with his fingertips. His brother was the last of his family and the keeper of his wards. Their lifelong bond formed in childhood which withstood many tests over the years. He barked, "Does anything else look funny, Julian? Please don't hold back. I want to help bridge the discussion if I can." Julian's sigh signaled more issues. He closed his eyes, hoping for the best.

"My brother, the ID I built for him must not have been to his liking because my source of new identities said he was approached by Rodrigo asking to buy a new identity." Julian cleared his throat and added another sigh. "When I asked my source who, he gave me the name of that new ID I sent to Rodrigo. If I had to guess, I'd say Rodrigo is getting ready to run and vanish, going from one ID to another. My source is reliable if you need to contact him."

"Send me copies of the duplicate invoices," demanded Mateo; then he swore under his breath. "I'll meet with Rodrigo." He shook his head, feeling the burden of the operations crushing him. "I thought things were going too well. In this business, that usually signals something's wrong. I will let you know, my brother."

Mateo paced a few minutes more, taking time to cool off, then poured two fingers of whiskey and threw it down his throat. He sat and mentally reviewed the details. Rodrigo, whom he had trusted for years, was going rogue? Yes, Rodrigo had become more insistent with his ideas and not steered him wrong. He had made money from them. Julian looked out for the best financial interest of the operations and never asked for anything.

He was helping care for his wards so Mateo could sell them for an exorbitant sum to the prince Julian had introduced. Would one of these men betray him? Loyalty meant everything.

Pacing, Mateo caught his fist in his hand and sent for his security chief. When he arrived a few minutes later, Mateo ordered, "I must get over the Rio and to Laredo tomorrow. I want to see how Rodrigo is finalizing the lab project. I want maximum security to get in and back to my hacienda in one day."

His security chief raised his eyebrows and challenged, "Sir, you're still a wanted man in the States. I'll take all precautions. However, if you are spotted or ratted out by a competitor, we will be firefighting with people who want you in jail or dead. I recommend we send someone to inspect. You should not take such a risk."

Mateo slapped his desk with the sound reverberating off the walls. "That's exactly why I will go. I must see if my trust has been betrayed. As my chief of security, ensure no one knows our agenda or timeline."

"Alternatively," suggested his security chief, "send for Rodrigo and have discussions here. Security is job one. Here, the authorities work for us."

"Thank you. I appreciate your advice. I will see more if I show up unannounced and find the operation is not as I ordered. If he journeys here and I ask questions, his responses can be truth or lies because they are only words. Besides, I want this to be a surprise meeting, not a fabricated response while in transit."

Seeing the apprehension in the eyes of a man who had protected him from birth, Mateo assured, "This is not a social call. Treat it like a full-scale hit if it comes to that. Make the necessary arrangements." He paused, then turned back. "Oh, and bring Javier along."

"Yes, sir."

CHAPTER 38

Take the Shot

Marian tried to stifle a yawn but made it more pronounced as she inhaled enough to make her ears pop. She blinked, unsure of her steps, exiting the plane into the chaotic Puerto Rico terminal. As her mental faculties cleared, she muttered, "That flight was almost as bad as the one they shoved me on leaving Afghanistan, except without the sixty-pound rucksack." She rubbed her face and eyes to erase the sleep. She looked at the signs and said, "I wonder where I get my bag and go through customs?"

Taking note of the two text messages on her main phone screen, she noted the location of her destination and a note from JJ. "Ah, good. I'll have Judith or Xiamara pick me up so we can debrief."

She watched the baggage carousel circle the luggage, looking for hers and dialed JJ's number. "Hi, JJ," she said as he answered. "I'm in San Juan. Are there any new hits on the beaconing flip-flops? And did you find Brayson? I suspect he's popping in and out of satellite surveillance with no alarms."

"Marian, Judith, and Zee were near the beacon signals. We don't know if the teens in the jam-packed bistro were our missing girls. Frustrating, yes, I know, but at least you're there to help identify them. That's the good news. The bad news is that you can't let Sophia or Elena know you're there until we can arrange to take down the organization that stole them. You walk up and say, *let's go home, girls*; we lose the first mover advantage. If you can spot them and remain undetected, then we can gather needed evidence on the human trafficking scum that stole them and bring them to justice."

Marian felt let down. "JJ, I understand, but I don't like it. Because we received a signal in a cafe filled with teens, I suspect they've been turned into harvesters. I shouldn't be too angry because if Sophia and Elena had already been sold off, we wouldn't have gotten this chance to find them. This whole business is vile. I don't believe we have much time before the situation shifts. We need to move quickly before we lose them permanently."

"Marian, these are thin leads," cautioned JJ. "I think you are right. We don't have much time. Smart criminals seem to know when to zig and then zag to stay safe. We'll move quickly but need hard evidence to eliminate this group."

Marian sighed. "My old drill sergeant pounded into me, *'Kid, you alone must know when to take the shot; Never too early, never too late.'* JJ, I'll make that call."

JJ grinned. "Agreed." Then he added, "As for Brayson, he just surfaced in Monterrey. We are hoping he's in a position to deliver our parasite cryptocurrency code to the traffickers for transport."

Marian asked, "If that happens, can we do an extraction? If he thinks he's delivered the crypto code to its source, he has no reason to stay in the caravan, right?"

"Marian, that's his call based on the circumstances. If he sees value in staying with the human traffickers and remaining out of danger, then that's what I'd expect. We're prepared to do an extraction when it's needed."

Marian grumbled, "I hope he makes the best choice for a win and comes home."

"Yep."

Judith and Xiamara rushed through airport security an hour before Marian's Houston flight was scheduled to arrive. Passengers from all over the world landed at the bustling airport, making it noisy. They decided to grab a table with a reasonable view of the sea of travelers at El Mesón Sandwiches to wait for the text indicating she had cleared customs. They ordered drinks and a few leftover breakfast items.

Marian rolled her bag near the table. Her voice boomed in the sudden drop in the noise from the last wave of tourists. "Hello, I bet you're Judith and Xiamara. I'm Marian."

Startled, their drinks bobbled. Judith's half-eaten bacon and egg bagel fell onto her lap. Judith huffed, then glared at the woman.

Xiamara giggled, all smiles.

Judith hissed, "You were supposed to text us and arrange to meet in a commonplace. We had no idea what you looked like."

Marian shifted on her feet innocently, making Judith think, "oh gosh, ma'am," scenarios from old movies and growing more irritated.

Her eyes shifted between the two. "I was told to look for two impatient but pretty ladies acting like they have everything under control. That is JJ-speak for, try and impress upon them that they can go from hunter to hunted in a heartbeat in this business."

Xiamara hung her head and moaned, "That obvious? No situational awareness, sitting here gabbing about nonsensical things, and making ourselves targets?"

Judith lifted the bagel, placed it on the plate, and wiped her hands on the napkin, which, fortunately, was in her lap. Then, she laid it next to her plate. She sipped coffee and griped, "Great, so you're here to deliver a tutorial on stealth? I find it irritating that JJ saw fit to belittle us. Still, it's unconscionable to receive a lecture in an airport from another team member who also happens to be a woman. Next, you'll tell us how to dress, do our makeup, and walk."

Simultaneously, their cell phones chirped with an incoming text message.

> You're on terminal cameras, obviously arguing. Take the discussion to a quiet area and call me.

"I don't know why he has us around if he already knows everything," complained Judith.

Xiamara added, "We're always in trouble with JJ. We can't do anything right."

Marian smiled and reached to pat each of their shoulders. "Not to put too fine a point on it, girls, but if he didn't have confidence in your abilities, he wouldn't care. He cares about safety and provides aircover, when possible, to ensure we succeed. We're after some ruthless people who think of humans as commodities. I was in the service as a leader, so I know how he feels. The enemy kept planting IEDs around the air base. My job was to make that impossible. I'm glad he backs me up, especially when he says, *'Hey, you're in a minefield, so step where I tell you.'* I'll take that kind of support any day of the week and twice on Sunday."

Fighting to keep her tears in check, Judith saw that Xiamara was too stunned to speak.

Judith felt she'd reached an inflection point with Marian and looked at her. "Zee and I have hustled for ourselves forever. Sometimes, our pride makes us overlook valuable support. We're not used to it." She stood, gathered her trash to pitch it, and inclined her head to Zee to do the same. "Nice to meet you, Marian."

Marian winked. "Right back at you, Judith," she added, grinning. "You too, Xiamara. I like your Zee nickname."

"Thanks," Zee grinned, flipping her curls on the right side of her face. "Feel free to use it."

Judith paused to do something with her phone. She liked the response. "Come on, our rideshare is this way," she indicated with a sweep of her arm.

Zee snagged Marian's bag. "I got your luggage, partner."

Marian mused aloud as she exited the terminal. "I hope you won't think me too presumptuous, girls, but since I'm here as your backup, we should do some situational awareness training." She cleared her throat. "I think some basic self-defense moves. I checked out the hotel's amenities. Let's meet in the workout room at five-thirty in the morning. Please wear appropriate workout clothing."

Xiamara stopped, wide-eyed.

Judith scowled and complained, "How about nine-thirty?"

Marian smirked, "Oh, that's right. Criminals always worry about what's convenient for the victims."

Judith glared. "We'll be ready."

CHAPTER 39

Empty Chamber

Rodrigo's two-way radio connected to his belt crackled alive, conveying a potential altercation at the entrance to the Laredo compound. He called the gate guard to get the details. Disconnecting the call, his eyes rolled as he muttered, "An unannounced visit from your boss with his security team can't be a good sign."

Rodrigo exited the building, watching the black SUV pull to a stop adjacent to the steps. Mateo's security team inspected the area to verify that everything was clear. Rodrigo's men appeared edgy. He moved down the four steps with his stomach doing somersaults while he forced a smile.

One of his guards asked, "Rodrigo, are we good?"

Exuding a confident tone, he responded, "Go back to your tasks. If I need you, I'll let you know. This is business."

He quickly looked around, pleased that Mateo would see that the living quarters of this remote location were neither rundown nor lavish. He made a mental note to add the low-maintenance groundskeeping to his following report.

He approached Mateo and extended a hand. "This must be important for you to risk coming here. Let's go inside, " he said.

Mateo nodded and jerked his chin to Javier to stay close. Sensing something was off, Rodrigo ushered them through the entry to an office with folding tables containing neat stacks of papers. Several chairs were positioned for easy access. Rodrigo offered, "Would you like to sit?" His hands indicated the chairs.

"No."

"Mateo, what brings you here instead of a phone call?"

Mateo's lips thinned while his expression darkened as he pulled out his cell phone and scrolled through the screen. Stopping, he tapped the screen to enlarge the image, then turned it around to face Rodrigo. "Julian said you're sloppy with your expenses. He has me wondering why you're asking for more money than we discussed. Care to explain?"

Rodrigo grunted, faced Mateo directly, and stated, "Boss, I have to deal with people who only accept cash and don't provide a bona fide receipt to use on your income taxes. I have to manufacture a receipt, which takes longer than we have to operationalize this place. So, I sent the same receipt for the second expense to show I spent the money. Julian didn't like my shortcut, huh?"

"You didn't bother to clarify it with him or me." Mateo, appearing angrier by the minute with his eyes narrowing, took another step closer. "What about the fresh ID he sent you that was used to buy another fresh ID but not through Julian?"

"I wanted my guy to test the ID to see if it would work as advertised or if it was flawed." Rodrigo added, "If it's good, then I have a standby, but if it isn't good, I don't get tossed in jail. Anything else?"

"Julian suspects you're lining your pockets and getting ready to run with your two fresh identities."

Rodrigo stood taller. Sensing rage course through his body, he clenched his fists at his sides. "I'm not ripping you off or getting ready to run."

Mateo bellowed, "One of you is lying!" He pulled out his semi-automatic 9mm berretta, pressed the barrel to Rodrigo's forehead, and pulled the double action trigger to bring back the hammer to fire. The hammer fell but only made a sharp click.

Rodrigo didn't blink. Out of his peripheral view, Mateo watched Javier pale from the act but remained silent.

Mateo's breathing slowed as he placed the weapon into his shoulder holster. "I wanted to hear you tell me to my face, Rodrigo. From now on you tell me what you need. I'll have it delivered."

Rodrigo suppressed a satisfied smile, "Thank you, Mateo."

Gracie apprehensively accepted the incoming call. "Hi, JJ. Is this good news or a bad news call?"

"We've got some insight into the human trafficking trade, but it's not what I would call good news. The U.S. Border Patrol shut down all train traffic coming from Mexico through Eagle Pass. The deluge of people seeking entry, whether legal or illegal, is at epidemic proportions. Mexican nationals are joining in the flight out because the cartel wars are raging. People claim they're terrified to go to their jobs because they may be kidnapped and forced to work in the narcotics export business. Even the Mexican army has to think twice about bringing order to northern Mexico."

Gracie's mind raced through the last week of escalating reports. "Yes, I'm seeing the update feeds from JW's team and the regular media. The whole situation's completely insane."

"It gets worse. Brayson met with his sources on both sides of the border before going undercover. He saw evidence that the human tsunami heading north into Mexico toward the U.S.

confirms ten to twelve thousand people crossing the border daily. Furthermore, officials on the U.S. side are convinced t hat experienced criminals are succeeding in establishing the distribution of narcotics to major cities. All under the guise of helping immigrants. Seems more like wolves in sheep's clothing pushing their wretched product inside the U.S."

Gracie moaned, "Good grief. Our project to stop Mateo sounds petty compared to the other issues."

"Sis, the support team is suggesting that the drug cartels are directing the illegals to focus on certain points of entry to overwhelm the U.S. Border Patrol deliberately. That leaves wide stretches unprotected. The cartels are using the poor unfortunates as human shields so they can move product over the border unmolested."

"They aim the people at border crossing areas to swamp the authorities and run over to open areas to complete their supply chain service of killer narcotics. It sounds like we're only targeting a small cog in a giant wheel of corruption."

"Desperate people just trying to run to a safe place to live are stopped at the U.S. border and told to go home. They become easy prey for the cartels who force the able bodies into their supply line of shipping illegal drugs. The other fate they face is the human traffickers picking off their kids as inventory for the sex trade. We were trained to fight this kind of injustice."

Frowning, Gracie admitted, "The answer to my question is it's bad news."

CHAPTER 40

Treasure and the Hunt

Light poured through the floor to ceiling windows on one wall of Julian's expansive office at his San Juan six-bedroom estate. Cream-colored ceramic tiled floors were topped with a few Turkish rugs that complimented the blue walls. The elegant furnishings extending his work area contained the neat stacks of papers and plans under review. His fingers clicked across the keyboard as he added items to the spreadsheet for staffing requirements and needed materials for his new data center.

He leaned back in the glove-soft brown leather chair, glancing at the butterflies dancing around the flowers surrounding the pool patio. Setting aside the last stack of papers after extracting the items, he texted Ryu to join him and bring a mug of tea. His cell phone rang. He noted the caller ID and ignored the call. Ryu knocked and then entered with the tea.

"Thank you, Ryu," Julian said as he rolled his shoulders. "I have our list completed, but I wanted to review it with you."

Before Ryu responded, he pulled his vibrating phone from his pocket. He threw his hand dismissively at the caller's information. He turned the screen toward Julian. "It's him again. I'm next on speed dial when you don't return his calls. What do you want me to tell him?"

Julian softly chuckled. "Don't answer. I'll call him back so he won't get his feelings hurt. Now and then, he makes progress."

Ryu shrugged. True to form, the caller left a frantic message begging to talk to Julian, which Ryu played on the speaker.

Julian took a sip of his tea and pursed his lips. He picked up his phone, pressed the number, and held it to his ear. "Harto," Julian said in a patronizing tone, "what news do you have?"

Harto's enthusiasm increased vivaciously until his voice boomed, forcing Julian to hold the phone away from his ear. "Sir, we are hot on the trail. Salvage teams have mapped the wreckage of Nuestra Señora de las Maravillas, which sank in the shallow waters of the Little Bahama Bank. You said it was salvaged to death, but people keep finding more metals. Coins, silver bars, and cannons are signposts to the magnetometer fish towed behind the research ship. They do measure metal, but not gemstones. I've located two additional gemstones where they're trolling. I know I'm right."

Julian's heart pounded at the mention of gemstones. He took a deep breath and motioned Ryu to leave as he rose and walked close to the windows. "You've kept this quiet? We don't need to share our finds with the silly governments who want a part of our action without investment."

Harto's giddiness forced Julian to slip into a favorite movie character and quoted, "Oh no, oh no by Jove no." Julian grinned, then asked, "Have you begun to mine the target area for more jewels discreetly?"

Harto took a breath. "I need more divers and more equipment, but that means a larger ship which will attract unwanted attention. Julian, I know you're in a hurry to add to your collection. Still, if I significantly increase the activities, it could draw more notice from the authorities. If they get involved, they'll demand a piece of the action or kick us out. We have our target location for the disbursed payload the Maravillas carried. I recommend we maintain our cover of amateurs poking around. I need additional time to experiment with the infrared spectrometer to spot the gems. We don't want to dredge and sift several nautical miles of the ocean bottom to have someone ask, '*what are you doing?*'"

Julian impatiently asked, "When can I see the gemstones?"

"They're already on the way," said Harto.

"Keep at it the way you've explained. Send me what you find for my evaluation. I'll have them polished and added to my collection. Thanks, Harto." Julian was elated, realizing he was nearing the pinnacle of his goals. As he returned to his desk, he texted Ryu to return. The girls would return from school in a few hours, hopefully bringing friends to enjoy their pool.

"Sorry for the delay, Ryu. Look at the list. If it appears complete, please print out a copy. Then we can meet with my new contractors and explain the setup I want in the data center cage."

Judith and Xiamara were delighted to have the opportunity to speak with Julian and hear about his plans. They both dressed in casual business attire of lightweight fabric, as rooms in the hotel tended to get warm.

"He must feel confident about us to have checked our background and called the professors about our abilities. I promise I won't say anything before listening," said Judith.

"Good. We are the experts, and we need this job. It will keep us close to the girls and maybe help get a lead on Mateo."

Both smiled at the door when Julian greeted them. He'd reserved the conference room in the hotel where they were staying. The room had a conference table, six chairs, one large whiteboard, and laptop connections for presentations. An array of beverages and food items were available on the smaller counter built into the side alcove.

"Thank you, Julian, for inviting us. We're excited to be a part of your private data center vision," said Judith. "Please tell us what you have in mind."

Julian grinned. "The comments about your capabilities from your references were quite good. Let me tell you what I have in mind, and we can go from there."

Julian launched into his plans, outlining the number of servers he wanted in the hosted data center cage. Judith shifted in her seat, itching to get up and modify some of his lines on the whiteboard, but Xiamara's silent look made her stop. After what seemed like an eternity, Julian wound down and asked for questions, looking quite pleased with himself.

Xiamara delivered a pleading look before Judith started into lecture mode.

Judith took a breath, tilted her head, and schooled her face into a serious expression. "Julian, we have extensive experience building out a server room or cage hosted by someone else. Today, with the capabilities at our fingertips, no one does that anymore. Spinning up virtual servers in a hosted data center is cheaper and faster. They provide perimeter security and Internet access; the hardware runs on reliable power. We simply remote into our virtual server stack, select the operating system flavor needed, and the programming creates what we need. Then we load your applications, and they are up and running. If we want some servers to be load-balanced or mirrored, it is a click in a checkbox. If we do it our way, you'll be online this afternoon or tomorrow after getting the contracts and commitments completed."

Xiamara bobbed her head, making her curls dance. "It will take weeks to build your environment if we use your old-school method, and it won't be as reliable. We are describing a cloud-hosted data center. We rent what we need based on answers to questions. It's more cost-effective as we don't buy what's unnecessary."

Judith got worried, thinking she'd said too much, when Julian's face darkened with annoyance, and he stood.

Pacing, he blurted with annoyance, "I want to touch my servers with my hands. Putting my data in someone's cloud data center is disadvantageous to me. I don't have your level of confidence. I want it where I can see and touch." He ruffled his hair and sat. "Umph."

Xiamara stared directly and calmly added, "Using cloud providers, telecom pipes, redundant electrical lines, and equipment permits you to access your data anywhere. You mentioned that your business could be quite fluid, so we recommend you build it to allow it to be moved quickly from one location to another. A viable hosting provider meets the criteria."

Judith soothed, "Julian, if we get you into a cloud provider you dislike, we or you can export everything to another host. The design we are recommending is both secure and supports mobile businesses. Most of the edge infrastructure we get with a hosted provider is stuff we would build. Using the telecom pipes takes a couple of weeks to order and configure. The cloud host has everything built and ready for us to plug into simply. You said you were in a hurry. This is how we resolve that concern."

Julian thumbed his chin, thinking. Judith breathed, thinking they were over the challenging part.

He asked, "How do I know it's safe? Some people…uh are corrupt and would try to steal my information. How do I protect against threats?"

Sensing his resistance was dissolving, Judith pitched, "We will lock everything down using two-factor authentication and give you God rights to all the systems. Nothing can be performed without you granting access rights to the applications, areas, and data. That includes us on your system. We always use secure tunneling to get to the systems so nobody can enter the door behind us."

The turmoil inside Julian seemed apparent, but he looked at his watch and said, "I need to leave. Draw this out so I can see how it will work. We'll talk again in the morning at nine. I'll have the hotel replace the food and leave the boards for you to use. That's all for now. Thank you."

When the door closed behind him, they rushed to grab some refreshments and started to work. "That was interesting," Judith commented in between bites.

"You were marvelous."

"Thanks, you too."

CHAPTER 41

Alternatives

Gracie enjoyed the morning light growing over her Manhattan office panoramic view, revealing the buildings opening for business. The spoon tinkled against the side of her coffee cup in her stirring, swirling the cream and dash of sugar. The clock ticked off the seconds, nearing the top of the hour when she expected the call. Gracie answered, "Hey, JJ, thanks for calling. Let me add JW so we can discuss your e-mail."

Moments later, Gracie verified, "Everybody here?"

"Yes, ma'am."

"Good, JJ, your email is thorough but fairly alarming. We're working to stop Mateo's group, but the trafficking maelstrom you depict dwarfs what we can solve as an organization. We don't have the resources to deal an effective blow to the import of fentanyl or human trafficking. The human tsunami racing to the U.S. is camouflaging the influx of illegal drugs. Political tensions keep the military forces of both countries on high alert. Armed conflict seems a possibility with average people caught in the middle."

"You're right," said JJ. "Our family assets, accumulated over four generations, aren't enough to slow this mass migration. You want us to stop this vile business, and I agree. However, we're outclassed in this particular game. We can share our intelligence with the Mexican and U.S. governments and simply back away, but I think your response would be no way. We need a different attack vector."

JW offered, "I wish I could disagree with him, Gracie. There are too many issues and people dedicated to their evil businesses. The governments are stalled in trying to combat the immigration of desperate people and organized crime. Honorable people are losing. Things might have been easier to control if some digital clown hadn't invented cryptocurrency for cartels to launder their profits. It's a perfect storm of misery."

ICABOD interjected, "May I make an observation? You seem to focus on the liabilities, looking for ways to beat them. Yet, everyone on this call knows it cannot be done. Approach the problem from a different angle. Under the current circumstances, the best strategy is to make the immigrant problem an asset. If you remove them from the problem side of the equation, the other issues are easier to focus on."

Gracie drummed her fingers on her desktop, tossing the idea around and weighing the options. "Of course. The border patrol is stating that ten to twelve thousand illegal immigrants are being intercepted a day. Instead of turning them back, they need to put them to work. We push for Mexico to designate economic zones to build manufacturing plants and small cities at the border. Instead of Mexico saying, Texas, it's your problem, they get a new tax base."

JJ added, "These people want to live and work somewhere, so putting them to work building their jobs and homes would shorten their journey. They were headed to look for work anyway."

"They're going to need shelter," suggested JW. It makes sense for them to make housing construction quick and cheap. Then, after the initial crush, slow the pace to build higher-quality housing. It follows that if the immigrants have jobs, a purpose, and a community to be proud of, the traffickers will find it harder to extort money from them to cross the border. They can apply legally and get accepted over time."

Looking out the window, Gracie's imagination painted the future. "We help get the new cities designated as economic zones, making receiving international loans for business development easier. Established manufacturing companies would appreciate a functioning community with a ready workforce for new plants to expand sales to viable markets."

"Guys," JW said, "even if we started tomorrow, it would take decades to build what you're suggesting."

ICABOD challenged, "There is a precedent for mobilizing many people into a building frenzy if properly motivated and managed. In 1942, the U.S. decided to go forward with the Manhattan Project. They located their manufacturing plant on the Columbia River based on the logistics and water needs. The city of Hanford in Washington State became the home of the first atomic bomb. The city was established in early 1943 as part of the Manhattan Project to produce plutonium for national defense. By 1945, over 40,000 people were working and living in that area."

JJ agreed, "A large workforce of desperate families and individuals willing to work to build lives for themselves would make it harder for the cartel infiltrators to move across the border to link up with their drug distribution pals in the U.S. The human immigrant camouflage used by the cartels would vanish. Border Patrol resources could spot and stop bad actors with more time to vet those crossing."

ICABOD summarized, "I calculate a sixty percent reduction of immigrants with this plan. The original process of asylum requests could slowly return to normal. With viable work and suitable living conditions available on the Mexican side, many will elect to establish their families in those communities."

JW reasoned, "I expect better screening and more pressure on the cartels on both sides of the border."

"In my role at the World Bank in the international lending division for business development, I have some ideas on where funding could be obtained. I also have friends at the United Nations and the International Monetary Fund who would camp onto the humanitarian angle this solution poses."

JJ advised, "That leaves the big problem of the fentanyl trafficking and teenagers being seduced into the sex trade, underwritten with cryptocurrency and the illegal mixers."

JW chuckled, "JJ, I just got word from the team that some of our crypto parasite tags got picked up when Brayson sent it to another wallet. Our plans to track are active. Is the rest of the team ready to launch the next phase of the plan?"

They all cheered.

"I need a favor, Gracie," said JJ. "I need a nice corporate shell company to be my Cloud provider."

Beaming, Gracie stated, "Contact Jeff. He can make that happen."

Jeff sat in his home office in his New York apartment, working on two projects due today. He'd completed the research but was finalizing the report required when his watch notified him of an urgent email. He then saved the document on his laptop and opened his email application. Pleased at the notation and link, he straightened his tie and joined the conference bridge. "JW and JJ," he grinned, "Nice surprise. How can I help?"

JJ smirked, "Jeff, you look all professional with that cool tie. Tell me you're not working in your home office in the slacks and Italian suit that Gracie likes, too."

Jeff laughed. "Nah, cutoffs I've worn for years, comfortable as heck."

The guys laughed.

"Gracie and I have come up with an idea," said JJ. "We need a private corporation created for a longer-term investment to help migrants who need to flee their countries but put a dent in cartel activities." He explained the vision of funding for community development on the southern side of the US border in locations near Texas and Arizona. "I need you to establish articles of incorporation with the best tax advantages with you as the legal counsel. This is all above board. You, Gracie, and I will work out the details for this private entity. That's the long-term project. In the near-term…" JJ cocked his head as if trying to find the right words.

Jeff arched an eyebrow, scrutinizing the guys on the screen. He could see a bit of Gracie in JJ's features, which made sense since they were twins. JW had chiseled features with startling blue eyes that seemed to drill into one's soul.

JJ grinned. "I need you to immediately create a shell corporation that can pass almost microscopic scrutiny and an attorney with superb negotiation skills for a special project. The company Magnolia Bluff Cloud Hosting needs to look credible, have a history and have an outstanding reputation for reliability from top-tiered experts. JW and I will help place the information wherever you direct in case someone goes snooping."

"What do you want to do with the shell corporation, and who needs the convincing that it is real?"

Jeff kept his eyes on JJ, watching as he formed his response.

"In a confidence game where you need to con someone who steals for a living, the opportunity or investment must be bulletproof when scrutinized. In this case, we will offer a secure private Cloud instance to the target, a man named Julian. We don't yet know how diligent or connected he is, though we are working on gathering intel on him. We suspect he will check the details from all angles to ensure that our hosting entity is reliable, secure, and with a significant track record. We make it verifiable from his research efforts and not just clicking a weblink we provide."

Jeff said, "I presume you can build the whole website of this private corporation to hold all the relevant information."

JJ nodded and continued, "The shell corporation must have been in business for years, say four or five; some customer testimonies, bios on the key people of the organization who have come from other plausible companies, some financial information elements, though it's not required of a private corporation, that shows their world is growing by leaps and bounds but still satisfying customers as job one. Soundbites on their investment strategies from a well-known now deceased investor that we can reference."

JW added, "I'll build multiple data points for background and references of users who contribute to its history."

Jeff opened his eyes, feigning shock. "Are you guys asking me to do something quasi-legal to scald an evil suspect?"

JW grinned innocently and offered, "Yes, but only in the pejorative sense."

Jeff laughed. "Why didn't you just say so? Count me in. I'll start now."

CHAPTER 42

We Had a Deal

Santiago wanted to finish this trip as soon as possible, especially since he was already spending the bonus Mateo indicated when he texted that the transaction was completed. Waiting on the side of the main road for his team to return with his golden goose gave him a headache. He crushed the wrappings of the lunch that he and his driver grabbed on their way through Monterrey and wiped his mouth. He spotted the text from Mateo.

> Flores was short one laborer from his contract. I said I had an extra if he could meet you. His team should arrive in under twenty minutes.

Santiago was satisfied with Mateo's solution. He rubbed his neck; the guy was too good to be true. Opening the passenger door, he said, "Keep it running. I see our SUV, and we are waiting for another one. I shouldn't be too long." He pulled out his revolver, climbed down, and strode toward the back of the trailer.

The SUV stopped, the passenger door opened, and the man was pushed out and bounced on the highway before ending in a lump. After a few heartbeats, Santiago released his breath as the man got to his knees and struggled to gain his footing. Santiago waved at the departing vehicle and approached Brayson with his gun raised.

Santiago waved the gun a bit, and Brayson raised his hands.

With squinted eyes, Brayson cracked his neck by moving his head from side to side, then appeared confused. "I take it the extra five thousand wasn't enough?"

Santiago smirked. "It was enough to get you back here alive. But your story's not quite right. You won't be riding in the trailer."

Brayson complained, "We had a deal—ten grand to the border and another payment to get me over. I agreed to the same for my friend. The twenty-five grand was transferred. Your guards witnessed it. What changed?"

"Friends of my boss called in a favor, and you won a new line of work. We've got so much inventory to get across the Rio that we can afford to be generous with some extra suspicious cargo. Don't worry; they'll get you over the border. You aren't all tattooed up like the young boys who get stopped by the U.S. Border Patrol and denied as gang members. Flores requires a few workers who can get past the security checks."

"And if I refuse?" Brayson said with a defiant edge to his voice.

Santiago guffawed. "This road has no human resource department. Either you get through security to move their fentanyl, or they shoot you through the head and then dump your body in a mass grave. After a little backhoe and dozer action, you never existed. Follow the rules, and you live. I think it is a no-brainer, Señor."

Brayson's shoulders slumped, but Santiago wasn't confident the man was convinced.

The guy shuffled his feet, and Santiago nosed the gun up.

"Señor," he implored, "I've got crypto and can pay more than they will if you get me to the border. Same as before for my friend and his family."

Santiago sighed. "If only it were that easy. The deal's done. I don't buck orders from my betters. Plus, I have no idea how to deal with digital currency. This way my boss gives me a bonus. It would have been different if you had gold bars that I could use. They'll be here in a few minutes. Work hard for them, and you'll live. That is unless the U.S. drug police catch you. As for your friend, it's a shame his teenagers will be the only ones to make the journey. But they may find you looking for a source." Santiago maniacally laughed and watched the emotions play across the man's face.

The long-awaited minivan pulled up alongside. Brayson got yanked in by two men, and as the door closed, Santiago saw them binding his arms.

Judith and Xiamara worked in the conference room for several hours, drawing out the data center's proposed connectivity and listing the expected security protocols. They exchanged three versions with JJ, making his suggested changes each time. Pleased with their results, they sat back in their chairs, sipping the last of their tea.

Judith wiped her hands and said, "Let's ask Marian to join us. We can show her what we're doing. Perhaps she can fill us in on the girls a bit more?'

Xiamara picked up her phone and sent the text. The reply was immediate. "She's on her way."

Moments later, a crisp knock sounded on the main door into the room. Xiamara rose and went to open the door.

All business, Marian entered and looked at the drawings on the walls. "You two have been busy." She slid into one of the chairs. "I was hoping you might call; I was getting a little stir-crazy waiting for information. I looked at the photos you sent JJ. The Sophia you met is one of the girls. I didn't see her best friend, Elena." She sighed. "I hope all is with her as well. The Julian name doesn't mean anything to me.

"Do you need to do any more on these drawings? I don't want to delay your work," asked Marian.

Judith shifted in her chair. "No, we're all set for tomorrow morning. We hoped you might tell us how you know these girls and why they are so important to you. It's still a bit of a mystery."

Xiamara nodded with a smile.

Marian shifted to get a little more comfortable. "Brayson and I helped with the case last year on the cruise ship. It was a messy case with lots of bad actors. One guy was named Mateo, and he brought the two young ladies to dinner. Based on their eyes and mannerisms, they were on some drugs. I was convinced he was grooming them as high-end escorts with table etiquette and conversation with others. This man controlled them so that when Gracie spoke to them, and they replied, he whisked them out of the dining room. They later surfaced, very drugged in an awful situation, and we rescued them. They were brutalized, abused, and manipulated to comply with demands. They were too young to choose what they did if you read between the lines."

Judith's eyes filled with tears. "What a shame. I can tell you that the Sophia we met and took a picture of looked like a clean and sober teen having fun. She was sweet and extremely talented, with a virtually operated keyboard, a quick smile, and nicely dressed. She spoke highly of Mr. Lafleur."

Marian nodded with a wry smile. "I hope she's safe and Elena too. They were both stolen from Brayson and me outside the port terminal in Miami. I gave them the shoes on a gut instinct

I hoped I never had to count on. I feared they'd been sold, which may be the case with Julian as the buyer."

Xiamara gasped. "That's the story behind those two. Sold into the sex trade, brokered by some low life, and rescued by you and Brayson, then taken from you. Wow."

Marian nodded thoughtfully but appeared sad. "JJ said I couldn't approach them until other things were in place." She slapped her hand on the table. "And Brayson's tracking beacon has stopped beaconing along the border between Mexico and Texas. It's not a good day."

Judith shook her blonde hair and complained, "You are connected to them, and JJ doesn't want you to be spotted! Why can't we get assignments where success is humanly possible?"

Marian shrugged. "Ladies, I'm your backup and guardian angel, but I need you to be my eyes and ears. Whenever you leave the hotel, please set your phones to Wi-Fi enabled to accept any Bluetooth beaconing signal. I know it will eat through your battery life. If you bump into that signal, I'll text you to shift to video mode, pretending to create a social media post. I'll watch and maybe see both girls here. I know this isn't your assignment, but you can help me clear my mind that I let them down. Tomorrow, I will go secure a rental vehicle for our extraction."

They threw their hands in a high five, reaching across the table.

Judith stood, shook out her outfit, and stretched. "Come on, girls. Let's visit the hotel restaurant, drink, and talk trash."

Marian laughed. "I like you two."

CHAPTER 43

Eyes on the Prize

At that exact moment, Satya and Auri announced, "Bingo!"

Satya cast a questioning eye towards Auri.

She admitted, "Okay, you saw the trail first. I like saying bingo."

Giggling, Satya asked, "JW, are you on Gigazon?" Looking at Auri, she giggled again. "That sounded cool."

"Yes, Satya, I'm on. Are you two cutting up?"

"Yes, sir," Satya replied, hanging her head in fake remorse. "We have movement of the crypto parasite from Monterrey to San Juan, Puerto Rico. They're running the Ethereum through several wallets, but we can see their movement and map the stops. They even ran our coins through a mixer, but we still have eyes on the prize."

Chuckling, Auri said, "You just did it again, Satya."

She nodded and sucked in her bottom lip to keep from bursting into laughter.

JW appeared on everyone's screen, rubbing his eyes. "Good work. The crypto parasite is doing what we hoped. Is Granger on?"

Granger cautiously entered the Gigazon and politely asked, "I'm here. I didn't scare anyone this time, did I?"

JW grinned. "Do we have eyes on Brayson somewhere near Monterrey, Mexico? He got the needed parasite infection, but I'd like his status."

Granger frowned. "I received a partial message from his Zoleo fifteen minutes ago in Monterrey, but it looked incomplete, so I was waiting for more. His clothing beacon signals show him on track toward Texas with a straight line toward Fronton Island at a fast clip. I don't believe he's in the 18-wheeler anymore."

JW's face drained of color to the point that Satya was worried.

JW asked, "Can you and ICABOD speculate on his abrupt direction change? He gave them the cryptocurrency to get transported to the border. Something's changed."

ICABOD's avatar showed in the corner of their screens. "Several things are possible. The first is the cryptocurrency bribe got him special transport considerations like a luxury tour bus or…"

Granger moaned, "They didn't buy his story and killed him. Or another cartel grabbed him—lots of buying and selling of humans are occurring in this region. Sex, drug smuggling, and scapegoat are likely options. But which cartel? Who knows? His text mentioned Santiago, and we are trying to cross-reference the name and create a profile."

JW closed his eyes. "I'll alert JJ that the cartel is not following our plan to snare them."

Judith and Xiamara smirked at the name Magnolia Bluff Cloud Services and the logo JJ displayed on the screen.

"Don't you have a property in that location, JJ?" Judith asked.

JJ nodded. "Sort of, but this is way different. We have a foolproof corporation that can be verified from every perspective possible. The pricing is attractive, and your time to complete the setup is attractive, secure, and expandable as the business grows."

Judith tilted her head and glanced at Xiamara. "We do the research and provide him the top three companies. This one is in the mix and ends up on top for every category."

Xiamara bobbed her head enthusiastically. "Sweet."

"You know the drill once the contracts get signed," JJ clarified. "Spin up what Julian needs to do his cryptocurrency services comfortably. Provide whatever level of security he demands. Put the monitor code on each virtual server as you spin it up. It will cloak itself at ring zero and allow us to observe all transactions. It's your failsafe if things go sideways."

Xiamara chuckled. "What happens when it is invoked?"

JJ replied, "It is a scorched earth routine that destroys all their data by erasing all data blocks, then passes bogus ones and zeros into the data blocks. No forensics can salvage the deleted data. It starts with one word, which you can decide later. It needs to be a word he can use in a pinch, but not every day. Then we have one recovery word he doesn't get."

Judith felt reticent and remarked, "Doing it correctly will take significant effort. Time we may not have if things go sideways."

JJ replied, "It is a two-step process. Suppose you are put on the spot. The first step moves all the pointers to the data, and the operating system reports to the operator that everything is gone. Then you get time to bargain. If things go seriously wrong, you can replace all the pointers, and life goes on. If everything goes to plan, you set the program in motion, we do your extraction, then the destructive program goes into overdrive, and his data is toast."

Xiamara asked, "And you're sure the crypto parasite landed in a wallet here in San Juan under that missing youth named Lisbeth?"

JJ appeared serious. "The parasite has bounced around through several names of people on our missing list. We must learn the process they use to sanitize and mask the owners. All the evidence points to Mr. Lafleur, but we need more concrete proof to turn over to authorities."

"Wow," Judith said, reaching out to hold Xiamara's hand. "Either this a false lead, or we are heading into the highway danger zone with no lifeline. Is that it?"

"Correct. We need to catch Lafleur with his hands dirty. Marian will watch your backs."

Xiamara commented, "She also has us hunting for signals from Sophia and Elena. If this comes together in a tidy package, do we help retrieve them?"

JJ moved his hand's palm up. "Packages are not neat with these types of criminals. Let's get everything we need to bring justice to the situation. If this Julian is the money handler for Mateo, as we suspect, then we are in a position to cripple Mateo's vile business model. That could include saving some innocents. Please be careful; you're important to my team."

Both of the ladies grinned as they disconnected the conference call.

CHAPTER 44

Quest and Discovery

Class ended for the day at the high school. Most of the students scattered, some toward home for studying, others headed toward the best place to hang out. Sophia and Elena strolled, stretching the time before their car arrived. Each looked around the immediate area for anyone who might overhear their private conversation. They paused, facing one another, eyes roaming to catch the movement of anyone approaching.

Sophia softly asked, "Did you get anything on them? I tried the kinetic eyeglasses I've been illustrating to book kids for interviews to place them, but I can't break through the admin control settings."

Elena shook her head with a defeated expression. "I went to the library computers and accessed the applications. Their last entries on social media were the day we came here. I reached out to one girl from school in St Kitts. When I asked her about Lisbeth, Maria, Consuelo, and Raul, she got mad. She said they hadn't been seen since we left. Everybody believes they came with us to San Juan. I'm so confused."

Sophia felt confused, and her stomach unexpectedly churned. "We know they didn't come with us. But, if no one's seen them, where did they go?"

Elena changed her expression by widening her smile; Sophia shuffled her books, grinned, and turned.

Madam Chloe, concerned as she approached, greeted, "Girls, is everything all right? I became worried when most of the others passed by."

Sophia giggled and admitted, "I thought I forgot my assignment from class, but Elena helped me find it. Do I need to work the bistro crowd again to get you more people to interview? Are any kids I sent to sign up working out for selling the devices or the part-time modeling jobs you and Nohea are trying to fill?"

Chloe chuckled and hooked an arm with each girl to begin the trek to the car. "My dears, we make the introductions to the hiring agency. The agency works to get the kids placed during the auditions. If the auditions go well, they progress to the photo studio and more interviews. Once they become billable models, we get notified. It can take weeks or months to hear back. I think you're doing a great job. I was notified that some received assignments allowing them to travel."

Elena casually added, "Madam Chloe, we keep wondering what happened to our friends from St. Kitts who wanted to join us here. An old classmate reached out and said they disappeared."

Sophia noticed Madam Chloe's expression blanched for a heartbeat. She waved to Nohea to open the passenger door.

"Now, girls," soothed the governess, "I explained they chose not to go with us. That doesn't mean they didn't leave for something else. They were unhappy at home. Nice-looking teenagers getting hired off islands in the Caribbean as models or spokespeople for selling products may jump at the highest bidder. That's their choice. You'll probably see them soon on some streaming television movie or ad."

Handing Sophia into the backseat, followed by Elena, she added, "You'll see them and say, *'Hey, I knew them when.'*" Then she slid in beside them.

Sophia sighed, "You're probably right. They weren't happy and just wanted more. I hope they get all they deserve."

Elena nodded her agreement but said nothing.

Madam Chloe breathed. "Nohea, let's go home. The girls have homework. Grades are job one. Right?"

"Yes, ma'am," Elena said.

The following morning, Xiamara and Judith, dressed for success in tasteful slacks and tops, arrived early in the conference room, delighted that the hotel buffet table was replenished with coffee, pastries, and fruit. Judith filled a couple of plates while Xiamara connected her laptop to the room's projector. Their confidence rose between the drawings placed on the walls and the presentation they planned. Judith would explain their approach to the project while Xiamara would demo each of the three options.

Judith took a few grapes and closed her eyes, enjoying their sweet juice sliding down her throat.

Xiamara bit a custard-sweet roll and signed, "This is going to be fun."

Judith nodded with a grin.

Julian arrived with Ryu in tow. "Good morning, Judith, Xiamara." He looked around. "Did you work all night?" he said with waggling eyebrows.

Judith straightened. "No, sir, but we did complete our research. We found some options to show you and can make some recommendations."

Xiamara added, "Please grab some of the delicious goodies, have a seat, and we can begin. Oh, and thank you for getting the buffet filled. It's terrific."

Julian deferred his head, poured coffee, and took a seat. Ryu excused himself and left, closing the door.

"Let's see what you put together."

Judith rose and flashed a smile. "Mr. Lafleur, we felt you might be more comfortable with a leading-edge Cloud hosted solution if we reviewed all the details. You understand the technology and have some concerns we felt we could address with a demonstration and explain some of the changes we have experienced."

Judith took him through the slideshow of connectivity to the cloud and linearly discussed the issues. An attentive participant, he made a few notes on his tablet and asked a few questions.

"I appreciate the details, Judith," he said. "Now what?"

Judith knew the next step would be received exactly as they hoped and handed him the three proposals. "We put together packets of information on the three top industry runners to solve your business need as we understand it. We'd like you to read them over. We are prepared to demo any of them after you finish."

"You aren't going to give me a recommendation?"

"You are a man who likes making decisions; am I right?"

He nodded, and a satisfied grin bloomed. "I'm glad you recognize that. Let me read these." He brushed his hand toward the sideboard. "Have some coffee or tea. Take a seat while I review the superb information you have provided."

Judith resumed her seat after filling her cup and adding fruit to her plate. She discreetly winked at Zee and received a smile of agreement in return.

Julian started flipping through the pages of the proposals. Each outlined its capabilities, pricing, guarantees, and reference comments by industry leaders. In the two loser proposals, a negative element was subtly placed. Xiamara expertly read her customers and knew precisely which items would kick the proposed option out. It worked in every scam they'd done. Both girls grinned quietly, watching his expression shift when he found the problems.

He looked between them.

Judith's confidence rose with his pleased expression. "Mr. Lafleur, which of the offerings would you like to see first?"

"Ladies, thank you for this education. I can see all my operational needs are accommodated easily with these options. I appreciate being able to compare the options. You've shown me security procedures, mirroring techniques, ease of operation, and pricing options lower than my original thoughts of having all the equipment myself. Plus, reliability and uptime are key factors. I found one, the Magnolia Bluff Cloud Hosting service, to have the best recommendations, competitive pricing, and superior options for incremental expansion. Would you agree?"

A knock interrupted Judith's response. She stood and opened the door.

Ryu said, "Julian, I apologize for intruding, but I have a call from Chloe for you. She says it can't wait."

Julian accepted the phone. He stepped outside but left the door ajar.

Judith and Xiamara both strained to hear his conversation.

"Yes, Chloe, what is so important you called?... Oh, that's good to know…Any idea how they were contacted?... Did you check their phones?... Well, that's good…Have them do their homework, and I'll remind them of the rules and to keep their curiosity in check…I must complete this meeting. I'll let you know if I'm bringing home dinner guests…Talk later."

Judith eyed Xiamara, and she raised her shoulder, looking as concerned and confused as Judith felt.

Julian rushed in, closed the door, and sat. "Sorry about that. Where were we?"

Judith said, "You were going to tell us which option we should demonstrate first."

He leafed through the proposals. "After reading the details, only one of these is worth my time seeing in action. Magnolia Bluff Cloud Hosting, or, with your permission, MBCH, seems to be the best option. Show me what it can do, please."

"Xiamara," said Judith. "Please establish a secure tunnel, and the show is yours."

Zee logged into her system, ensuring everything appeared on the big screen. She bit her lip as she peered at him. "I previously established an account in each solution to make the demos flow. You would get your account and tell us who should access which features."

She spun up a couple of virtual servers and added standard applications required before any customization. She walked through the entire process and indicated where their custom programming could augment different standard applications.

An hour and a half later, they finished. Julian grinned like a puppy who was getting a treat. "You made it look so easy. Wow. I think I could easily learn it, don't you?"

"One hundred percent," replied Xiamara, her curls bouncing.

"Can you please assemble the pricing and contracts for us to pursue tomorrow? I want to bring the accounting online first, then establish a bank of servers for digital coin mining. Is that doable?"

Judith eagerly indicated, "Yes, sir."

He smiled at them both. "Also, include your fees and hourly rates as I see good news in your future. I was hoping to invite you for dinner tonight, but I have a couple of matters that will take up my time."

He scribbled some information on a piece of paper and handed it to Judith, adding a kiss to the back of her hand, inhaling her scent. "Bring the documents to my home around three tomorrow. I can review it, and you can stay for dinner. I have a pool if you would care to swim before we eat."

Xiamara stood to say goodbye. He took her hand and gently kissed the top.

"It's been a successful day, ladies. Thank you."

When he left, they hip-bumped and started to remove the documents and secure their equipment.

"Let's find Marian, and then we can call JJ," Xiamara said.

CHAPTER 45

Closing the Sale

The victorious young women returned to their hotel and changed into casual clothes. Judith danced around singing childhood ditties after texting Marian to join them. Xiamara filled the room's refrigerator with the leftover goodies they had grabbed on their way out of the conference room. She was crafting a plate with the excess items to share when they heard a knock at the door.

Judith rushed to let Marian in. Bubbling with excitement, she said, "Come on in. We have good news."

The room had a nice balcony, so Judith opened the door to let in the fresh air. Marian grabbed fruit and a napkin and slid into a cushioned wooden chair. Xiamara followed suit.

Energy radiated off Judith as she paced. "Marian, it was textbook perfect. We provided the education layer with the relatable elements of new changes. He soaked it up like bread with milk. Zee did a fabulous demo with…" Her hands flew up, tapping her forehead to knock loose the memory. "Wait, we need to get hold of JJ, so we don't have to tell this twice. Zee, can you launch a conference bridge and request him to join?"

"On it." Minutes later, the secure bridge was launched, and the image transferred to the ginormous wall-mounted screen, courtesy of the hotel.

JJ's face appeared, "Xiamara, your demo was perfect. I suspect that Judith's presentation and the options packets worked since you didn't access the storefronts of the other two contenders."

Judith beamed, "JJ, it was perfect." She wrinkled her nose. "However, in the middle of the meeting, Ryu interrupted, and Julian stepped into the hallway to talk on a phone. We overheard a portion that sounded like a problem. Maybe the girls had done something wrong."

Zee added, "Yep, something about his needing to remind them of the rules."

Judith nodded. "He has more than one. We know he helps Sophia, so perhaps the other is Elena, Marian."

Marian appeared pleased, but Judith thought she saw the wheels turning.

"Anything else on that?"

"Yes, someone named Chloe. I'm not certain who she might be. A wife, housekeeper, or nanny is possible. It was around the time of school dismissal. Then he mentioned he might bring dinner guests, but he would advise her later. It was weird."

"When he returned to the meeting," Xiamara explained, "he reviewed the proposals and asked for the MBCH demo. When it finished, he recounted how he viewed it and requested a full-price proposal and our salary requirements to be delivered tomorrow afternoon. He gave us an address." She waved the paper in the air.

JJ grinned. "I heard that part, and your proposals are almost complete. I want to take one more view of them before sending them. Based on your location, I found a custom printer three blocks over. Marian, perhaps you can make certain it is put together correctly."

Marian nodded.

"Did you also hear about us being invited to his place to present the numbers and maybe swim in his pool? I'm betting his place is spacious," said Judith.

"Yep, and I can use that address to do more investigating of our Julian Lafleur."

Xiamara hung her head in shame as she sent the address information via chat. "We did good, boss."

"True that. You can check it out firsthand as long as you're careful. Take selfies to keep your memories of the experience forever. Don't be too nosey." They all laughed at the statement.

Marian looked at the screen. "JJ, send me the files and the printer's address. Let me see if we can make it the most professional proposal this man has ever seen."

"It shouldn't take me too long. If you find something glaringly wrong, use your judgment to make any changes," added JJ.

"Thank you," said Judith before she closed the video bridge.

They chatted about things they should do if things progressed as they hoped while waiting for the document.

Judith said, "Zee, we've got a good chance to get those girls rescued and keep our jobs."

"I think you're right," she replied.

Marian looked down as her phone chirped. "JJ sent us a copy of the proposal. Let's review it."

They opened the file on the screen and read it line by line with no issues.

Marian closed the file and copied it to a thumb drive. "I'm off to the printer. I'll be back as soon as possible."

"We'll be here," Judith promised.

Marian shut the door behind her, and Judith stretched. "Let's review this proposal until Marian returns. We'll memorize it chapter and verse." She pulled up the file and displayed it on the room's screen.

"I didn't want to comment before, but this is well done," commented Zee. "I've done proposals for software and services by us before, but this is the next level. It's got options for annual, multiyear, white-glove support, and all our costs per hour with additional per diem if we travel. It's everything he asked for and additional references for us outside the university."

They spent the next two hours reviewing the details and testing each other. It felt like they were back in school. When they agreed, they were prepared to cite the contract contents chapter and verse; they began to plan their outfits for the meeting the next day.

"I'm getting hungry. When do you think she'll be back?"

Judith looked at her. "How can I guess any more than you can? You can text her if you want to know."

"Yep, you're cranky and ready to eat like me." Xiamara grabbed her phone and sent a message.

A knock sounded at the door. Judith laughed as she went to open it. "That was good timing."

Marian came in with a bag, appearing pleased with herself. She handed it to Judith and said, "Open it up, and tell me what you think. Gary at the print shop said he'd be there for another hour if we needed changes. It turned out pretty good, I think."

Xiamara took one of the copies reverently and marveled, "Marian, it must have cost a fortune to have these printed with the gold embossed lettering, the heavy bond paper, and the saddle stitching for the spine. It looked good when we read it on screen, but I've seen coffee table books that weren't this nice."

Marian beamed, "You two cannot come off as cheesy floosies with a proposal handwritten with a crayon and then stapled.

Your professional status and acceptance depend on this proposal's extra polish. Oh, and I bumped your price per hour to two fifty with a minimum of forty-hour blocks. If he chokes, then strike through it and agree on a price. We need you in there, so haggle, if necessary, but not too hard before you accept his offer."

Judith chuckled. "You're willing to bet he won't quibble, right?"

"You had him at *'let me show you why our solution is better.'*"

Xiamara nodded and stated with her hands on her hips, "Are you as hungry as we are, Marian? I'm ready to eat. I want to take you to this little place to enjoy fish, beer, and live music. It's adults only."

"Good idea. We celebrate tonight because tomorrow, you professionals will stick to tea and coffee. You'll need to keep your wits about you when you are there. He's a potentially dangerous adversary who appears to launder money and is possibly involved in buying and selling human beings."

The chilling statement had a sobering effect on Judith and Xiamara. "Let's go. We'll be careful tomorrow." Judith promised.

The stinky, worn SUV bounced along on the almost paved Mexican road with the guards talking among themselves, ignoring their captives.

Brayson kept chattering in Spanish, trying to get a response. The cable ties secured his hands firmly behind him, making the ride insufferable. The two guards with him seemed uninterested until one held a knife to his throat.

"Shut up," he demanded.

The view outside told him they were headed away from Monterrey into the barren countryside. The few shacks they passed marked the homes of the very poor, who were likely taking siestas in a spot of precious shade. Checking the sun's orientation convinced him that they were heading northeast into cartel country.

A few hours later, Brayson petitioned, "Hey, can we stop? I need to pee. I don't want to spoil the car."

The guard in the first bench seat leaned over and asked the driver to pull over. The driver nodded and stated he could also use the break.

The SUV slowed and pulled off the road, stopping to accommodate the nature call. Brayson added, "Can you cut these cable ties? I can handle the situation myself. If not, would one of you help?"

Brayson was dragged out, and they cut the cable ties.

Brayson smirked and muttered to himself. "Don't worry, even though the cave is open, the beast is asleep."

The armed guards took a passing interest as Brayson relieved himself. After zipping up, he returned to the vehicle, where they waited to add his restraints. He decided to make a break for it and take his chances. He cracked one guard in the head with his elbow and tried to wrestle the weapon from him only to receive the gun butt to his head by the other guard, sending him lights out.

The standing guard sneered. "I figured he'd do that. You all right, man?" he asked as he helped his buddy.

The dazed guard shook his head, trying to recover from the unexpected blow, and delivered a kick to Brayson. They cable-tied his hands and tossed him into the SUV. The driver eased onto the road to continue their journey.

CHAPTER 46

Reality Chicks

Entering the estate's driveway, with white and pink flowering bushes on both sides, Judith was reminded of a fairy tale sequence in which the princess wannabe dreams of riches. Xiamara seemed just as excited as she pointed out her favorite plants and rainbow-colored tropical parrots. The rideshare stopped at the front house gate to the estate.

"Sorry, this is as far as I can go. Step up to the speaker, and an image of you will be sent to the house to validate your admittance. It's worked before, and a golf cart will carry you to the estate entrance."

"Thanks," Judith said with a grin. "Zee, I am certain this will be first-hand lifestyles evidence of the rich and famous."

Zee grinned and gripped her friend's hand. "I know. Even looking through the gate, it's unbelievable."

They climbed from the rideshare. Zee sent off a quick text on her cell phone to verify Marian could hear the conversation. Holding up her phone, she took a few photos of the plants and caught one of Judith and the driver.

"These memories are going to be special," Zee remarked.

"I know."

A text confirmed the question.

Judith completed the verification at the gate with her name and a photo of the agreement. The gate swung aside, and they entered, oohing and aahing at the stunning blooming plants, a skittering iguana, and a child who giggled and disappeared with a shout from its presumed mommy, who was close by tending to the grounds.

The promised golf cart, driven by a groundskeeper, arrived moments after they had confirmed who they were and whisked the pair directly to the front entrance. A lovely dark-haired thirty-something beauty appeared at the entrance. Judith felt scanned from head to toe in a brief moment.

She clapped with glee. "You must be Judith and Xiamara, the amazing geeks for cloud computing."

"Yes, ma'am, I'm Judith, and this is Xiamara," Judith said, extending her hand. "And you have us at a disadvantage," she added shyly.

"My apologies. I am Chloe, the governess of Julian's two wards, who will be down shortly. Come in, please."

Judith entered confidently, though internally shuddering after meeting Chloe. She recalled her fears after first hearing the line of a childhood poem, *said, the Spider to the Fly."* She smiled as she eyed the brightly tiled flooring, which offset the pale walls graced with paintings reflecting the islands and local workers. "This is beautiful. I've never been in such a lovely home." She pointed at a large piece of art and excitedly asked, "Can I get you next to me and take a selfie with that painting of the woman and her child behind us?" Leaning conspiratorially, she added, "I don't want ever to forget this."

Chloe smoothed her hair with her hands, loving the attention and moving alongside. "Of course, I'd be delighted."

Judith raised the camera, but Xiamara interrupted. "Hand me the camera, and I'll take the photo."

Xiamara snapped several photos, felt her phone vibrate, and heard the muted tone she'd set for the shoes' beacon signal. Without thinking, she swung around with the camera in hand, taking photos of the walls, when two girls wearing brightly colored belted summer dresses entered, giggling.

"Girls, our guests have arrived," Chloe announced. "Come meet them, please."

Sophia's eyes registered recognition, and she rushed to them. "Ms. Xiamara, I had no idea you were the guests tonight." She motioned to the other girl to join them. "This is Elena, my heart sister and best friend."

Judith spotted similar qualities in Elena: youth, pretty features, close to the same height, and flashing shoes. "Hi, I'm Judith. Nice to meet you. Do you work the kinetic eyeglasses like Sophia? That's how we met her at the cafe."

Elena shook her head. "I can't quite get the hang of that, but I'm great at math and science. Madam Chloe doesn't need to tutor us on our classwork, but she checks everything."

Xiamara reached out. "Hi Elena; I'm Xiamara, but friends call me Zee."

Chloe suggested, "Let's go to the patio. We have beverages and hors d'oeuvres available. If you wish to swim," she checked her watch, "we have time before supper is served."

Judith watched Chloe almost usher the girls and wondered if she controlled the teens. She made a mental note to mention that later when they debriefed. Xiamara lagged a bit and nodded at Judith to join her. She handed back Judith's phone. "Sweet, you have open Wi-Fi connection here if we need to check anything."

Judith acknowledged seeing the image and verified that Marian's app was still alive. She thumbed through the pictures and realized Chloe was looking at the screen beside her.

"Ladies, is there a problem?" Chloe asked.

Judith swallowed. She was grateful she hadn't been caught sending the photos. "We have some great shots. Look, Chloe," she pointed at one and nudged the woman's shoulder, "you have such a lovely smile. Thank you for making a memory for me."

Xiamara quickly added, "I wanted to verify she liked the photos. Apologies for dawdling. After you, ma'am."

Chloe halted. "Oh, your desire for fun photos inspired me. Would you mind if I take a couple of candid shots?"

Before Xiamara or Judith could object, Chloe captured them both with her phone. "Please, this way. You can relax before discussing your contract with Julian at some point." She looped her arms through both of theirs and headed out.

Julian entered the patio from a side area. "Welcome, Judith, Xiamara. Ah, I see, you've met everyone. If you have your proposals, please step into my office." He gestured at that doorway. "We can discuss business and hopefully celebrate an agreement."

Judith gave Zee an encouraging nod, and they entered his inner sanctum. Judith saw the view from his office of the girls outside dangling their feet in the water. Chloe kept a watchful eye. "I bet the pool sometimes calls to you, Mr. LaFleur."

Julian chuckled as he nodded. "Please, you two need to call me Julian. I expect we may be working together. The mister is an unnecessary formality. Judith, you're right, however. It can tug at me in the middle of tense negotiations. But this data center is of utmost concern. Did you bring your proposal?"

He indicated chairs for them with their backs to the pool. Once seated, Xiamara smiled and handed over his copy of the proposal.

"Julian," she began, "we assembled the costs and options for the contract of one, three, or five-year commitment for the services. Then, in the next section, we have our service costs, which include any custom programming you need and per diem expectations if you need us to travel to the location. We estimate it will take at least ten days to set up the environment, do the custom programs you alluded to, and test."

Julian read through the document and paused. "This looks good, though the hourly cost is higher than expected."

Judith interrupted Xiamara from caving on the amount. "Good tech support and creative programmers are hard to find in Puerto Rico. You checked our references, plus we added others, and you know we're two of the best."

He laughed, "Quite an adept negotiator, I see." He eyed them both. "If you can complete the initial tasks within seven days, I'll sign for the amounts indicated and begin with a one-year contract on the service. One of the reasons I preferred MBCH is because I can move everything to another service if needed."

Xiamara penned and initialed his change on her copy and exchanged it with him to complete the modification on his version. She grinned. "We can do that."

Judith asked, "Where is the location for this work, Julian?"

"It's in the adjacent building on the other side of the pool area. It contains guest living quarters and the same Wi-Fi connectivity across my estate. You can eliminate drive time and the cost of your hotel by staying here until the project is complete. Meals are my treat," he smugly added.

Judith felt a shiver move up her spine but ignored it. "I believe we have a deal. We can celebrate over dinner and return tomorrow with our things. I am sure the hotel will be happy to store our things for a week to let our room to tourists. It's a great location."

Julian smiled and signed the documents with a flourish. "Perfect." He texted Ryu to join them. He entered through an inside door moments later.

"Yes, Sir."

"Ryu, I need you to sign on the witness line of this document. Judith and Xiamara will reside for a week in the guest house. After supper, I'd like you to drive them back to their hotel tonight and pick them up at nine in the morning."

"Yes, sir. I'm glad they can help you with your project, Sir."

Judith grinned. "Can we get a group shot of my memories of this occasion, please? We are excited to begin your project, Julian."

"Ryu, please take the photo, then we will enjoy a nice dinner to celebrate."

Hours later, Judith and Xiamara returned to the hotel. Minutes after they were settled, a knock sounded at the door.

Marian rushed in, closing the door behind her. "Let me see the pictures, you talented pros."

Judith gave her the phone. Marian was delighted with the photos of Sophia and Elena. Judith saw her eyes fill with tears she refused to spill. She breathed heavily, gripped Judith's arm tightly, and muttered, "You found them; thank you."

In her exuberance, Marian gripped Judith harder than expected.

Judith winced. "Hey, easy on the merchandise. I'm not looking for any warranty work on that arm yet."

Marian caught herself. "Sorry, I didn't mean to hurt. You have photos of Julian, this Chloe character, and the missing girls." She tapped the photos to forward to JJ and copied them to her device.

"You don't know how relieved I am to see they are alive."

"We can't liberate them until the rest of the project is complete," advised Judith. "We've got to set up shop in the guest house, aka hosted data center, and prowl for clues for Julian as the money launderer for Mateo. We need some information on the Chloe chick. I wouldn't trust her for a second; she's too smooth, and she keeps a close watch on the girls. Something's off."

Zee nodded. "Agreed. Now, we need to stay there around the clock while fast-tracking the solution without getting caught while setting the trap. I'm not into being sold into slavery. It appears that Ryu is Julian's right-hand guy. We didn't see any other guards and a groundskeeper drove the golf cart from the gate, but the estate seemed secure, except for the wide-open Wi-Fi. The estate is massive; however, other guards could be scattered. The man's got an ego and air of confidence we've seen in men who think they own the world. We'll take care because we don't want to get sold into slavery, too."

Xiamara studied Judith apprehensively for a moment. "Is this where you'll complain that we don't get enough exciting and dangerous missions?"

"I think we are deep in the danger zone," retorted Judith.

Marian deadpanned, "I don't know why JJ thinks you two are adversarial. But I can provide boxing gloves if you feel they are needed."

"Naw," smirked Xiamara, "This is just our way of chicks doing reality checks at full emotional throttle. I always try her patience, knowing she has none."

Before Judith could comment again, Marian interjected, "Let's loop in JJ, so he can ask questions. I just sent him what I heard and the photos. He might have some fresh insight to incorporate into our next steps."

JJ immediately joined the conference bridge, and the girls updated him.

His face showed concern. "That's a lot to get done before we can extract the five of you. Marian, if Elena and Sophia discover you are here, we could be in trouble before we have enough evidence. I'll get some information on Chloe. I want to understand her role. Her photo helps. We'll run it through our facial recognition program. Thank you for the address on Julian LaFleur. We searched the property records, and he has estates on three islands, including St. Kitts. Each of these is sizable. He has social connections on all the islands. His photo was captured in the case with my sister. He's somehow connected to Pliant, who we put into jail for illegal dumping. Pliant was connected to Mateo. We're looking for the thread that ties Julian and Mateo together now that Pliant is jailed. These are dangerous people. I don't like you two on his property overnight."

"JJ," Marian said, "I have a small app on their phones that, when activated, I can locate them and hear most conversations. I will monitor it closely when they are at his estate."

JJ frowned. "Okay, someone, please send me Julian's phone number and any other numbers you have. We are going to track his call records to find out his connections. I'm sure his phones will have additional encryption, but I'll work through that. He also must have security people somewhere. He's too wealthy only to have one guard. We need proof that he's the money guy for Mateo, and I think we are running out of time. If we properly link Julian to Mateo and commandeer his finances, we can bring all five of you out."

Marian moved her hand with two fingers pointed to her eye and then to each of them in turn when she advised, "I'll keep a close eye on you." She handed them a device. "See if you can set up this remote camera for the data center creation so I can watch what's happening. I need you to stay together and let me see you often while you're working. Carry your phones with you even if you go for a swim."

Judith and Xiamara both groaned.

JJ growled, "You are in the lion's den once you arrive tomorrow. If we lose contact, we'll assume you're compromised. At that point, we will scramble to rescue and extract you. If things have gone sideways, I'd like us to be close. Are we clear?"

Judith replied, "Yes. But if we are heads down working, don't jump on a false alert. Marian, we will try to talk more to each other than we normally do. Don't jump unnecessarily because that will also put us in danger."

"Don't miss some sort of communication flow. Tell them your den mother worries about her chickens if they see you texting."

Judith complained, "I didn't like it when he smelled my hand like he'd do an appetizer. What if he wants to paw me as well? How much must I put up with before I deck him?"

Xiamara said, "JJ, I saw him enter her personal space like he was shopping in the produce section. It was creepy."

JJ laughed. "I know you are both self-reliant. If the situation goes sideways before the appointed check-in, please text the code word *sniper*. Marian will launch the rescue protocol activities."

CHAPTER 47

Touch Point Options

Julian, pleased with the contract to get the data center up faster than anticipated, phoned Mateo from his office after the girls retired for the evening.

Mateo answered. "Julian, how is it going? Do you deem my girls ready to be sent to the prince? I only have another nine days before he'll be at my hacienda to see them firsthand."

Julian grinned and said, "My brother, they are improved. I also have them positioned to attract new resources for your other business. Chloe tells me she had Nohea take four new candidates to Alvaro a few days ago. I expect him back tomorrow."

"That is good news. I will call him when we finish."

"Plus," Julian added, "I think I've two suitable options for the prince in case you want me to continue to leverage Sophia and Elena. I sent the photos to your special email address a few moments ago. They are slightly older but quite charming and beautiful, and the blonde one has an aphrodisiac aroma and is multi-lingual in English and Spanish. I need them to complete the data center setup for our digital currency transactions, and then I can have Ryu transport them to you. What do you think?"

Mateo grumbled, "You still want to keep Sophia and Elena there, right?" He studied the photos and observed, "They're a little older than he likes, but the blonde is stunning, so he may not object. The brunette isn't his type, but if I tell him they play together in a way he will enjoy, he'll go along. But bring Sophia and Elena along to be on the safe side. Who knows, maybe he'll take all four. With a big bankroll and insatiable desire, he's always looking for new acquisitions, so he says."

Julian argued, "Come on, Mateo. I found suitable replacements and let Sophia and Elena find you candidates. If things get too noticeable here in San Juan, I have locations on two other islands."

Mateo bellowed, "Do it because I said so. You don't question me when I tell you what I want. How long before transport?"

Julian ground his teeth, frustrated. "I can be there in a week, maybe eight days. Does that work?"

His temper now in check, Mateo clarified, "The prince can't get here any sooner than nine days, and it might be two weeks. If you can ship them earlier, then do so."

"Yes, Mateo." Julian disconnected and cursed the phone.

CHAPTER 48

Day Laborers

The sun beat down on Brayson as he sputtered and choked on the water, hitting his open mouth and face.

He smelled the dust of the desert drifting on gentle winds and heard the thud of an object land near his head. Then, the familiar voice of the guard reminded him he was a captive. In Spanish, the voice advised, "Are you still going to demand to speak to your lawyer?"

Brayson wrapped his arms around his head and whimpered, "I have a headache; what happened? Where am I?"

The guard smirked, "You were uncooperative, so my commander, Jose, clocked you upside your thick skull. He thinks you may be ex-military based on your defensive moves. Your build is one he prefers in his recruits, provided they work as directed. We normally don't offer second chances, but we are shorthanded. Your only option to live is to do the work he assigns you, and no more backtalk. Comprende?"

Holding his head, Brayson tried to open and shut his eyes to clear his vision. He struggled to a sitting position and groaned, "After all your hospitality, it would be poor manners not to offer to help in your noble cause of drug smuggling." He took a deep breath. "When do we start, chief?"

"Name's Arturo," he chuckled. "I don't know what government you are running from, but never forget you won't be able to outrun us. You are in our squad in our deployment, and we shoot deserters. The device for geolocation, likely used for your trip to our country of Mexico, is gone, as are the other metallic pieces sewn into your clothes. We believe recruits are more committed if no one else knows where they are."

Brayson swallowed his new reality, realizing the team would not find him. He nodded and rose to stand, ready for instructions. Arturo motioned for him to follow. They walked to waiting trucks, where Brayson joined several other unfortunate people also nursing bumps and bruises.

As they loaded, Arturo mockingly announced, "I love it here. Every burrito is a feast. Each recruit is a blessing. All loads of fentanyl are a fortune we share. I love being a member of Sinaloa." He laughed as he closed the door to their transport van.

Brayson closed his eyes and sadly said a prayer that Marian would forgive him when he recognized the name of the most vicious cartel operating in Mexico.

Granger hit the enter key repeatedly and insisted, "ICABOD, the signal on Brayson just died. Can you confirm?"

ICABOD responded, "You are correct, Granger; we have lost his beacon. JW, I recommend you contact JJ and update him on this situation. I will get a map of our positioning for the last twenty-four hours and have that to you momentarily."

JW announced into the Gigazon, "Everyone stays online while I conference in JJ. We need to get our direction at the same time. Thanks, Granger, for the fast call out."

A few minutes later, JJ entered the conference bridge. "What do we have, JW?"

JW advised, "JJ, we alerted you that Brayson's signal went rogue for some reason. Now we have no signal at all."

JJ quietly speculated, "If he were killed, we'd still see the beacon transmission. Battery life is not a problem for those devices. They might have discovered and destroyed them. He's likely alive and incarcerated, but that doesn't mean he's behind bars. We have no idea about his location."

"JJ, ICABOD loaded his tracked travels for the last twenty-four hours."

With tears shimmering in her eyes, Satya interjected, "I calculated the direction and speed of the signal, and we lost him maybe three hundred kilometers from the U.S. border. He stopped for roughly an hour, and then the beacon moved a short distance away before the signal weakened and disappeared. ICABOD, can you confirm that, please?"

"You are correct, Satya."

JJ rubbed his face. "Satya, Auri, can we intercept any satellite shots of the area and get close enough to see people?"

"We'll try and get back to you shortly."

"Thanks. We can't extract him if we don't know his crossing point. Have any more of the crypto parasite markers surfaced? If they do, that would indicate he is still alive and is trying to alert us to keep looking for him."

JW faced hope in JJ's eyes, even as his stomach roiled in worry about a missing teammate. "Good point. We'll keep looking. If the kids get some decent sky views, I'll share them with everyone. It doesn't make sense to alert Marian yet. We have nothing to tell her, and she's needed exactly where she's at."

JJ groused, "Sometimes you and your observations are a real chore, JW. I do tentatively agree."

Granger commented, "I read in a couple of places that there is an increase in single men crossing. Many are stopped or rejected as gang members based on their tattoos or attitudes. Authorities believe those are potential laborers to transport drugs. Some have been caught with drugs on them. Does Brayson have any tattoos or markings which could be misconstrued?"

JJ perked up, digesting the comment. "No, he has none. But you have a good point, Granger; they could have forced him into their service. That would check the boxes, too. I'll make another inquiry for help. Please let me know if anything changes on your side."

CHAPTER 49

Favors Owed

JJ's call to Agent Gabriela of the J-CODE agency went straight to voice mail. He left almost half his message before she returned his call.

Relieved, JJ brightly offered, "Hi, Agent Gabriela. Thanks for the quick call back. A conversation is easier than the clumsy voice message I was leaving, so you can delete it. The nice young couple who visited you a while back, Brayson and Marian? We had him infiltrate the recent migrant wave of immigrants to hunt for clues on the traffickers. He may be in trouble as his tracking signal has gone dark. He may be dead, or he may have been inducted into the cartel's drug distribution. We'd like him back if anyone spots him. If I send you his photo and specs, can you help locate him?"

Gabriela grumbled, "JJ, we're stretched to the breaking point. Frankly, I don't see how we can help. You want us to locate one man out of the thousands we see daily. That doesn't count the thousands we don't see because of cartel smuggling. It's not like TSA screening at the airport because the illegals choose lots of entry points. How likely will they cooperate by crossing in the right place so our facial recognition programs work?"

JJ countered, "I'd like you to have your team be on the lookout for Brayson. His last mapped trajectory had him pinpointed for crossing toward Fronton Island. That strip of land is a cartel stronghold at present, right?"

Gabriela protested, "JJ, we're not in the search and rescue business, especially in that locale. The Border Patrol would have a better chance…"

"I called you because we collaborated well. I've got suggestions to potentially stem the flow of illegals. I know you can't do a maximum all-out search, but I'm asking for a little help that might save his life."

Gabriela sighed heavily before she admitted, "If it were one of my people, I'd be asking you the same thing. Send me his information. I'll see what I can do."

Marian answered, "Hi, JJ. I'm on track with the girls; they're fine. Is that what you called about?"

JJ exhaled and said, "I've got a tough problem and need your help."

Marian swallowed hard to squash the fear in her heart. "I know that tone means we are in deep doo-doo. Let's hear it."

JJ calmly said, "Brayson's tracking beacon went dark. We believe the cartel grabbed him, but we doubt he is dead or in jail. We think he is being used to support the drug transport operation. I've asked for support from the J-CODE agency. They are drowning in their problems but did agree to try. Frankly, I'm not counting on it."

Marian lamented, "Damn. You hesitated to tell me because you think I'll dump the assignment here in San Juan and look for him. You worry if I stay here to extract our team and our missing girls, I'll hate myself for not rescuing my husband. You know, you shouldn't have told me; that way, I wouldn't be distracted from the assignment here."

JJ admitted, "Sorry, there's no right answer, but I couldn't keep it from you. Nobody but you can cover Judith and Xiamara while they arrange Julian's digital demise. Then they grab Sophia and Elena to complete their extraction, but if you bolt and go to the Texas border, that rescue scenario is gone."

Marian offered, "We need more people to help those we care about."

JJ considered, "Perhaps I ought to go to the border. I'm just sitting here answering the phone for bad news, and we have a MIA team member."

"JJ, you're the master planner of the CATS team, not search and rescue. You'd be going up against cartel guns while trying to stay in covert mode. Brayson and I have seen you on the firearms range; we need someone else."

Marian studied the situation momentarily, then bargained, "Let me call in a favor, JJ. I might have another solution to add to the pot."

CHAPTER 50

Vertical Markets

Mateo smashed the answer button on his mobile phone and snapped, "What is it, Flores? I've already started shipping recruits to you for grunt work."

Flores angrily retorted, "My guys told me that you're holding back on the precursor fentanyl shipments. Then, I heard about a new lab being set up in Laredo. Your people weren't smart enough to buy their gear from someone I don't know. Nothing occurs in my territory without me knowing. I own this part of the world, Mateo."

Mateo's nostrils flared as he stood and began stomping around his office. "I know! You're getting all the precursor fentanyl you ordered. It makes sense to provide downstream finished products to boost my profits. What's the big deal?"

Flores barked, "The big deal is I'm the only source authorized to distribute fentanyl. Since you're my precursor supplier, I'm prepared to make it worth your while. I understand you're in business for profits, just like me. I'll purchase the lab, property, and people to avoid an inner war over your indiscretion."

Stunned, Mateo reeled back his anger when he realized Flores' offer was generous. His troops were far more formidable. Still, he gently bargained, "Do you still want me to cull good strong backs from the human migration for your use? I can for the same price as the last few."

Flores calmly stated, "I need you supplying and supporting me, not as competitors. I'll pay your reasonable fees but stay out of my patch. Are we clear?"

Mateo took a breath and returned to his chair. "Yes, we're good. I'll alert my man in Laredo to the change in our position. We can transfer the knowledge of this lab if you have someone to trust and run what we've set up."

Flores roared with laughter. "The people I trust are still alive. I'll send in my lab engineer, Manny. Just give him the keys and passwords."

"Flores, your product and mine is coming through to Fronton. My load is destined for Laredo for the first production run. I want payment for that as well."

Flores grunted and demanded, "You were out of bounds with the lab for your profits. I suggest you donate the product as a gesture of goodwill."

Almost shaking with rage and barely under control, Mateo cooly offered, "Then let me sweeten the deal, Flores..."

Rodrigo gripped his chest, confused when he noticed the incoming call. "Yes, Mateo?" he said.

Trying to contain his annoyance, Mateo snarled, "Where are your loyalties, my friend?"

Surprised at the tone, he replied, "I told you where my loyalties were while you had a 9mm pointed at my head. What's going on?"

"I was forced to sell the lab in Laredo to Flores. Otherwise, it would be a range war I would lose. I don't want to sentence you to his organization. I'd rather you stay with me, but you don't want that. You've served me well. Set someone to run the lab. Once Flores's guy, Manny, has everything operational, they will shoot whoever remains outside their group. If you don't want to return, I'll send you money and tell you to run into the U.S. and leave all this behind. Maybe you can land a teaching job again. This offer is a point of honor for me."

Rodrigo smirked, "A point of honor in this business, who would have thought? I have two false identities; may I keep them both? I would be grateful for the coin, Mateo."

Mateo chuckled. "Sure, they won't do me any good. Check your phone. I've provided a link to a crypto wallet with twenty grand. Are we good?"

Rodrigo sighed. "We are. Goodbye, my friend."

"Goodbye, Rodrigo."

CHAPTER 51

Engineering Rescues

Auri delightedly announced, "Ah ha! I show our parasite crypto moving to Laredo." He looked hesitantly at Satya in the image displayed in Gigazon. "Uh, unless you saw it first, Satya."

Satya laughed, "No, you won this round. I was busy trying to crack into the cell calls from the numbers we received from our team in San Juan. The Laredo number is new to our list, but I believe it is part of the Mateo circle. Our target endpoints reach from San Juan to Miguel Alemán, down to the Sea Port of Manzanillo, and now Laredo, Texas. Let's wake up JW to tell him what we have."

JW snapped, "I'm on, Satya! It's not that late here." JW brushed his hair behind one ear and asked, "What's up?"

Auri looked between the two and grinned. "I tagged our crypto parasite in quantity at Laredo, Texas. It's in a wallet we haven't seen before. Oddly, the funds show all at once, not piece-meal like the other transactions. It didn't go through a mixer. I suspect it might be an emergency transaction with this urgency and lack of safeguards."

Satya waved her hand wildly to gain attention and exclaimed, "I got into one of Mateo's latest cell conversations with someone called Flores. I'm having trouble getting their Spanish, expletives, and everything translated. Mateo is selling his drug lab to this character."

JW advised, "Flores is the main instigator in the big cartel. He is the dominant bad actor near the U.S. border for fentanyl production and transport. Interestingly, crypto flows in from Mateo's group to a freshly built lab being turned over to a rival gang. I suggest that JJ look into this location because something isn't right. Why would you add funds if I had sold a property just coming online? I would have thought it would outflow."

ICABOD interjected, "Even in criminal organizations, bonuses might be available for performance. However, the transfer would have made more sense to a wallet located in San Juan or Miguel Alemán for a valued employee. I see a high probability that the recipient will not return to Mateo's organization, which is unusual."

"Well done," JW praised. "You can reach out anytime you spot something, Satya. I'll alert JJ."

His voice was loud and clear as he announced, "Lieutenant Austin Stevens, Texas Border Patrol. How can I help you? I have no number displayed and you're not marked as SPAM."

Leveraging her perky, disarming voice, she replied, "Hi Austin, it's me, Marian. I've got my operations control manager, JJ, on the call to fill in some of the background to my request for help."

Austin pushed back his Stetson. "Uh-oh, sounds like you need a favor."

Remaining upbeat, she chuckled. "I see why you're the go-to official with the Border Patrol. We've lost an operative who went undercover and joined the human tidal wave heading toward the Texas border through the desert. His primary objective was to understand how the human trafficking slimeballs prey on the migrants in the caravan. Our intel points to him being drafted into the cartel. He's able-bodied and lacks tattoos, so he might be tasked under threat of death to bring in fentanyl. Our last known path showed him heading north toward Fronton Island."

Austin felt blindsided by the call. Before he could protest, JJ interrupted, "Austin, I'm JJ, the department director of this group. I want to share details that make things look worse. We got word of a cartel transaction a short time ago. It involves Mateo Hernandez, who we are focused on. He broke out of a supermax prison in the United States, and we can position him in Mexico. Our suspicion is that our operative got forced into labor and is heading toward a new fentanyl lab being built on the northeast side of Laredo. The cartel manpower on U.S. soil running this lab prevents our team from rescuing him. Can you help?"

"Austin," Marian said, "The operative is Brayson Morris, my husband."

Austin felt the burden of emotional weight roar through his senses. He shut his eyes and mentally said a prayer. "I wish you'd started with the last piece of information first, dammit. We might locate him at the crossing into Fronton Island, but we have a higher probability of catching him at Laredo. Is that your thought? You know, arrest warrants and handcuffs on these wretches are like using harsh language and water noodles from a pool. Areas hot with fentanyl traffickers shoot first and skedaddle. I need a better reason to go in than one unauthorized man. Marian, don't take that personally; it's just a fact."

JJ's hand getting slammed on the desk echoed on the call. "Sorry, I'm frustrated. We know precursor fentanyl is coming through Fronton Island to be manufactured in a new lab on the outskirts of Laredo. It's a big load. I would submit that hammering them just as the lab is gearing up for production would be an important setback to their operations. I think I can pinpoint the address for your team. It's an ideal ambush if your team can pull it off."

Austin roared, "What do you mean IF WE CAN PULL IT OFF? Listen, JJ, we've been fighting this drug scum for years. If we can believe it, your information would allow us to hit before they ramp up. And, yes, we'll try to find Brayson, preferably alive. Marian, I owe you at least that much."

CHAPTER 52

Celebrating

Julian hit the buzzer to admit Madam Chloe. She entered the data center to deliver a tray with coffee and sweet bread snacks. Judith and Xiamara were busy at their keyboards, with Julian off to one side. Chloe set the tray on a table near the girls and moved toward Julian for some privacy.

She quietly remarked to him, "They're here and lounging around the pool." She appeared concerned. "Sophia and Elena seem a little on edge but are socializing with their friends."

Julian nodded. "We'll be ready for a break in twenty minutes. I'll meet with my wards privately in my office. You and Nohea begin the inventory processing steps on the candidates. I have Ryu arranging transport for Saturday morning."

Chloe nodded and left the room.

Xiamara looked up from her keyboard, grinning with delight. "Oh boy, snacks. Just what I need to pad my posterior."

Judith focused on identifying the items on the snack tray and frowned. "Zee, you promised to curb that appetite for calorie highballs. Good thing we're almost finished with the data center build. The constant flow of coffee and treats has become too tempting, Julian."

Julian chuckled. "What's wrong with a light snack to reward your hard work? We're almost done with the build, and I'm pleased some of the applications are already operational. How much longer on the digital currency mining servers?"

Xiamara advised, "Julian, you can start right now. Profitable crypto mining is all about how many servers you can run in parallel to crank out more coins. As your electricity bill doesn't eat you alive while the investors buy in, you can keep adding servers to run the mining program. Please remember we said the mining program will have your servers running at full capacity, so expect to see processor failures requiring replacements. We have documented the process so you can have a junior tech spinning up new virtual machines as needed."

Julian nodded, pleased with the brilliant duo who would do well where he sent them. He grinned. "We're almost done. I want to celebrate with a dinner in your honor this Friday. I'll have my data center. You will be well on your way to your next contract. I don't want to let you go without a proper goodbye. Think of it as a bonus. Please tell me you will permit me this moment to honor you."

Xiamara smiled, and Judith nodded with a worried expression.

The data center oversight work was finished for the day. Julian met Sophia and Elena in his office overlooking the pool. "How are both of you feeling? I am pleased with the number of candidates you've lined up for Madam Chloe's modeling placement business. She's thrilled. She also tells me your grades are perfect, and you have received teacher praise."

Both of the girls beamed with the good news and words of praise.

Julian continued, "With next week's summer school break, I thought we might visit Mexico and see my brother, Mateo. I have gifts that I need to deliver."

The girls sported worried looks with apprehension in their eyes.

Julian promised, "We won't be gone long. We'll return with plenty of time for you to have fun with your friends." He laughed. "That's unless they pursue modeling careers. Don't you feel good about helping your friends achieve their dreams of modeling careers? You have helped so many kids achieve success. You should be proud of yourselves. I'm proud of you."

"Julian," Sophia said, "please don't leave us with Mateo."

"You will return here with me." He crossed his heart and smiled at his wards, who he felt were his not his brother's. "Go get ready for supper with our guests."

Sophia and Elena left, chattering and giggling.

Julian nodded to Chloe, who entered as they left. "I'm taking inventory with me Saturday morning to Mateo. Make sure all is in readiness. Ryu has air transport lined up. We leave early. Ensure there is no trace of the kids being here in case someone inquires."

Chloe replied, "Nohea and I will ensure they are properly neutralized for the flight and not spotted by Sophia or Elena."

Julian smiled, "Good. I'm hoping once Mateo gets the two new whores, he will stop hounding me for my wards. This calls for a celebration."

CHAPTER 53

We Got This

As they returned to their quarters, Xiamara discreetly scanned the area and asked, "Did you get it placed?"

Judith grabbed her friend's hand with a reassuring squeeze. "Of course, Zee. I'm an old hand at this cloak-and-dagger stuff. The stealth audio/camera is high enough in the data center to capture almost everything for transmission to Marian, including audio and video. I wish we had a way to plant one in his study, but I don't see that happening. I received a text message from her saying the signals are presenting perfect images and sound."

Xiamara stuck out her tongue at her friend. "Last time I checked, you have about eight minutes more experience being stealthy and secretive than me, which means we are neophytes. Our team members have the needed gear, know how to use it, trust us just enough not to screw up, and direct us on what to do next. The only thing we are old pros at is great programming skill for pigeons wanting to get plucked and getting into trouble."

Judith stopped and placed her hands on her hips like a challenge. "Hey, we got this. You and I are not some laughable clowns but sharp ladies adding to our resumes with each success. We discovered where Sophia and Elena were stashed, got into the lion's den to build a fake data center, and are about to put the squeeze on Mr. Enchantée. We've gotten this far with our superior skill and cunning. Stop dissing us."

231

Xiamara sighed. "I feel better having a camera and audio watching over us while we work. I'm not sure I can take much more of him coming close enough to smell us. It creeps me out."

Judith smirked. "Agreed. I bet Marian's laughing her butt off, watching us trying not to squirm when his breathing invades our personal space."

Xiamara mused, "Do you think we need another camera for the dining room for the gala dinner he insists we attend?"

Judith commented, "It wouldn't be bad if we had an extra. Anyway, we've only got one more day before the dinner, and then we are out of there."

Xiamara lamented, "I almost wish JJ would let us release the code and pull us out now. I'm tired of hourly text messages to Marian. The longer we stay in this gig, the less I like it."

Judith patted her friend's arm. "Come on, we're almost there."

Ryu knocked at the office door and waited to receive permission to enter. He was nervously fidgeting with a handwritten note. Finally, Julian waved him in. Ryu discreetly passed the note to him yet said nothing. Julian, puzzled by the irregular action, opened the note.

We need to talk outside, not in here.

Julian folded the paper and placed it into his pocket. They retreated to the patio and waited for the access door to close.

Julian growled, "What the hell is wrong? We need to come outside to speak?"

"Sir, you have me watching your back and eliminating problems. I found a problem. As a precaution, I always scan the premises when guests are in for extended periods. I found an electronic eavesdropper signal from your guest house/data center. It showed on the house Wi-Fi router in transmitting. The signal is encrypted, preventing me from seeing what is being transmitted, which means it is military-grade. It wasn't there last week, but it is there now. Sir, that is the room that those two contractors have been working in for the last seven days. I believe they introduced it when you were out of the room."

Julian stomped around the patio and fumed. "I've been duped. Someone is attacking me, using Judith and Xiamara while they program the data center. Dammit. If I wasn't sure about taking them to Mateo, I am now. I must have you and Nohea hit them tomorrow after the last server is spun up. I was going to treat them to a nice gala dinner before taking them, but that's off the table. Hit them and store their drugged bodies until the Saturday flight. Make sure they are heavily drugged before they get loaded. I'll have Mateo deal with them so they never bother us again."

Ryu stated, "We can't remove the electronic bug because it will alert the listeners and they'll run. You must pretend all is good. Don't say anything that will give our operation away."

"Yes, you are correct. Will you be ready to grab and sedate them when I give the signal tomorrow?"

Ryu acknowledged, "We've got this, sir."

CHAPTER 54

Hope is Not a Strategy

Brayson was despondent. All he could think of was escaping back to Marian. She had been his rock and reason to work so hard. He was not at the top of his game and feared he would be eliminated as they moved the precursor material into the rubber rafts. The second carton he dropped earned him a bruised rib from the butt of an AK-47 rifle.

"Mister, perfect Spanish, drop another one, and you'll be floating face down in the Rio Grande, sucking water into your lungs."

Arturo bellowed, "Pick up the pace to cross the Rio and order dinner. You won't get fed if you make me late for food from my favorite taco vendor."

The early evening crossing was uneventful. They hauled the product onto the waiting trucks. One of the vehicles was a food truck labeled *Roach Coach*. Everyone ordered food. Arturo dropped a pint-size bag of the in-demand capsules into the hands of the vendor, who grinned at the bonus payment.

Arturo completed a head count and swung his AK-47 around to aim as needed against resisters. He barked, "Everyone in the trucks; it's time to drive to work."

Brayson assisted one of the older men into the storage area. The man was short, early forties, and on the verge of tears. He nodded and clasped Brayson's hand. "Gracias."

Arturo sneered. "You are way too helpful. Get your ass in there, Mr. Boy Scout, or I'll blow it off in two shots."

Everyone was loaded and perched into an opening with the cargo. Arturo raged, "You volunteers are here to work, and we'll feed you if we get the effort required. Sluff off so someone else has to do your bit; you get a bullet. Comprende?" He stared at the older man who needed help getting in.

Brayson struggled to mask his anger, wanting to choke the life out of the man with the gun. He nodded in acceptance to avoid the fight with Arturo until the odds were in his favor. The doors closed, then padlocks clicked locked. No one would leave unauthorized.

The volunteers, up before sunrise, started to nod off to sleep in the cramped confines of the truck. The bumpy, rut-filled roads did nothing to wake the exhausted men. Brayson overheard that it would be a few hours' travel to get to the new Laredo compound. Brayson was awake enough to pray for an opportunity to escape, then chided himself, recalling that hope was not a strategy.

Brayson was almost asleep when the truck lurched to a stop. Voices were heard outside, and the padlock was removed so the doors could swing free. It was late afternoon, with twilight soon approaching. After the lousy truck ride, the volunteers crawled out and tried to stretch their tired, aching muscles. The two trucks loaded with precursor fentanyl were repositioned to back into the unloading area. The volunteers watched, and the security guards watched the volunteers.

Arturo was greeted by Emiliano, the compound lead, who had only recently achieved the honor of being in charge of this f acility. A third man joined their conversation. They fist-bumped as a show of comradery, letting everyone relax.

As the sun set over the wooded compound, Arturo swung his weapon and instructed, "Manny is our lab person assigned to understand your production process, Emiliano. My orders are to get you two connected, unload the precursor fentanyl for processing, and then head back to the border for more. Our volunteers will work to move the raw material into the production area and then transport it to our distribution center where…"

A voice, fully amplified with a bullhorn speaker, demanded, "Throw down your weapons and put your hands in the air. We're U.S. Border Patrol, and you are under arrest."

Brayson noticed Arturo was not going to go quietly or even at all. The security guard cursed and swung his weapon to fire while running for cover. Brayson lunged at the volunteers, yelling, "Get down and start crawling out of here. This will be a range war with us in the middle."

The wild, sporadic fire from Arturo's guards hardly matched the precise, controlled fire from the Border Patrol. Half the eight guards were down in seconds, with the others pinned down by a crossfire. Brayson made it to cover behind a truck only to discover that Arturo had joined him.

Arturo, somewhat rattled, asked, "Brayson, you've got military training, but can I count on you to use it?"

Brayson growled. "If I don't, I'm gonna die. Give me a weapon, and let's fight!"

Arturo jumped as a bullet bounced right next to him. He pulled out a semi-automatic with two clips and pitched them to Brayson as they both heard another bullet whiz over their heads. Brayson pulled the slide back to check it was loaded, and fiery eyes grinned before he said, "Let's do this."

But rather than square off against the Border Patrol people, Brayson turned and fired twice into Arturo, killing him instantly. One of the last security guards had made it to his cover area, and he was also shot, falling dead on top of Arturo.

The gunfire exchange dropped off from both sides, and the voice over the bullhorn demanded, "We have the area surrounded. Throw out your weapons and live."

Two weapons sailed out into the open, and moans were now audible.

The bullhorn voice then instructed, "Is there a Brayson Morris here? If so, announce yourself."

Brayson was startled, uncertain how to respond. He whispered, "Here."

The voice bellowed again.

Brayson screamed, "I'm here! Brayson Morris is here. Don't shoot."

The bullhorn voice cautiously demanded, "We are looking for the Brayson who can correctly answer the passphrase, *Are you a turtle?*"

Brayson, stunned by the old Air Force pilot drinking challenge, muttered, "I'll be go-to-hell. Yes, Marian, I remember. Thank you, honey."

Brayson, loudly chuckling, yelled, "You bet your sweet ass I am."

The bullhorn voice replied, "Response accepted. If you have a weapon, bring it with you and stay low in case any stray cartel members are still alive. We hope we got them all, but hope is a poor strategy."

Brayson smirked and muttered, "Copy that."

CHAPTER 55

Change of Plans

Graceful fingers delivered the final keystrokes, timed like the last act of Swan Lake, when Xiamara announced, "Ta-Da! Julian, you have a solid cloud-hosted data center ready for business."

Judith handed him the final documentation binder. "I've added post-it tabs to the changes discussed during your final test. The manual has everything you requested and an online folder with all the current instructions. I am sure you will grow and modify it over time."

Julian accepted the manual and set it aside. Grinning broadly, he graciously stood and clapped. "On time and within budget. Together, you delivered everything you promised and," he looked down with a boyish smile, "included my wild changes without complaint."

Xiamara chuckled, "Changes are a part of technology. You can run this with minor support, but call us if needed."

He withdrew envelopes from his pocket and handed one to each of them. "I had this ready to present, knowing you'd be finished today. You're that good. Smart and lovely. Half in U.S. dollars and the remainder in individual cashier's checks."

"Thank you." They responded in unison.

Smiling broadly, he said, "Let me open a nice sparkling wine and toast to a job well done."

Chloe entered the data center shortly after he summoned her with a tray of three glasses and an opened bottle of almond sparkling wine. Smiling at the group, she silently left.

Julian poured and joked, "I still have to catch myself and refer to it as sparkling wine rather than Champagne. A sommelier once chided me for using the terms interchangeably, which I have not forgotten."

He handed a full glass to Xiamara and Judith, then raised his, toasting to a finished project and good health. His sip was interrupted by the musical tune of a call to his cell phone. He set his glass down to retrieve his device and answer the call. Using his hand, he motioned for them to continue as he turned to gain a small amount of privacy.

They sipped the bubbles and giggled between the sighs for the delicious, light flavor.

Julian listened to the caller and turned to face them with a grin. "Let me ask them. Ladies, do you favor this beverage? My chef is asking because we need to order more for tomorrow's festivities if you like it. Are you still coming?" He pointed to the phone. "He is going all out to prepare a quintessential Caribbean feast."

They each swallowed the remainder of their flutes and then licked their lips.

Xiamara gushed, "This is excellent, champ…I mean sparkling wine. I'd like a little more in my glass, please."

Julian looked to Judith, who nodded in agreement, extending her glass.

Julian shook his head slightly and loudly laughed before he replied to the caller, "Judging from how fast this bottle is going, better make it a full case. I need to catch up; they're way ahead of me."

Julian disconnected the call, and the phone slipped from his hand to the desk, knocking his glass over the edge and onto the floor. It shattered. "Oh, bother." He grabbed a linen napkin used earlier to dab up the liquid. "At least I missed the documentation with my clumsy move. I'll ring for another glass and ask to have this spill mopped up."

Suddenly, Xiamara uttered, "Excuse me, I need to run to the lady's room."

Alarmed, Judith followed right behind. "Zee, are you okay?"

In the hallway to the guest quarters, they ran into Nohea and Ryu, who quickly pressed chloroform-soaked washcloths to their faces. Moments later, they were silent.

Ryu softly chuckled, "Between the drugged wine and chloroform, they'll be out for a while."

Julian casually strolled into the hallway to watch his men load Judith and Xiamara into wheelchairs and whisk them out the back entrance to the waiting van. Ryu returned to gather the ladies' possessions and stuffed them into their satchels. He'd cleared the bathroom earlier and wiped it down. He looked around in their sleeping quarters one more time. He grabbed the two bags to leave but stopped short to do a two-finger salute toward the camera location before exiting via the hallway to the van. The entire house was deserted shortly after Ryu entered the van to drive. Madam Chloe, Sophia, and Elena were in a vehicle closely following.

Marian loudly squealed as her heart sank, causing her to drop to her knees. "What the hell? No, it can't be." Tears formed in her eyes as she punched the speed dial number on her mobile phone, calling JJ.

He answered, "Yes, ma'am. Is the project completed?"

Marian, breathing like she was running a five-mile marathon, gulped air, trying to speak. "They failed to check in, JJ. I saw them cheering like the project was finished. Julian applauded. He had Chloe bring in crystal flutes and a bottle of wine. Julian was distracted by a phone call. Both of them drank and seemed to be having a good time. Zee set her glass down and rushed toward the sleeping quarters with Judith on her heels. Julian picked up the documentation binder Judith had presented and, a short time later, left in the same direction as the girls. Ten minutes later, one of Julian's security people gave the camera a smirking two-finger salute as he left the data center. I think they've been grabbed and maybe drugged from the wine. Julian did not have a chance to drink his. You can watch the playback in case I missed a detail."

On their conference call, JJ presented the floor plan of the guest house the team had located during the property's title search. He noted the hallway and exit door to the rear entrance. "They could have left out the rear door. With the salute, I guess the camera was discovered at some point. Julian wanted his project completed."

Marian stood and wiped her eyes, getting ready for instructions. She heard his fingers on his keyboard.

Seconds later, he said, "Yes, Xiamara set the track code earlier today, which means they finished. We know from bits and pieces of cell phone surveillance that Julian was planning a trip to Mateo's hacienda. He likely bagged up all the girls and will take them to Mexico."

She heard his fingers clicking again while she stuffed her gym bag with a few clothing items, a passport, and toiletries.

JJ sighed. "He's going to run fast. He has no idea who or what he's up against. We don't know when he found the camera, so Julian's had time to plan something. There it is; I'm checking for private aircraft flight plans out of San Juan. Ah, hmm, nice. I found a fast jet that could hold ten and has the range to fly non-stop to Mexico, leaving tomorrow afternoon. I'll see if we can locate a charter contract and flight plan if that's the one. Marian, any noise from the secondary transmitters you stashed in their computer bags?"

Marian stomped her foot. "I forgot all about those. I am looking now. I have a bad feeling about these signals. They are a few hundred yards away from Julian's home but not moving. That can't be good."

JJ advised, "Can you go and check on the signals, but don't get too close to be spotted. You're too important, and they have no idea who they're messing with."

Marian jumped into her rental SUV. She was on her way, closing in on the signal destination. Marian pulled the vehicle up to stop within yards of the signal, advising, "JJ, I am going to check this out, but I'm leaving the call open just in case I get jumped."

JJ agreed: "Prudent thinking. While you hotfoot it there, I will see if we can intercept Julian's air transport so he can leave earlier."

Marian was moved rapidly. "Leave earlier?" she said. "What are you thinking, JJ? We need more time to think and organize, not less."

JJ chuckled, "Rule number one in warfare is that when the enemy is in range, so are you. Translated, this means the more time we take, the more time our enemies get to escape."

Marian sighed, "True, that. JJ, I'm almost on top of the signal and…rats! It's coming from a dumpster behind a street of food vendors. I'm putting the phone down to look. Be right back."

A few minutes later, Marian confessed, "JJ, it was just their bags and computer gear. Julian probably figured they did not need computer gear where they were headed. There is a high probability Judith and Zee won't need PCs for their next gig as sex slaves. That's four girls I've let slip away while on my watch."

JJ chided, "Boy, you and Brayson with your *'it's all my fault thinking.'* I'm looping in some folks to help. I need you to head to the airport and connect with the security team."

Marian felt relieved to have a task. "Thanks. On it."

CHAPTER 56

Almost Home

Julian sat comfortably in the front passenger seat of the luxurious limousine headed toward the airport. Sofia and Elena were seated in the back, with Madam Chloe in between. They looked defeated, which made him sad, but he had no choice. "You will be quiet unless I or Madam Chloe ask you to speak. Do you understand?"

The girls nodded, eyes brimming with tears.

"You will not cry or do anything to draw attention from anyone. If you do, Zee and Judith will pay for your failings."

They both inhaled deeply, nodded, and said in unison, "Yes, sir."

His cell phone rang, and the screen indicated Mateo. He closed the privacy screen and faced forward. "Mateo, we are staying the night at the airport suite I reserved. I'm trying to change the flight plan to first thing in the morning. I…"

Mateo interrupted, "Brother, I need the girls to arrive tonight. You will remain in San Juan until tomorrow or the following day."

Verifying the privacy panel was shut, he shrugged toward Ryu and shook his head. A glance out the window confirmed they were behind the van Nohea drove. Julian suspected he had misheard, so he paused to collect his thoughts, then soothed,

"Mateo, I don't understand. I told you I have chartered our flight out tomorrow afternoon to arrive tomorrow night. I will try to change it to a morning departure. You mean you want the girls to fly, but I stay here? I don't get…"

Mateo roared, "I don't need you to think. I've several things in play. The problems I'm facing are easily cured with money. You're my finance expert. I insist you remain connected and available to complete the funds' transfers when ordered for the next twenty-four hours. This is not up for debate, Julian." Julian heard Mateo slap his desk before he continued. "Put the four females, the governess, and one guard on the flight number I texted to you. I must have my inventory tonight! Get connected, then stand by for my instructions." The phone went silent.

Julian frowned, then took a breath and read Mateo's text. "Ryu, contact Nohea to head toward the far side of the airport. The Learjet, tail number ending in 2WT, departs in forty minutes. We'll help get them loaded, and then you and I will go to the airport suite I reserved for tonight to await instructions."

Julian lowered the privacy screen. "We are making a change, and your flight is leaving shortly. We're headed to the plane. You will board without a fuss of any sort."

The girls nodded and looked down. Madam Chloe appeared confused.

"Chloe, take them safely to my brother."

She nodded.

Ryu followed the van to the private jet ramp with two individuals on the ground waiting. Julian decided it was the pilot and co-pilot in their aviator sunglasses. He appreciated his brother's attention with a professional crew smartly dressed in black caps, aviator sunglasses, and blazers with matching slacks, white shirts, black ties, and black shoes shiny enough to reflect the afternoon sun.

Julian rushed to the gangway and met the captain, who extended his hand. "My apologies, captain, but a couple of our guests overindulged. Can you assist Nohea here with getting them seated?"

The captain chuckled. "Certainly. This isn't the first time we've helped partygoers get home safely."

Madam Chloe shepherded her charges past the crew who were unloading the wheelchairs. The girls focused on their feet walking up the ramp. Chloe hissed, "Girls, this is what happens when too much wine is consumed. We're taking them for a much-deserved vacation in Mexico before they begin a new project at the hacienda. They will be fine after a few hours of sleep."

The ground crew helped load the remaining passengers and luggage. Julian walked up to verify everyone was securely belted. "I'll see you tomorrow or the day after."

The flight crew removed the chocks and boards. The co-pilot shut the door. Seated in the left seat, the captain finished the pre-flight check and began the sequence to start the engines. Headphones replacing flight caps, the captain checked with the tower and nudged the plane toward the taxiway.

A few minutes after the plane started moving, the captain announced, "Folks, this is the captain. I've got a red-light condition on the instrument panel. We are instructed to head toward our maintenance hangar on the other side of the runway for remediation. I don't expect it will take long to correct."

The plane aligned with the company's hanger. The pilot shut down the engines. After the co-pilot released the door, the ground crew lowered the gangway. The captain allowed airport security to board the plane. They seized and cuffed Nohea and Chloe, escorting them down the gangway to the emergency vehicles inside the hangar.

The captain and co-pilot stepped aside so EMS personnel could enter the cabin to evaluate the condition of both Judith and Xiamara. Following a quick evaluation, they were loaded onto stretchers and carried to the waiting ambulances.

Sophia and Elena were silent with wide eyes as the captain and co-pilot approached. The co-pilot removed her cap, shook out her hair, and grinned. The girls shrieked in recognition, undid their seatbelts, and threw their arms around her.

The captain chuckled, "I guess you have this handled, Marian."

She looked over and nodded, with tears riveting down her cheeks. "I do now."

Marian cried, "You're safe. Home free."

CHAPTER 57

Practicing Patience

Ryu jumped out of the chair where he'd been napping as Julian stormed around the suite and yelled, "What the hell is taking so long? He said to get connected and wait for money transfer instructions. It's been hours."

Ryu cautiously offered, "Text him? It's less intrusive than a call if he's busy."

Julian scowled yet nodded at the logic and quickly typed.

> Mateo, I still stand by to transfer funds, but it's been hours. When were you to call?

Moments later, Mateo called, "What money issues? What phone call? I haven't spoken to you today. Are you losing it?"

Julian's eyes widened with alarm. "Mateo, I got a phone call from you almost three hours ago demanding that the four girls I was bringing tomorrow get sent on a flight today. The plane was waiting on the tarmac where you said. You said I should stay here to complete critical transfers. I'm at the airport suite waiting. Tell me…"

Mateo shouted, "What? I didn't call you or tell you anything. We deal in narcotics, but we don't sample them what we create in the lab. That shit makes you sound crazy like you are now."

Julian paced, sweat beading on his forehead. He yelled, "Don't use that tone with me. I got a phone call from your phone. You made your demands, and I followed them to the letter. Are you the one sampling?"

After a few moments of silence, Mateo closed his eyes, fearing the worst, and stated, "We've fallen for a fake. We've been hacked."

Julian shook his head. "We found a camera and microphone hidden in the data center. Ryu felt certain it was introduced by the female contractors I was bringing to you. Whoever was smart enough to impersonate you and your phone likely already has all the girls in their possession."

Mateo asked, "What exactly were those contract girls working on for you?"

Julian stared at the screen. "I had them working on our cloud hosting solution." He logged to the home page. "I can't get into the system. They gave me all the login passwords for everything, but I can't log in. I am only getting a message about a 404 file and website not found." He closed his eyes. "Our accounting records, banking info, and my new Bitcoin servers aren't reachable. I swear I tested them."

Mateo raged, making sounds of things being thrown and kicked. "Julian, get control of our funds, or I will have you killed. Call me back in two hours with what I want to hear."

Realizing that the call had been disconnected, Julian threw his phone onto the desktop. "Ryu, we need to run. Whoever got those geeks to sabotage our money systems must have us targeted, too. Find us untraceable transport while I make one more call."

Julian paused a moment. "Don't use anything we've used before. We need a clean getaway."

Ryu nodded. "Yes, sir."

CHAPTER 58

Bargain Hard

The orange and red tendrils announced the sunrise on the horizon when the gates protecting Mateo's compound exploded. Shots were exchanged between shadowy figures. The opening was cleared, and three vehicles raced toward the main building. Many of the hacienda's security guards littered the path with blood seeping into the earth. Flores's men burst through the front door, shooting two additional defenders. Flores strolled toward Mateo's open doorway. Mateo struggled to strap on his shoulder holster and pistol.

Flores wickedly cackled, "Don't bother putting it on, Mateo. This isn't a social call."

The two weapons on either side of Flores drew Mateo's attention. He slowly slid the holster and 9mm off his shoulder and laid it on his desk.

Flores recognized Mateo's fierce anger and determination, reflecting his internal turmoil.

Flores spat. "You set me up, el bastardo! You knew the Laredo lab was targeted, so you tricked me into buying it. Border Patrol agents swarmed the place as the precursor was delivered. Too many of my best people are dead. I want my money back."

A storm formed on Mateo's weathered face. He maniacally laughed. "You expect me to write you a check? Then sit at my table and have breakfast like old times?"

Flores stomped forward and pressed the barrel of his semi-automatic against Mateo's forehead. "You conceited el cabrón. Your games are over. I want my money back. You're out of business. I'm taking it all."

Mateo took a breath, stared Flores in the eyes, and smirked. "Flores, get that gun off my head. My contacts are getting your drug products into this country from China. They only deal in cryptocurrency. You don't have anyone smart enough to handle digital financing."

Flores lowered the weapon but remained toe-to-toe.

"You don't have people able to broker or place the young people to fill the insatiable thirst for sex, but I do. If you're that unhappy …."

Flores growled, "I've got three of your best working for me. When Javier lost two fingers during the discussion, he decided to help make shipping connections for me. My people in Houston said the feds got to Alvaro before we could. The whore house is closed for now. Santiago was regrettable, but the rest of his team joined me. I thought we'd get Rodrigo in Laredo, but he was never found."

Beads of sweat formed small rivers from Mateo's forehead and neck. "I'll pay you. I don't have that kind of cash here. Everything's converted to my digital money accounts. Shoot me, and you get nothing. My brother manages it in a cloud hosting company…"

Flores uproariously laughed. "That's exactly what Julian told me you'd say. You know you pissed him off, grabbing his two wards. He cut a deal with us and agreed to do the buying from the Chinese for me. Goodbye, Mateo."

Flores raised the gun and sent a round through Mateo's skull. He commented to the lifeless body. "Rest in hell."

CHAPTER 59

A Small Win

JJ peered into the Gigazon portal. He smiled, seeing everyone abuzz in anticipation of their special guest. Auri and Satya were bouncing in their chairs with grins. JW wiped his sweaty hands. Granger was busy coding a new program to enhance his artificial intelligence application.

JJ joined the bridge.

Everyone fell silent and appeared attentive.

"Well done, all." JJ grinned and added, "The poisoned code has trapped Mateo's accounting system, which is being exported to the authorities for prosecution. Mateo is out of business."

Marian and Brayson joined the conference bridge. "Brayson, a little worse for wear, having put himself at risk to expose the human trafficking angle, is back with us."

Brayson smiled and waved to everyone. "Thank you for helping the authorities locate me. It was scary."

JJ continued, "Marian, thank you for your brave actions. Your quick thinking while everything looked like it was going downhill at a gallop made the difference."

Marian chuckled. "We got Judith and Xiamara back, but they're still in the hospital for observation. As a bonus, the two human trafficking victims, Sophia and Elena, were recovered. They are receiving medical treatment."

JJ said, "That is great news, Brayson and Marian. You can rest easy; no more blamestorming yourselves."

They both nodded and leaned their heads together.

Gracie clapped and raised her thumb. "The U.N. peacekeepers and on-site contractors have intercepted the human migrant tsunami to begin building the new economic zone in Northeast Mexico across the border between Piedras Negras and Nuevo Laredo. Construction materials will come over through Eagle Pass and Laredo on the U.S. side. The immigrants are all being recruited as we speak."

Satya and Auri could no longer contain themselves. Satya said, "Gracie, tell us how you tricked Julian. We gave you the phone number you requested, but how did you convince them to put the ladies on the earlier plane?"

Gracie smirked, placed her phone closer because of the Gigazon camera, and launched the deep fake application. Gracie admitted after playing the voice segment, "We had a voice sample of Mateo that you had copied from the call you hacked into of his. We ran it through the voice synthesizer, creating a voice exactly like Mateo's."

Auri impatiently argued, "We know how to do it, and I could've done it. It's not just the voice."

Gracie chuckled. "You're right. We had to get into Mateo's character to bark at people. I had to make whoever I was speaking to believe it was Mateo. With the correct persona for the voice deception, I added a mask number app to display his number on the receiver's cell. I barked and demanded like Mateo and added vulgar words in Spanish."

Auri acknowledged with a smile. "When I heard his voice demanding the girls be loaded on an earlier plane, I believed it was Mateo shouting the orders. Har! Har!"

Gracie admitted, "It was JJ's idea. I role-played and became Mateo for a phone call."

JJ chortled. "Gracie tricked me like that one time when we were teenagers. I never forgot it. Thanks, Sis. That's all the good news. The bad news is that the money man, Julian, and one bodyguard vanished. We trapped Mateo's accounting books in our MBCH area, but most of the funds were gone. We think Julian got away with it. He may start up something in the future. Thanks to Judith and Zee, at least we have his information."

Brayson interrupted, "JJ, we've received word from the Mexican government that Flores wiped Mateo out in a range war at his hacienda yesterday. Gracie, it seems you got your wish. Flores is ascending the throne of power with his army and branch of the cartel. The battle is over. The war is not."

Discussion Questions for

Enigma Forced

Book Club Leaders …contact Charles and/or Rox to participate in a special meeting to discuss the book; the concepts; and the evolution of the series. We always encourage readers to post individual reviews on Amazon.com. And thank you.

In-person gatherings are possible if you are in the North Texas region. Otherwise, Zoom is always an option.

Group Discussion Questions

Did the ending pull you in? Did you want something different?

- Would you have preferred Mateo survive?
- What did you think of his hacienda, and what should happen to it?
- How did you like Julian and want to know what he will do next?
- What was your top takeaway from Enigma Forced?

What do you think of Gracie's role in leading the R-Group?

- Do you know anyone like her?
- Do you think that there are women like her today?
- What would you have liked to see more of?

What do you think of JJ leadership of the CATS team?

- Do you know anyone like him?
- Do you think that there are men with honor and commitment today?
- Do you think a caste system remains between men and women in technology?

Who was your favorite supporting character?

- Why did you like them?
- Did you find them believable?
- Did they have relatable character flaws, or were they too squeaky clean?

Do you think Mateo was a realistic antagonist? Is he better or worse than Pliant and Julian?

- Did he get his just desserts?
- Have you crossed paths with evil people like this?
- What would you do in a similar situation if you were the leader?

What risks did Marian take that you liked?

- Should she continue to help Zee and Judith?
- Should she and Brayson continue to have a place in the stories?
- Was she a hero, a victim, or both?

What themes surfaced in the story?

- Have you ever been in a situation where you needed someone to save you?
- Have you ever been in a situation where you did not want someone to save you?
- What was your favorite part?

**Breakfield
and Burkey**

Enigma Jewels

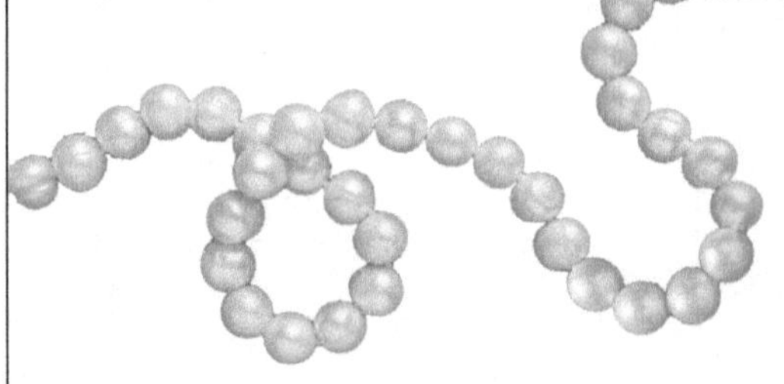

3
Enigma Heirs
Thriller Series

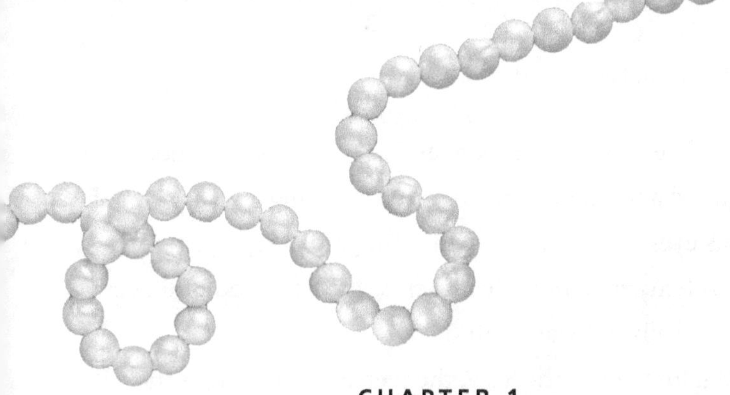

CHAPTER 1

Ride Share

Flashing lights and the screaming siren pierced the night as the cop dropped his car into gear, speeding after the black SUV as it squealed past. The officer shook his head. "Jerk!" he said, realizing the chase was on as the culprit surged forward and took a radical right at the next corner. He notified headquarters and then focused on the pursuit.

Being a seasoned pro, the officer laughed as he closed the distance and pulled onto the left side of the Tahoe. The driver jerked the wheel to the right to evade and clipped the curb. He overcorrected and then braked to miss the police car. Losing control, the car careened into a commercial trash container, pushing several feet with a crumpled front end.

The officer pulled his car to a stop and jumped out with his revolver drawn. He clicked his shoulder radio, reporting his current status as he rushed to the driver's door and tapped the gun's muzzle on the window.

"Get out of the car. Keep your hands up," he shouted, trying to see through the tinted window.

Moments ticked by before the heavy SUV door began creaking open. "Don't shoot," the male voice cracked. "I'm hurt and can't open the door any wider. I'm not armed. Can you help, please?"

The officer kept his weapon level as he grabbed the door with his left hand and opened it. Surprised at seeing a young teen, he rolled his eyes. "Kid, who are you? This vehicle is registered to Julian LaFleur, not a punk teenager. Why didn't you pull over when you realized I was behind you?"

Struggling out of the SUV, the teenager moaned as the officer pulled him over and then made him face the vehicle.

"Some dude pulled up to my friends and me, flashed the cash, and said there could be more if one of us volunteered to tear around the city fast. He said to meet him at noon tomorrow at Tiki Bar in San Juan. Then I'd get the money since I was the dumb ass who let him and his buddy walk away with their briefcases."

The officer clicked on the handcuffs. "Didn't you think something was wrong with doing this? You're lucky you didn't kill someone or yourself."

The teen winced. "His buddy laughed, saying only a man would take the dare. I couldn't resist the hundred bucks."

"Describe the two men."

"One was an older man with greying blonde hair who smelled of cigarettes. The tall, muscular man was younger and tougher. They were betting which of us would bite down for the dare."

"Where were they headed?"

"They headed toward the San Juan Bay Marina."

The officer spun the kid around by the arm and pulled him toward his patrol car. He opened the back door, helped him in, then shut the door. He tapped his radio and transmitted the facts he'd learned, annoyed at missing the expected tag.

0101010101100101

JJ ran his hand through his black hair in frustration. He clicked the contact on his laptop to connect the call. "Gracie, we had a lead that Julian LaFleur escaped while the targeted plane was stopped and the girls secured. We're trying to get possible locations to provide authorities."

"JJ, we've got eyes on San Juan, looking for the cryptocurrency parasite we introduced into Mateo's organization to track him. With Mateo dead, we expect to see more activity directly from LaFleur since he was Mateo's accounting money man. Your group engineered the bogus hosting infrastructure that allowed us to seize and copy Mateo's records."

JJ laughed. "I wish I'd seen the *astonished, we're screwed* look on his face when he tried to demo the system to Mateo."

Gracie sighed, shaking her reddish blonde hair. "The authorities saw no trace of him at the airport. They are trying to determine where he might have gone. His compound was deserted except for several local groundskeepers who loved LaFleur, according to the authorities who interviewed them. I'm not sure how we might locate him, dear brother."

"He's on the island. No one's going to airlift him out. That only leaves a charter boat service. The team is running down those leads. We didn't get his crypto when we searched his cloud information. He must have it in other wallets. Maybe we are tracking the right ones if we are lucky. Since we haven't analyzed the accounting records yet, we don't know how much cash he has. He appears to favor cryptocurrencies, so we hope to see the infected crypto we introduced as he tries to exit the island. He's boxed in."

She tapped her pen on the desk in a staccato beat. "Whenever we think we have these jerks ready for gift wrapping, we find an empty box. He and his lieutenant must know we are onto them. They're changing their patterns. Did you start backtracking to St. Kitts, where we got the first blip on the beaconing signal?"

"That's a good idea. I can do some digging there. We might locate something. His best option is to set up shop somewhere else. A smart, black-hearted rabbit always has another exit from the burrow. Gracie, can you have JW and the team begin hunting for other properties in the Caribbean that he owns or has access to?"

Gracie smirked. "Yep. I don't know if we can understand his alternate aliases."

JJ chuckled. "True. Don't be surprised that he didn't use his real identity to arrange these safe houses for himself. After all, one of his resume highlights is identity theft."

Gracie groaned. "It's like looking for a needle in a pile of rats."

"That's what our R-Group and CATS team does best."

Gracie smiled. "How are Judith and Xiamara doing after we secured them from the plane? You sent me a message that Brayson was ready to return to Luxemburg, but Marian wanted some downtime for him to recover. I think she was more scared than she let on of losing him," she sighed, understanding Marian's feelings. "Are you still in Europe, too?"

"Yes, I don't plan to return to Brazil for a week or so. Judith and Zee were released yesterday," he continued. "They weren't pleased to hear Julian escaped and wanted to help search the islands. I asked them to return here. I'd rather they work from here for the time being."

"Good. They are tough ladies and good team members."

"Yep, we are lucky, Sis. I'm going to get some rest. I'll check in with Brayson in the morning."

CHAPTER 2

Short Term Reprieve

"Ryu, how much more of this evasive action are we taking?" Julian fisted his palm with his right hand while he stared intently at the bodyguard's square chin and focused on the road. He was grateful to have this tough, intelligent, devoted man beside him. Though they wore black jeans and tee shirts, they had changed after getting to the car, so it was easy to spot the brawn. He combed his longish blonde hair with his fingertips, then insisted, "I told you we need to head to Saint Martin." His French accent was more pronounced because he couldn't control the situation.

"I know, sir. You also said we need not to get caught. I am trying to make sure we can't be tracked. This old Chevy isn't as fast as your Tahoe, but we can reach San Juan Bay before authorities connect the dots."

Julian frowned with tightened lips. "You're right, but it will never be the same." He pulled his laptop from his case, powered it on, and then tried logging in. "Hey, pull into the next local bank parking lot. I must secure a quick Wi-Fi connection and do a fast ATM transaction."

Moments later, Ryu located a bank without deviating from his route. He watched Julian complete his activity and input the keystrokes required for the ATM withdrawal. He handed the wad of cash to his boss.

"We need one other withdrawal, then we can go."

Ryu completed the instructions as directed and passed the additional U.S. currency.

"Perfect, let's go."

Ryu shifted the Chevy into gear and sped toward the marina.

"When I phoned my buddy, he said two fishing boats were in the harbor. We should be able to buy a passage on one called Ruby's Slipper. The captain is known for keeping a secret for a price."

"Good, we have some cash. I have access to our funds, and you protect me. Let's get off Puerto Rico as quickly as possible. I still don't understand how they found out about the transport. They must have tapped our phone calls. Thank goodness I have a couple of burners to use."

"You taught me long ago, Julian, to have backup plans. This time, we used them."

Dark settled over the area as Ryu pulled into the far side of the parking lot.

The night sky crackled with lightning and thunder, promising a heavy storm was approaching the island. They located the Ruby's Slipper tied to the end of the pier. Julian saw the grizzled captain chatting with the marina owner and walked toward the pair. The marina owner returned to his shop.

Julian approached the captain. He noted the dark, shaggy-haired man's baggy, stained pants and grey, full-sleeved woven shirt. He figured the man was over six feet and then noted the worn dark boots. He inclined his head as he stated, "We'd like to purchase passage to Saint Martin. We were told you liked fishing in those waters, Captain."

Julian felt the man's once-over appraisal. He grinned, picking the last chunk of dinner with the worn toothpick from his teeth. "My name's Shaughnessy, and you are?"

"I'm Jules, and this is Ryu," he extended his hand, enveloped in the man's massive, rough hand but not hurt from a show of strength. "Nice to meet you."

"What takes you to Saint Martin? Wouldn't it be easier to fly?"

"Possibly, but," he clasped his midsection. "I get air sickness but am fine on the water."

"I can take you. It'll cost you a thousand U.S. each."

Julian looked at Ryu, who shrugged.

"No problem." He pulled a small wad of bills from his jeans pocket and counted out twenty Franklins. Only a few were left, so he added them as well. "Here, take it all. Consider it a tip for taking us on such short notice."

Shaughnessy grinned, showing his white teeth brightened by the first streak of lightning. "You can stow your sacks in the cabin below deck, which will also serve as a place to rest." He looked into the sky. "Make yourselves at home while I check on the storm."

Waves began to slap the fishing trawler harder, driving it back against the dock buntings. Winds increased, making it hard to hear. Julian yelled, "This is the best you could do?"

Ryu shouted, "We weren't safe at the airport, and if they knew your name, we would have been caught in the terminal. The only other option was a reliable watercraft. This fishing trawler carries enough fuel to get to Saint Martin and potentially travel around the storm."

"What if this tub won't go fast enough to outrun the storm?" Julian asked, tamping down the fear from showing in his eyes.

Ryu fatalistically replied, "We'll probably drown."

Julian laughed. "We've dodged them so far, thanks to you. This is our best chance."

The pair returned topside from stowing their gear below deck. Julian watched as Ryu cleverly blocked their spot by moving crates of supplies. Rain began to hammer the dock area and boat deck, increasing with each flash of lightning and deafening clap of thunder. Julian felt the warm rain as it drenched his hair and headed toward his toes. He shouted, "Can we tow the cigarette boat behind us as an insurance policy?"

Ryu wiped a hand across his face, clearing his eyes. "We could, but it would slow us down. We could slice through the waves faster to get around the storm, but we wouldn't have enough fuel."

"Where could it get us to?"

"The Virgin Islands, possibly."

"Damn. I don't have nearly the same connections in the British or U.S. Virgin Islands, but maybe just as a weigh point to stop and refuel."

"Sir, this boat isn't elegant, but no one can trace it to you."

"You're right. Whoever these guys are, they have the girls, Madam Chloe and Nohea. The girls don't know enough, and the other two will resist talking for as long as possible."

Julian watched the captain approach them. "Gentlemen, we aren't going anywhere. This storm is massive. The Coast Guard issued orders to secure boats for about twenty-four hours or until the storm passes. We're safer here than out on those growing swells expected to exceed fifteen feet. It's not a hurricane-class system, but dangerous. We aren't going anywhere tonight."

"Shaughnessy, I paid you for room, board, and discretion."

"That you did, Jules. But not enough for me to want to risk death on a fool's errand. There are slickers in the hold if you need them. I'll fix us some grub after securing the ropes for the night."

Julian nodded.

0101010101100101

JW rushed to join the virtual conference room. He pressed a key to add JJ. "JJ, are you there?"

Half-awake, JJ fumbled to tie his bathrobe before pressing the key to join the Gigazon. "Why don't bad guys sleep on my schedule?" JJ stopped long enough to retrieve the missing slipper for his left foot.

JW yawned. "I feel your pain, sir. Granger was doing some update work on ICABOD when the crypto parasite surfaced. He woke me here in *Zürich*. After I reviewed it, I thought you'd want to know."

JJ strained to look awake and cleared his throat. "Is this going to be a pot of coffee discussion, or is it some sort of imaginative material that will keep my mind spinning half the night?"

Granger interjected, "We got a cryptocurrency exchange for some hard currency at an ATM outside San Juan that converts Ethereum to dollars. Our parasite code was part of the transaction. JJ, it's gotta be Julian doing a quick conversion to flee the island."

JJ frowned. "I'm hearing short imaginative material. Rats!"

"I'm Sorry, JJ." Granger apologized. "He also made a secondary transaction minutes later for more hard currency."

JW complained, "The good news is he stopped long enough to alert us he was converting digital funds to U.S. Dollars. We lost visibility on him as soon as the exchange was completed."

JJ rubbed his face to wake up. "That's inconvenient. So, he's not trying to leave San Juan using conventional methods. He'll buy his transport and their silence. The switch-up escape methods are getting old."

JW cleared his throat. "I thought this was important so we could collaborate on the next steps he might take."

"I'm not angry with you or Granger, only the situation. It was a good trap on his activities, and I'm glad you woke me, so I can think of options. I need to brew some coffee and make another call. You both try to get some sleep. When I have some options, I'll let you know. Thanks again."

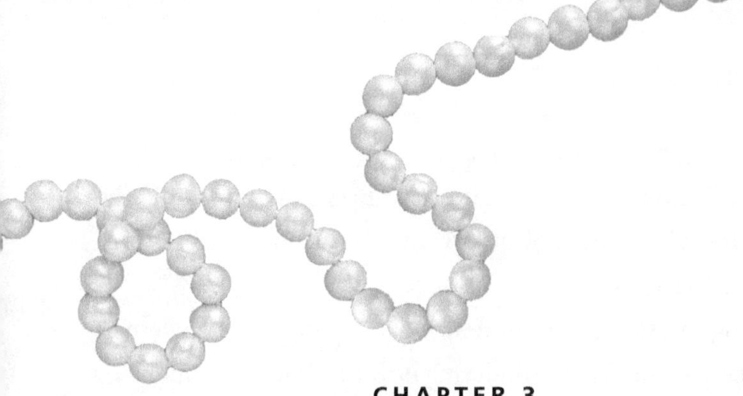

CHAPTER 3

A Fool's Errand

The low, black storm clouds spewed heavy rains for hours making the night appear darker. Winds buffeted the fishing boat against the rubber fenders, adding periodic thuds to the booming weather concert. Little by little, it eased as the worst passed Puerto Rico on its way to soak other islands. Julian, Ryu, and Shaughnessy awoke to loud voices saying they were harbor security. The three exchanged glances, and Shaughnessy raced up the stairs to the deck.

One deep voice demanded, "We need to inspect your boat. We're looking for two suspects involved in a high-speed chase near San Juan."

Shaughnessy retorted, "Why would I assist you unless you help me bail the water left by the storm? Do I look like I'm running a hotel for fugitives? Get out of here before I call the police on you two prissy rent-a-cops."

Harbor security stepped onto the trawler, ignoring the burly captain.

"You have no rights on board my boat," Shaughnessy shouted as they began prowling the deck and under everything. After several minutes of searching, they clomped into the sleeping quarters and the hold below.

269

They stepped off the deck briefly, tilting it slightly away from the dock with a bob. "I guess our tip wasn't any good," the deep voice said. "Let's look at the other boats on the other side. I want that reward."

Shaughnessy raced around the boat looking for the two men, then scratched his head, wondering how they'd left without being seen. He took another turn around on the deck and noticed a heavy rope draped over the side. Tugging it, he discovered it wasn't dangling as he'd thought, but heavy. Moments later, Julian and Ryu bobbed to the surface, gasping for air. Smiling, Shaughnessy helped them back on board.

"Quick thinking, lads. I was afraid I'd have to give you up. Go below before you're seen. I'll get us underway."

"Thank you," they said in unison through clenched teeth.

"No problem. When we reach port on Saint Martin, you'll want to increase my tip to maintain my silence."

Julian turned with narrowed eyes, then shrugged and nodded as he headed below.

Shaughnessy laughed.

0101010101100101

JJ started on his second cup of coffee before calling Brayson, who answered on the first ring.

"Hey, JJ, tell me you need me back at work."

JJ chuckled. "I wanted to check on you, but Marian asked both of you to remain in Texas for a few days." Brayson's frown increased, confirmed by his rapid reply.

"I'm fine. I've had enough of Texas for now. I can book a flight back to Luxemburg and bring Marian along."

"Does she realize you're saying this to me?"

"I'll tell her if you approve it."

Marian's voice joined the conversation with an annoyed tone as if she were near Brayson. "Tell JJ I know now."

"I heard, Brayson. Why don't you put it on speaker so you don't have to relate?"

Brayson cleared his throat. "What can we do for you, JJ?"

JJ grinned, knowing Marian wouldn't let her husband out of sight again. "I wanted to know if you two might travel back to San Juan to search Julian's estate. We're reasonably certain he did not return to that location because the man was flipping off the camera. The camera is still transmitting, but no movement has been detected in the days since the abrupt departure."

Marian sighed. "I wouldn't mind retrieving the things I stored there. But why the estate?"

"Even if Julian shows up, he's not seen you or Brayson. You would not be a threat if seen. If you can get inside, I hope you find something to tell us where he might have gone. We don't have much on the man. It is possible he had an alternate home on St. Kitts since that was the location of the original beacon signal you trapped on, Marian."

Brayson said, "You want us to break in and search the place. Is there an alarm?"

"Honey, I have Zee's gate code and door automatic sequence. She sent them to me after they learned they were staying on-site," announced Marian. "Judith told me he had an office overlooking the pool. They were in the guest house with a few local servers for Julian's required data backup."

"What do we say if anyone asks who we are or why we're there?" asked Brayson.

"Judith said there were not many guards. A gardener drove the golf cart to pick up her and Zee from the entrance gate on their first visit there."

Marian interjected, "The grounds were maintained perfectly according to Zee, so there might be a permanent crew and maybe a housekeeper."

"If you gain access using the code at the gate and enter the house without setting off an alarm, you are Mr. LaFleur's guests. If you bring in groceries and overnight duffle bags, you can say you rented it from him for a few days as a private romantic getaway. Tell the help, if they bother you, to take a few days off."

"Marian, I am feeling improved thanks to your care. This doesn't sound dangerous to me. Let's see if we can find some information."

"I'm in, JJ. When can you get a flight booked from Houston?"

"You have two tickets booked on the next flight tomorrow morning from Houston Hobby to San Juan. I have a car reserved in your name, Brayson. I'll send you all the information to your secure email accounts."

Brayson laughed, and Marian chorused in. They caught their breath, and Brayson confirmed, "You must have been confident I'd do it."

"Not really," JJ admitted. "But I was certain Marian would go with you. I know you guys well."

CHAPTER 4

Loose Ends

The steady drone of the trawler engines should have made the two exhausted men sound asleep. Even with the moderate rocking of the boat, it didn't.

Julian whispered, "How much more to keep Shaughnessy happy and silent, do you think?"

Ryu calmly offered, "Nothing."

"Nothing?"

"You pay me to keep problems off your back. Shaughnessy is the needed savior until the next bidder arrives. We're going too slow to outrun radio communications from San Juan. However, he's just the opportunistic bastard to sell us out once we get to St. Martin. Julian, let me take care of the situation."

Julian thought a moment before he spoke. "When do we end our contract with him? As soon as we're docked or sometime earlier?"

"Earlier. Shaughnessy stated that the trip would be roughly less than two hundred nautical miles. At a little over ten knots, we have around fifteen hours to reach the coast of St. Martin. My waterproof diving watch says we've been traveling for thirteen hours. We are roughly two hours from land unless he doesn't know how to navigate. Sunrise occurs in an hour, a perfect time to take advantage of his tired state."

Julian nodded. "After Shaughnessy is dispatched, we take the dingy and row ashore?"

Ryu sneered, "No…I have something in mind with a little more finesse."

Two hours later, Julian gave one final kick that helped him reach Ryu's outstretched hand at the water's edge. Julian staggered as he struggled to his feet from the water, still breathing hard. He bent down to rest his hands on his knees while trying to get as much air as possible. Ryu was busy gathering the life preservers and their precious cargo items.

After several moments of trying to catch his breath, Julian asked, "Tell me you got our briefcases with the cash, jewels, and my PC."

Ryu chuckled. "Sir, everything is accounted for. I need to bury these Ruby Slipper life preservers, and then we can be on our way."

"On our way with no clean clothes or cigarettes? I've only got one shoe left from that long swim. Hell, it felt like we swam the English Channel."

"I sunk everything of ours that can be replaced. We will only be inconvenienced until we can buy more. We don't want to look like survivors from a shipwreck after we got off one. When the Ruby's Slipper shows up in St. Martin, they won't find evidence of us."

"Good. If we can get to the house, we have clothing and food. Thank you, Ryu."

Ryu announced, "Truck approaching. We must look and act like laborers heading to work who can use a lift. Let me do the talking. Avoid looking anyone in the eye or letting them see your face. We'll ask to be dropped close but must walk a bit. Safer that way."

010101010101100101

Brayson and Marian had an easy flight to San Juan. They took carry-on only, so they didn't have to wait at baggage claim. After picking up the rental car, Marian provided directions to the hotel. Brayson waited outside in the car while Marian retrieved her bags from the bellman and stored them in the trunk. Then they plotted their course to Julian's estate.

Brayson reminded, "When we arrive, we need to have a running conversation like this is the best trip ever, in case someone is listening."

Marian rubbed her hands together. "I agree. I'll be the wife in love, and you can be the hunk. It'll be so much fun."

Brayson pulled up to the front and stopped. Marian entered the code on the keypad, and the heavy black gate opened. They saw no one around driving up to the estate, where Brayson parked. They got out laughing and hugging, very much the couple in love looking for a delightful respite.

"I'll bring our groceries and luggage, honey," announced Brayson.

"Thank you, sweetheart. I hope this code works." Marian approached the door and fed in the code. Moments later, she heard the lock release and pressed the latch on the handle to open the front door. "You've got to see this place. It's more beautiful than Julian said. Oh, my goodness, the artwork. Wow. I think I'm in heaven." She pushed the door wider, holding it so Brayson could enter. She'd memorized the floor plan and led him to the kitchen to store their food and wine.

"Honey, you found us a great place." He turned a slow circle to see everything. "Not a dish in the sink, nothing out of place."

Marian poked her head above the refrigerator's open door. "We have condiments, a dozen eggs, butter, and wine here.

You're right, though; it's spotless. I can clean it when our long weekend ends." Methodically opening the cabinets, they each made comments.

"Honey, we can create anything with this array of pots and pans! It's like a chef wannabe's dream come true."

"Plates and glassware are so brightly colored. I bet the food looks way more enticing when served. I may not want to leave at the end of our long weekend."

"Let's look around the rest of the place, find our bedroom," she said with a sly smile and eyes he knew were mischief-filled.

They stayed close as they walked through the dining, sitting, and formal living rooms, peeking into nooks and crannies.

"If the weather stays nice, we should eat by the pool and enjoy the fresh air and beautiful flowers."

She nodded in agreement. "A swim before or after dinner may be in order as well. I brought the teeny bikini you like so much and sunscreen. I love how you apply sunscreen."

He laughed. "Come on, you feisty woman; let's find our bedroom and change into swimsuits."

The first four bedrooms were decorated in bright colors. Everything was neat. Marian mused aloud, "I wonder if there's a housekeeper. I forgot to ask Julian when I paid him. It would be great to know before we run around naked."

"I haven't seen anything that would account for anyone being here, but this estate is expansive. Look, this bathroom has an attached soaking tub with jets. The massive king-size bed is perfect. Since you weren't directed to a room, honey, let's use this one."

Marian spun around and then opened the closets. A few items of men's clothing were hung up with a shoe tree. She nodded. "I agree. This room is perfect."

For the next hour, they methodically searched the room while making sounds of passion in case there were microphones. They doubted any were in the master suite but didn't want to take chances. Brayson launched his stud finder application and began hunting for a safe. He shook his head, sensing defeat.

Marian squealed, "No, don't stop, sweetheart; it feels so good. I am so close," she added, with heavy breathing and intermittent sighs.

He joined the breathing along with determined groans as he used the stud finder in the closet. He grinned at her and arched his eyebrows.

"Yesssssssss," she screamed.

"You are mine, honey, all mine," he announced with a heavy sigh of release. He wiggled his fingers like he was typing and inclined his head.

Marian retrieved the laptop, crossed the thick carpeted floor soundlessly, and returned to his side. She connected to the bridge and typed, using her phone as a hotspot.

> We found a safe, and Brayson is opening it now.

> Good.

Brayson used his sensitive fingers to rotate the dial one way slowly and then the other. In under five minutes, the door swung open. He took photos of the entirety, then began moving out one thing after another, grabbing pictures. He paused to share them with Marian and continued itemizing the contents.

> Incoming pictures

Marian transferred the photos, which included stacks of U.S. currency, an ID with Julian's face but a different name, loose blue stones in various sizes, and a couple of silver pendants with the same type of stones mounted.

> I think the stones might be Larimar.

> The Blue Jewel of the Caribbean?

> The blue and white are very distinctive in color.

> Interesting. The man likes jewels.

> There are a lot here, plus a few diamonds
> and maybe Tanzanite

Marian flipped open the old book's pages and blew a long whistle. Her fingers went to the keyboard.

> A 1911 First Edition of The Book of Buried Treasure: True
> Story of the Pirate Gold and Jewels.

> That's impressive.

Brayson put everything back into the safe and locked it. He embraced her and said, "Honey, you are so good with me. Let's change and head out to the pool."

He carried a bottle of wine as they strolled toward the pool. He whispered in her ear, "I promise we will make that little show in the bedroom a reality later."

She laughed and spread towels on the loungers. He poured the wine and handed her a glass. As they raised them to toast, she took a sharp breath and shifted her eyes, so he realized someone was approaching.

"Excuse me," a woman's voice said. "Who are you, and why are you here? The master is out of town."

Marian piped up. "Hi, I'm Mary, and this is my husband, Bray."

Brayson turned and smiled at the woman.

Marian continued, "Julian rented us the place for the weekend for our romantic getaway. It's a lovely estate. Do you work here?"

"Yes, ma'am, I'm Emma. I wasn't told. I have no supplies."

Marian flitted her hand. "No worries, we brought our groceries and are happy to do all the cooking. Bray, here, promised he would clean up."

"Oh, okay. Do I need to open the guest house for you?"

"Only so we can quickly shower and change clothes before entering the house. I would hate to track anything in and give you unexpected work."

The woman appeared a bit confused to Brayson, so he added, "He must have thought he'd given you the time off as we have all the codes to get inside."

"All right," she said slowly. "If you need anything, pick up the phone in the kitchen and dial four. I live on the far side of the estate but am happy to assist anytime."

Marian grinned. "That is so sweet of you. Thank you."

The woman walked away after unlocking the guest house.

"Marian, did you find that a little strange?"

She looked around and thoughtfully replied, "Yes, but we don't know her background."

"If she is gone for twenty minutes, let's get into the guest house and take photos of what's left. Then we can clear out the safe and boogie."

"I agree. I would like to see if we can see anything on the servers in this room if we can."

"Fine, but I don't want to stay longer than necessary. I feel so uneasy, Marian."

A half-hour later, Emma hadn't returned. Brayson agreed that Marian could enter the guest house while he kept guard by the pool. She transferred a few interior photos to his phone as she moved around. Everything seemed fine until she approached the rear exit of the building.

His cell rang, and her Caller ID appeared. He slid the bar to answer and heard her say,

"Run, sweetheart."

KA-BLAM!

Breakfield – Charles works as a data/ telecom solution architect and supports digital security, blockchain solutions, and unified communications. He enjoys writing, studying World War II history, travel, and cultural exchanges. Charles' love of wine, cooking, and Harley riding often provides writing topics.

Much of his personality comes from his father who served in the military for 30 years and three wars. Charles grew up on multiple bases and different countries. The multi-cultural exposure helps him with the various character perspectives they bring to the series. His personal ambition is to continue to teach Burkey humor.

Burkey – Rox is a Customer Experience Specialist who works with businesses around the world. As a gifted speaker and accomplished listener, she bridges the chasm between business problems and technical solutions to optimize business productivity. She has written technology papers, white papers, but launches into high gear when plotting our next technothriller or short story.

As a child, she led the other kids with her highly charged imagination generating new adventures with make believe characters. She is proud of being a Girl Scout until high school, and contributed to the community as a member of a Head Start program. Rox enjoys her family, learning, listening to people, travel, outdoor activities, sewing, cooking, and thinking about how to diversify the series.

Breakfield and Burkey – began their partnership writing non-fictional papers and books. They formed a business partnership to share stories as fictional story writers. They recognize storytelling is an evolving method to share excitement, thrills, and insights to today's technology risks.

They are passionate about leveraging the real technology into fictional writing. The variety of characters have attributes from the many people who crossed their professional paths add that depth. Admittedly, Breakfield often asks interesting people he meets if they thought about being an evil cyberthug or femme fatale in their series.

Both authors have traveled to many places around the world. These travels are pulled into stories that requires real knowledge of specific locals. They enjoy well-rounded thrillers that include levels of humor, romance, intrigue, suspense, and mystery.

They love to talk about their stories at private and public book readings or events. Burkey conducts podcast style interviews with a couple of author groups, and enjoys extracting the tidbits from authors, especially new ones. Her first interview was, wait for it, Breakfield. You can learn where they will be from the calendar on their website.

EnigmaSeries.com has information on the Enigma Series, 12 books, 10 short stories, audio books, book trailers, and the newest series Enigma Heirs releasing in 2023. They have proudly earned multiple awards for their fictional creations.

We are also part of the Underground Authors group writing cozy mysteries/murders in the Magnolia Bluff Crime Chronicles. We are committed to providing an installment for Season 2 and Season 3 to accompany *The Flower Enigma,* released in Season 1.

Please provide a fair and honest review on Amazon and any other places you post reviews. We appreciate the feedback.

We would greatly appreciate if you would take
a few minutes and provide a review of this work
on Amazon, Goodreads and any
of your other favorite places.

More of the Enigma Heirs Series by Breakfield and Burkey
www.EnigmaBookSeries.com

Enigma Jewels coming 2025

MAGNOLIA BLUFF CRIME CHRONICLES SEASON 1

DEATH WEARS A CRIMSON HAT
MAGNOLIA BLUFF CRIME CHRONICLES
CW HAWES

EULOGY IN BLACK AND WHITE
MAGNOLIA BLUFF CRIME CHRONICLES
CALEB PIRTLE III

THE GREAT PEANUT BUTTER CONSPIRACY
CINDY DAVIS

YOU WON'T KNOW HOW ...OR WHEN
MAGNOLIA BLUFF CRIME CHRONICLES
JAMES R. CALLAN

THE FLOWER ENIGMA
MAGNOLIA BLUFF CRIME CHRONICLES
BREAKFIELD AND BURKEY

THE SHINE FROM A GIRL IN THE LAKE
MAGNOLIA BLUFF CRIME CHRONICLES
RICHARD SCHWINDT

DEWEY DECIMAL DILEMMA
BOOK 7: MAGNOLIA BLUFF CRIME CHRONICLES
LINDA PIRTLE

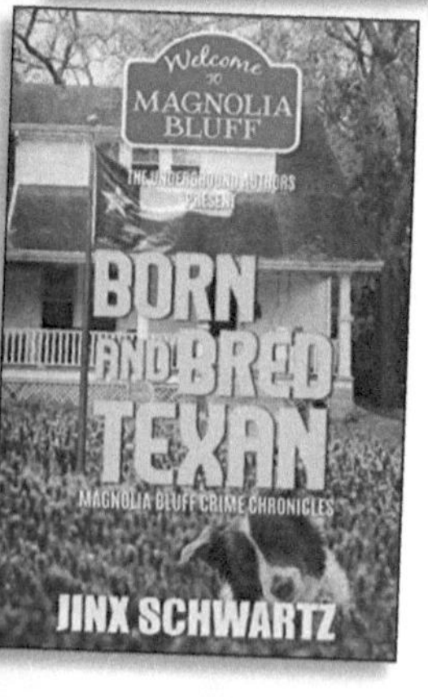

MAGNOLIA BLUFF CRIME CHRONICLES SEASON 2

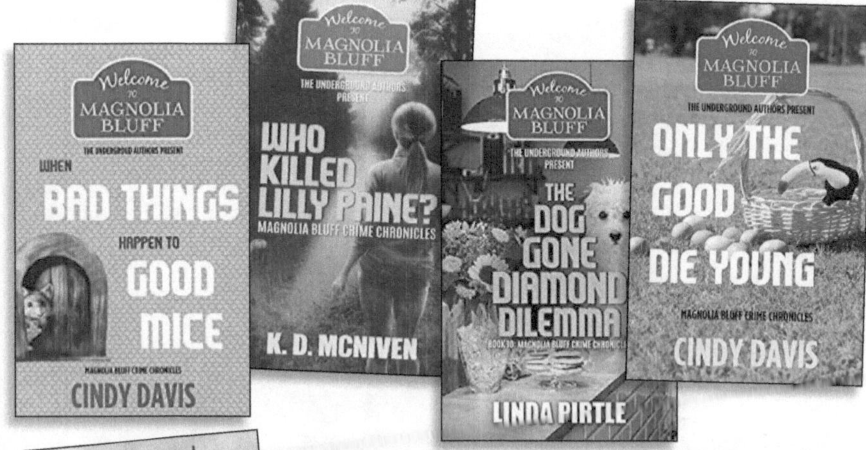

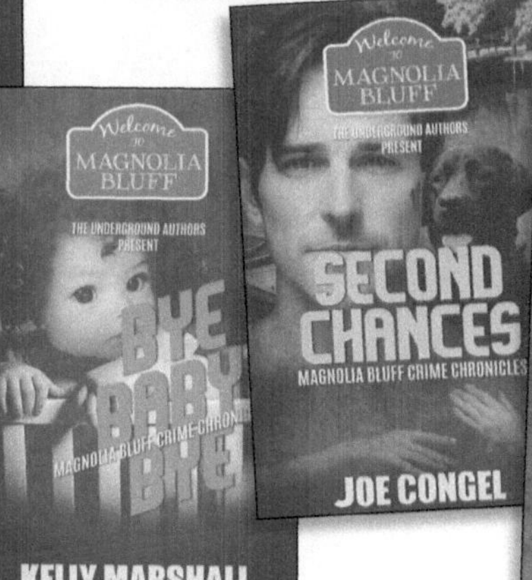

MAGNOLIA BLUFF CRIME CHRONICLES SEASON 3

www.ingramcontent.com/pod-product-compliance
Lightning Source LLC
Chambersburg PA
CBHW061652190726
48289CB00006B/1844